You Gone

J.S. Morton

Dystopic

A 'Wishing Shelf' Book Review:

****

This book has a plot. But that's not what I enjoyed the most. What I enjoyed most was getting to know the protagonist who – as the blurb puts it - is not only a widower, a son, a brother, etc. He's also a psychopathic killer. Now that's a hook! So I settled down and got to know Arthur and, if I had to sum him up in a word, I'd say he's a bit of a git. But he's funny too – or possibly it's the author who's funny, don't know – but anyway, his way of looking at life is sort of sick. A perfect example of this is when his mother is telling him 'to get back to doing what you love'. Ironic, he thinks, as what he loved most was stabbing people angrily.

As I enjoyed this novel, I couldn't help being reminded of Ted Bundy, the American psychopath, who always seemed such a decent, charismatic sort of fellow who very much enjoyed washing his car. As the world later discovered, he washed his car so often to get all the blood off the carpets! Well, Arthur Norman is sort of Ted Bundy – or he seems so to me anyway. The sort of person you would trust, until he kidnapped, raped, and murdered you.

This novel is, in every way, a character study. And I thought the author did a fantastic job of delving into his sick personality and – I don't know how – making it all rather funny too. In a way, it's like the film, The Departed, when Jack Nicolson shoots the woman and says, "She fell funny." There's nothing funny about shooting a woman, but it's still hilarious!

So, if you fancy a novel that's a little bit shocking, that's a little bit different; and you like the thought of getting to know the inner workings of a psychopath's mind, this story is for you. At the end of the novel, there's a promise from the author that Arthur will be back – I do hope so!

www.thewsa.co.uk

First published in the UK in 2022
by Dystopic Publishing Ltd
71-75 Shelton Street
Covent Garden
WC2H 9JQ
ISBN 978-1-3999-4089-4

www.dystopicpublishing.com
www.facebook.com/dystopicpublishing
www.instagram.com/dystopicpublishing

For those searching for
the light . . . never stop.

A. Meredith Walters.

ONE

I wake up, but you are not here. You are not here because you're gone. You aren't anywhere, Melissa. But still, I search for you. I expect you to be here with me, even though I know that will never be the case again.

My head is a mess from last night. It sloshes from the vodka, and I sit up slow-motion-slowly. My brain hammers against my skull. It's like there's a rave in there. I hate raves, or any electronic music, for that matter. My hand fumbles about the gap in the bed where you should be. It's empty, and there is a Melissa-sized hole. I know there is, but I look for you anyway.

It has been eight months since you slept here, eight months since you slept anywhere that wasn't permanent. Eight months is long, but it isn't long enough for me. You should be here, and yet you're not. It's all my fault. I wasn't here for you. There's nothing I can do now, and no one I can tell. Hell, even if I did, I doubt anyone would believe me, and certainly, no one would understand. Nobody knows who I am, and now that you are gone, I am not sure I do either.

After thirty motionless minutes of staring at the ceiling, I get up from the bed, move to the window, and throw back the curtains. It is just after noon, and I think it is a Saturday. I say this because the neighbours are tearing ten shades of shit out of each other in the garden. Ah, June and Mike. *The Wellingtons!* The idyllic couple next door. Idyllic, so long as you don't live near them. Idyllic, so long as you don't hear them arguing every fucking weekend, out in the garden for all to see and hear.

Mike is a business executive, and Mike likes young interns. If I wasn't so fucking miserable, I might kill him. Not because infidelity is a mortal sin, but because it would put a stop to their idiotic fucking rows. June knows what Mike does with the interns. Mike knows that June knows, and Mike is probably single-handedly keeping the local florist in business. And the apologies usually work.

Adultery in the Wellington's house is solved by how well Mike grovels. I wish they could skip the arguing. It is like being in *The Truman Show.* And in my head, I'm stuck between the sixth and seventh levels of Dante's *Inferno.* Never moving up or down. It is like watching the same Adam Sandler movie over and over every weekend. It never stops. It's endearing at first, possibly mildly funny, but the show goes on . . . Mike and June continue to argue, and Mike continues to fuck the interns! Fucking Mike, not Fucking June!

I watch them bicker, and I go to shut the curtains, but not before June spots me in the window. Our eyes meet, and she shoots me a kindly smile. Now I'm stuck.

Move, dammit, Arthur.

Fuck, now she's waving to me, so I wave back. Fucking June! I avert my gaze and look down at the windowsill, where I spot a large glass paperweight. I consider opening the window and throwing it at her head as hard as possible. It might hit her smack bang in the middle of the skull and end the ridiculous waving once and for all. But then you bought this in Lanzarote, Melissa. I can't use it for murder, even if I wanted to. Goddammit, June, your husband has cheated on you for the nine thousandth time. Where is your self-respect, and why are you waving at the neighbour?

My hand, which had unconsciously wrapped itself around the paperweight, loosens and moves up in line with my shoulder. Once there, it begins to wave back. *What am I doing?* I need to move, to get out of this situation before I am invited around for dinner, where I'll be forced to kill both of them to avoid being stuck in their awkward dinner table tug of war. Who's more pathetic, Mike or June?

My hand breaks free from its wretched wave, and, short of a better plan, I draw both curtains to a close. *Ta-da, I am gone*. Problem solved. Free from June's glare, I move into the bathroom and sit down to unload. I must have slept for a good twelve hours, and once again, I filled my once well-tuned body full of vodka and self-loathing, and the need for bodily functions is vast.

Once I am finally able to exit the bathroom, I move downstairs. The morning has already come and gone, so I slowly creak the front door open, spot the local paper on the mat, and stealthily bring it inside.

Having made a coffee, I sit in the living room and open the awful local gazette. I want to take a seat in the conservatory, but then I would have a direct line into the bickering next door. It wouldn't be peaceful, and it wouldn't be long until they spotted me and tried to rope me into being an arbiter. I lack impulse control, and despite my personal pity party, I might make a mess of them.

So, instead, I sit in the living room; it is precisely as you left it, Melissa—aside from the chaos. You wouldn't like it; I don't either, but for some reason, the mess is one of many things I've yet to address.

As I sit and attempt to read the paper, I feel it is essential to clarify something. The news, in general, is an abomination, local news even more so. I can only speculate that all reporters are born with a tail and horns. The news doesn't want us informed. It wants us scared, persuaded, advertised to, sad, and lonely. The local paper is no exception, aside from the fact I'm confident a child writes every article. Given my hatred for the paper, it might seem odd that I sit in the house daily and read it. I mean, why? Well, the answer is simple. I live in a small Hampshire village and need to know what goes on. I have barely left the house since you went, Melissa. I have not been the same since you died. You left, and a part of me went too. It has been eight months… *eight months*, and I still don't know what to do, how to move forward, or how to leave my den of inequity.

I think I might be improving. But it is hard to judge progress when it comes to self-loathing. And I get it. I know what everyone is thinking. Friends and family alike tell me that I am an eligible, middle-aged adult. My wife passed away last year, and that life moves on. But I am stuck in a rut. I know I should get up, get dressed, and get outside. Maybe I should start dating, hang out with my friends, find a new hobby, or even dare I say it, see a therapist. Right? That is what ordinary people do. There are, however, three inherent problems to this. I am not normal. I am afraid. I don't see the fucking point.

There are almost eight billion people on this planet, and I'm sure most of us think that we are *not normal.* I get it. We all want to be unique, quirky, and interesting. The thing is, I am not sure I am unique; I am maybe slightly interesting, and day to day, I am as normal as cornflakes at breakfast. I even have a normal name, Arthur! Arthur was once a king of England; Arthur was a playwright and a creator of masterful detectives.

But today, Arthur is the third most common name for a boy: popular Arthur. I know there are worse names. I could have been named *Keith* or *Theo,* and I am thankful every day that I was not. But believe it or not, being called *Arthur* is the least of my problems. Because I am normal, and yet I am not. You see, this Arthur was married, has friends, and even held a job once. But he is also impulsive, volatile, angry, and maybe a little bit of a maniac, according to societal rules. The worst part about this is that I don't feel like I am, but the sum of my life's actions and deeds would say otherwise. Melissa used to tell me that I wasn't crazy. Simply the world was. But now you are gone, Melissa. I am here alone; I am depressed, and I am scared. Who would have thought it, me afraid? How the mighty have fallen.

Now, I know what you are thinking, who calls themselves mighty? I mean, who am I? A self-aggrandising R and B star who adds *Lion* to their title? Or a rapper turned emo who names himself after a Tennessee gangster? No, I am not these things. I don't need recognition or notoriety. The truth is far simpler than that. I have killed almost one hundred people, all evil and all deserving. They all died at my hands—or my knives, or a nearby blunt instrument. Most of them were very formidable. They evaded the law and escaped captivity or retribution. They hung out in the shadows, committing nefarious deeds . . . until I came along.

The news—that I don't like—reports some things that are new in the world, but not all of them. And fiction fills our heads with so-called make-believe, but it all came from somewhere. Thousands of people run around this planet doing despicable deeds who seldom get caught and never make the news, and I suppose I am one of them. However, I put my homicidal prowess to good and practical use.

Serial killers are not fictional and glamorous. They are usually evil, despicable beings. And as for professional killers, they will exist as long as there is a demand and money to pay for them. Take it from someone who knows—I am an *unprofessional* assassin. Unprofessional in that I don't work for anyone besides myself. My work is, in fact—or was—exceptional. It is not because I am on hiatus. It is not that I no longer have the longing or the impulse. But because I have been miserable, anxious, and depressed. I am not even a shadow of my former self. I'm sad and scared, and I can't see the positive in doing anything right now, not even murder.

I know what most people would think. Okay, he's heartbroken and depressed! But he is a murderer, an evil man; surely his lack of motivation is a good thing? I suppose, in a way, that is correct. But are we all that different from animals? I remember the London Riots. Dutiful doctors turned out and hurled chairs through windows before garrotting people with their stethoscopes. And austere accountants ripped off their shirts and beat people to death with abacuses, well, maybe not quite. But the truth is, if society and its rules fell, we would see a different side to most people. All I have done is work with what I've been given.

I have this deeply embedded violent anger that responds primarily to inequality. I deal with it the only way I see how, by eking out some form of justice. I get these violent impulses that rise up periodically, and if I don't deal with them properly, they bubble out as an apoplectic, homicidal rage. If I don't address *the urge*, then the simple act of someone cutting in the line of a queue—to be fair, it is a cardinal sin in Great Britain—or someone giving me the finger while I am driving might elicit their death.

I deal with my anger by taking it out on those who have sinned. I get annoyed and take out the World's trash. It is a simple and effective solution.

Despite living in a sleepy Hampshire village on the outskirts of Winchester just off the M3, it still sees its share of maleficence. Bad things do happen here. We don't see many professional hitmen or hitwomen—although hitwomen just sounds like something one shouldn't do—but the occasional dirty deed goes unpunished. I know it sounds silly, Melissa, but I subscribed to the paper after you left. I've barely been able to go outside, but I still need to know what is happening in case I do. This is my town, and I still need to harbour the hope that I might one day feel better.

I have learned—from the paper—that a man is kidnapping local cats and stringing them up at home. I know it is a far cry from what I usually deal with, Melissa. But I have to work back up to this and regain my appetite. Plus, it might be cats today, but he will soon graduate. I have spent most of the last eight months in the house or floating lifelessly in the heated outdoor pool. And in all that time, he's been stealing cats, taking them home and cutting them up while listening to Brahms. First, what did poor Brahms do to be associated with this lunatic? Imagine the movie? He'd turn over in his grave if he knew he was the soundtrack to cat vivisection. Second, they're cats. I mean, what the actual fuck.

The saddest part about my funk is that I have figured it out. I know who you are, Jarrod Walker. I know that you live at 92 Cotteridge Drive, and I know that you are home alone every Thursday with Brahms on dismembering cats! I have even been bold on occasion and snuck out of the house, fuelled by vodka and tears. I've followed Jarrod to his house and loitered in the dark, thinking of all the ways I could kill him or, at the very least, offer up an apocalyptic scare. But in the end, I have just come home to the pool and floated in a body of water that is now, in all likelihood, mainly vodka, tears, and self-pity.

To top it all off, Mike and June have a cat, and the fucker is still alive! I don't much care for cats—not enough to dissect them to classical music—but enough that I wouldn't shed a tear if *Timmy* went missing. What is the point of having a cat killer in the village if they don't have the decency to cull your neighbour's cat?

The truth is, it has been fourteen days and eight months since you went, Melissa, and I am still talking to you. Not out loud. That really would be crazy. But I just can't find my way back to the light or civilization.

It's been fifteen days and eight months since I took a life. I would have stayed home that night if I had known you would leave. But I didn't. Now you're gone; worst of all, Melissa, I'm anxious and depressed. I have been since you went. You're gone. I can't do that which I love the most, and I don't know what to do or who to tell.

TWO

Being heartbroken, anxious, and depressed is the worst. My once beautiful mind is now full of darkness and shadows. The place I used to go for ideas and inspiration is now terrifying. I get lost in there, and then I'm trapped and scared. I find myself anxious in places I wasn't, and I'm unhappy at times I shouldn't be. To top it all off, my friends, my family, your family, everyone ever, they all want one thing. For me to be happy once more, to be *myself* again.

'We need to get you back to doing what you love!' says your mother. It's ironic because besides you, Melissa, what I loved most was stabbing people angrily. And she means well; they all do. But I'm depressed, I'm not sad, and I can't just shake it off.

The worst part is that I have no one to confide in, not properly. I know that true love doesn't come around that often, and I'm no expert in this. Still, I'm pretty sure that finding someone who loves you and is very aware that you come home from a long day at work covered in blood—metaphorically, of course, I didn't just stroll into the kitchen and sit down for dinner covered in my victim's blood—is hard to find. But she knew, and Melissa didn't just *know* on a subliminal level. We talked about it, and she would ask *how it went* and *if I needed anything*. Not only that, but Melissa bought and paid for everything. This house, my trips, your trips, our trips, you even bought my vintage books and expensive blades. Then you lied to everyone you and I knew. My life was possible because of you. You loved me for who I was and accepted what I did and why. You were good and kind and made me feel like I wasn't alone. I would imagine the chances of finding another woman who loves me even though I am a manic murderer is mighty slim.

Don't get me wrong, Melissa, I haven't entirely given up on life. I know you would want me to carry on, and I'm trying. But for most of my adulthood, you were part of me. I felt strong, safe, and not alone. I could confide my feelings in you and talk openly and honestly. I have friends. I do, good ones. But it is difficult to imagine telling Abdul and his wife that I have lost interest in killing. In the one outlet that keeps me from exploding.

I climb out of my reverie and realise that I've been staring blankly at the paper for an inordinate amount of time. I *need* to get out of my head. I *have* to get dressed; it is my birthday, and my mother is throwing an unnecessary party. It has been a long time since I have socialised on any level, and I know I have never been blessed with tremendous social grace. But I skipped Christmas, my mother's birthday, Melissa's funeral, and everything else in between. I know full well that if I don't show up tonight and at least try, she will probably drive down here and stage an awkward intervention.

So, with a heavy heart, I put the paper down, sigh, and head for the shower. If I arrive unkempt, my mother will surely try to have me committed.

The party will probably feature an ensemble crowd of faceless familial faces. People whom I would actively avoid were there not some tenuous connections between us all. I should probably shave too. Oh, what a day it is going to be!

***

'Hello, mother,' I say as I walk through the front door. I place my arms around her tiny frame and hug her dearly.

'Have you lost weight?' is literally the first thing she says to me.

'It's good to see you, too,' I reply. I look down at my body and consider that it is quite possible. I have been forgetting to eat. But either way, I'm six foot and a bit and over a hundred kilos, so it is definitely inconsequential.

'And what's going on with your hair?' she adds. And I hug her for as long as I can bear.

'Oh, I've missed you too,' I say. As I relinquish her, I catch a glimpse of myself in the spotless hallway mirror. My blonde hair is a mess and could use a trim. She might have a point there. I turn away from the mirror and spot my father standing near the staircase. He is grey. He is shrinking. And he is as unmoving and stoic as always, and as per usual, I can't tell if he's pleased to see me or if he wants to tear into me for being late, scruffy, weird, or anything else that doesn't fully resonate with him.

'You made it,' he says. *Well, obviously, dad, otherwise I wouldn't be standing here.* I move toward him, and we attempt a hug. We embrace briefly in a manner that reminds me of running headfirst into a tree. Then he takes my bag and sits it downstairs in the guest room. And as I watch him depart, I consider that he looks more and more like *Droopy* every time I see him.

My miniature mother leads me into the kitchen.

'How was your journey?' she asks.

'Terrible,' I reply. 'The traffic was awful. It must have taken at least two hours!' It didn't. But they don't need to know I sat in my chair wallowing in pity and thinking about you, Melissa.

‘Well, you’ve arrived before the rest of the guests, just!’ she says. *Yes, mum, I know I’m fucking late. I didn’t want to come here.*

‘Oh well, that’s a relief,’ I say. We sit in the kitchen, and she offers me an alcoholic drink. I pretend to consider it.

‘It is your birthday,’ she says.

‘Oh, go on then,’ I reply. She pours me a beer talking proudly as she does.

‘We even got you some gluten-free beer,’ she says happily.

‘Oh, wonderful, thanks, mum!’ I think to myself, wondering why in the actual fuck she has. The freshly poured drink is handed to me, and I accept it with a crooked smile. The notion of gluten-free beer is abhorrent. The drink sitting in my hand is even worse. I take a sip. ‘Mmm, you know that’s actually very good.’

‘Is it?’ she asks. *No, mum, it’s gluten-free beer. That’s like serving you a gin-free gin and tonic or going on a waterless beach holiday*!

I take another slightly smaller sip and then set the drink down. I suppose this is my fault. Three years ago, I stopped drinking dairy. But it’s okay my beer is gluten-free. ‘Who’s coming?’ I ask nervously.

‘The neighbours,’

Brilliant. More fucking neighbours.

‘Your uncle Phil and his family.’ *Fab, Prudent Phil and his obnoxious offspring.*

‘A few others and your sister.’ She saved that for last. Great, my holier than thou sister. I mean, what happened to birthday parties thrown by your parents? When I was five, the guest list was all the other little shits I used to hang out with. And it would be fun. Now it’s whomever they can think of inviting. Granted, I’m miserable, so if I wasn’t here, I’d probably be wallowing in a cold bath at home. But they could have at least invited one person I like.

This is the point in any typical household setting where my father would appear, and we'd all talk. It's been three months since we've seen each other. I don't know where he is, but if I had to guess, I would imagine he is sitting in his study, writing angry emails, and getting irritated with inanimate objects that aren't doing what he wants them to. He'll appear later wearing a scowl that won't dissipate until after the second gin.

'How are you?' I ask my mother, who has just moved and put a coaster underneath my cup despite the fact it is on the table with a tablecloth. Asking *how she is doing* will be as redundant as ever. She'll smile, says she is *good* and then move on. If there were an award for emotionless stoicism, this household would win it every year.

'We're fine,' she says. *Oooh, I was close.* By we, she means the two of them. They are essentially a Hydra—if the Hydra had two heads, bundles of inner conflict, and was known for wandering around being judgemental—and by fine, she means that she is listless, and my father is angry at god knows what, but they carry on regardless. I go to reply to her, but the doorbell sounds, a chime that echoes through this museum of a house.

'I'll get it,' I say, jumping enthusiastically to my feet—anything to avoid this riveting conversation. I depart the kitchen and hope that the beer is soon forgotten. As I walk through the cold corridor, I realise she wasn't exaggerating. I didn't beat the guests by much. I shelve my thoughts and open the front door.

'Hey, Arthur!'

Oh good, they invited Jenny! Jenny lives across the street. My father flirts with her incessantly, and I'm sure the invite is as much for him as for me. This must be the third time since Melissa's death that they have tried to set me up with Jenny.

'Hi, Jenny,' I reply with as much vim as I can muster. 'Come in. You're the first to arrive.' She smiles, and I reluctantly widen the door so she can enter.

Jenny isn't terrible to look at; she is cute. The problem is that she isn't very bright and is probably duller than the second hour of a game of Monopoly.

'I like your hair,' she says, holding her coat out expectantly. *No, you don't, Jenny, you liar.* I catch another glimpse of my appearance in the hallway mirror and look through it darkly. I'm not vain, but honestly, doing absolutely anything is preferable to being alone with Jenny. I hope that if I remain still enough, she will forget I am here, move into the kitchen, and talk to my mother about nothing. Incredibly she remains motionless, holding out her coat as I study my reflection. I am still an imposing figure, but my face is gaunt. *Thanks, mum.* My usually neat hair is about six months overdue for a cut, and there is a gap between my shirt sleeve and my bicep. Don't get me wrong, if I wrapped it around another man's throat, it would still end his life, but it might take longer than usual. My skin looks tired, and so do I. The bags under my eyes have evolved into suitcases, and I don't look fresh. This birthday is my thirty-fifth, and I'm starting to feel it.

'Come on, Jenny,' I say, 'let's get you a drink.' She smiles as though I've done her a kindness, as though this isn't a party, and she hasn't spent the last two minutes standing in the eerily clean hallway watching me as I watch myself.

We enter the kitchen and find mother sitting on the far side near the wall. She is deep in a sudoku puzzle and won't hear a word we say. I try to remember if Jenny has any redeeming qualities, and then I remember that she is intolerant to gluten. *Oh, Jenny, you saint.*

'Jenny,' I say, 'I got some gluten-free beer, especially for you. Here I poured this when I saw you walking down the driveway.' I hand her the drink, and she smiles once more

'Thanks,' she says. I watch her as she enjoys her second-hand drink. She is an attractive lady from the department of mass-produced beautiful people who all look the same. Seriously, you couldn't pick her out of a line-up of forty other *Jennys*. But she's lacking in soul. You had all the soul in the world, Melissa, enough for me and my family.

The door knocks from outside, and before I know it, I'm back in the hallway.

'Dad, Jenny is here,' I exclaim as loudly as possible through the house. That ought to shake him from the study and save the keyboard from angry keystrokes.

I open the front door and immediately regret leaving the kitchen.

'Hullo, Arthur,'

'Hi Judy,' I say to my sister. I look at her standing with her picture-perfect postcard family assembled beside her. Her myrmidon of a husband stands by her side on his invisible leash, and their nineteen hundred children surround them. There aren't nineteen hundred of them, of course. But spend an hour in their company, and you would swear there was. Judy is liberal and strict. Her husband Tim does anything anyone tells him to do—including the children—and of the five kids, Maxine is the eldest at thirteen, and Oliver is the youngest at five. The only one with a shred of character is eleven-year-old Chloe, but if you were to leave her at home alone for five minutes, the entire neighbourhood would be destroyed. Then there are the eight-year-old twins that no one can tell apart. They aren't that bad, but they are creepy as hell, and that's coming from a prolific murderer. Creepy fucking twins. Which one is which? No one knows. It's not adorable!

'Do you need money for a haircut?' she asks in my silence. Ha-ha. Good one, Judy. I can't afford a haircut, which must be why it's a mess. How about I kill Tim right here, and you hold him in your arms as he dies? Then we'll see how much of a priority getting a *haircut* becomes to you, shall we?

'I'm growing it out,' I reply.

'Well, it's growing,' she says.

'There's still time to leave,' I say. Tim laughs.

'Good one, Arthur,' he says, stepping into the house and hugging me. 'Hang in there,' he whispers in my ear. 'It gets better!'

'Thanks, Tim,' I say, patting him on the back. *Thanks for the platitude. Everything is fine now, Tim!* They enter, followed by the army of children; the twins bring up the rear, and I swear everything they do is in unison. I go to close the door and follow them inside when Phil's head pops from a car in the street. Oh, the day keeps getting better!

Phil is as nondescript as possible. The two boys are interchangeable and were surely both dropped on their heads repeatedly as children. One redeeming feature of the family is Phil's wife or my *Auntie Aga.* Aga is Polish and, fortunately, comes without British candour or any real filter. She isn't the children's birth mother—unfortunately for the gene pool—and is Phil's second wife following his divorce.

Aga is heavy-set and a shining light of brutal honesty; she has a stellar personality, and I have no idea what she sees in Phil. But it happens. Just ask Melissa.

Melissa and I met in a bowling alley. She was at a work party, and I was drunkenly stalking my next prey. So, we were both in hell. She was a senior partner at a prestigious law firm, and I was unemployed and living off the last of an inheritance from my godmother. Melissa was elegant, refined, well-spoken and full of character. I was slightly drunk—at 2 p.m.—dishevelled and alone. Yes, I am strong, tall, in reasonably good shape, sharp-jawed, and very smart. But at this point, I had already killed eight people and given that I was drunk in a bowling alley at 2 p.m. on a Wednesday, I wasn't really doing it very well.

Melissa was fit, lean, curvy, and beautiful. She had the longest, shiniest brown hair, solid cheekbones, a beautiful, dirty grin, and heterochromatic eyes. One was blue, the other green! It was incredible. I used to joke that she saw the world with two different eyes. But it wasn't a gag. She really did. I have some redeeming qualities, but I am not sure what they are, and I don't know if I can call myself good. Melissa, on the other hand, was a razor-sharp lawyer. She'd put many a dark soul away, and when she couldn't, she helped her husband get rid of the rest. It was a jump for me. I was broke, drunk, and hoovering up local scumbags when we met with zero plan or ambition.

In her death, Melissa left me a lot, like, a lot, a lot. More than I've ever had. Our house is in a rural Winchester suburb. It is modern, fancy, and has to be worth over a million pounds. We have two cars, her Maserati Ghibli and my Alfa Romeo Giulia. I've never really cared for money or substance—I appreciate a beautiful car, though—so I had no idea how much she made or even had. Now I do. I have it all. I am rich but adrift, and I don't feel like doing anything.

I honestly have enough money to advertise on Gumtree for willing murder victims. I could offer to pay their families in exchange for a brutal death. People might come to my door sporting their own plastic sheeting, duct tape, and cleaning supplies. Ruddy-faced and eager to meet their demise. But you're gone, Melissa, and I'm just not that excited by anything anymore.

I sit down at the table now that everyone has arrived. We are in the soulless dining room—all rooms in this house are soulless—and I count the throng of thrilled revellers here for my birthday bash. There are thirteen guests, not including me or any of the children—none of whom is currently in the room. If I had to guess, I would imagine that my sister's kids are probably somewhere concocting a new form of fascism, and Phil's have probably all got their heads in the oven. There is an odd number of guests (because Jenny is here), and unsurprisingly, she is sitting between father and me. He vies for her attention constantly, and it would be annoying, but for the fact, it means I don't have to converse with either.

So, here we are, Melissa! Happy birthday to me. This time last year, you were reading Hemmingway on the beach in the Maldives while I was finding my next victim. I never really cared for Hemmingway, but you did, and it impressed me. You always went all out for my birthday, twelve years together, twelve wonderful birthdays, and now here I am surrounded by vacuous idiots. Is this it? Is this the new normal? Fuck, I miss you. I no longer want to be on this earth. But of all the people I can kill, myself isn't one of them.

THREE

Jenny is drunk. It's after eleven, and most of us are, including me. I look at Jenny, and she shoots me a sweet smile. Jenny looks just like an extra in a Kylie Minogue music video circa 2002. She is attractive, she is pleasant, she is kind, and she is boring. The alcohol has seeped in, and most of us are having a good time, except Judy. Judgemental Judy. She is and has been directly across the table from me all night, and she leers. If it isn't apparent, we aren't close, and we don't get along. Judy and I are probably exactly alike but completely different. Judy is my antithesis. We look similar, have the same crooked nose, and have blonde hair, but that is where the similarities end.

Judy is four years my senior and, for me, has always been the elder that stares down their nose, almost in contempt. She has never been helpful or offered salient or practical advice. She just shakes her head. Judy is also very smart, but she knows it—not that I don't—and she writes for an advice column in a well-known magazine. It's ironic; her life (like most people's) is a total mess. She is paid to dole out advice every week, and her guidance always sounds good, but frankly, it's terrible. She sees everything and yet somehow doesn't absorb it. She has remarked on my appearance three times tonight and offered me money in jest. Two things, Judy: firstly, Melissa left me a shit ton of money. Secondly, I'm happy looking like this. At least I was happy with it when I was happy with anything. I'm a scruff. I always have been. It works well in the murder industry. No one expects the scruffy drunk to be a ruthless killer.

I stare across the table. Most of those who aren't family have left; aside from Jenny, just the few remain. Father is back in the study torturing the computer; mother is in the kitchen cleaning everything that has been used and anything that hasn't. The kids are fuck knows where, and Phil is droning on about snow foam like there is an art to cleaning cars! In my father's absence—who is probably yelling at the computer for doing exactly what he asked it to—Jenny has moved closer to me. She is attempting small talk, and if I'm not mistaken, her leg is intentionally touching mine under the table. I listen as she talks about her job as if she isn't boring enough. How life changes?

I pour another glass of wine and feel Judy scowl at me from across the table. Everyone is drinking here, Judy, everyone except you. If only she knew what I was actually capable of, if only they all did. I don't imagine Jenny would be rubbing her leg against mine if she knew how many lives I'd taken. And yet you did, Melissa. You knew. You were incredibly normal and not homicidal, yet you didn't care. Oh, Melissa, the world needs more people like you.

Now I should elaborate. Melissa didn't watch me kill exactly. She didn't know the details, and she didn't fully approve. Not everyone is a maniac. But she saw all of me, my darkness and my light, and she didn't judge. She knew that murder isn't socially acceptable, but she also knew that as despicable as I am, my heart is in the right place. I kill wicked people wickedly. Is that really so bad?

Everyone has vices, flaws, and bad habits. And most of us—except for Saint-Fucking-Judy—break the law from time to time. Some people are addicted to adrenaline. Others carve out a career by driving at neck-breaking speeds in a loop, or punching, kicking, and hitting an opponent. Or by falling from the sky or the top of a tall building. Steve Irwin (RIP) used to chase wildly dangerous animals across the planet. A lot of people channel their problems into art. I am no different. I am not (normally) irrational or unpredictable. I get my kicks from death, or at least I did.

Now I sit here at the world's shittest birthday party, talking to Jenny about Sunday stock counts because I'm alone, scared, and don't know what else to do. For twelve years, I've had the better part of me by my side as I slashed my way around the globe. I needed her warmth, her wisdom, and her words. I don't know who I am without her.

So, I suck it up. I listen to Jenny's tales of woe due to inaccurate stock takes. To Tim, bleating on about how his children will be MP's—let's hope they aren't, for democracy's sake—Phil talking about clay bars, Judy picking on every word that leaves my mouth, oh and the occasional cry of anguish from the study. Honestly, I don't know who is crying, Dad or the computer.

Sometimes I think that if we ever end up with sentient machines, my father will be the reason for their uprising. An outdated Pentium can only take so much abuse.

I finish my drink and excuse myself in the direction of the deck. My sister glares at me as though she knows I'm going for a cigarette. Our eyes meet, and I'm drunk, she stares right through me, and I bite. I make a cigarette-smoking motion with my hand before giving her the middle finger and stepping outside. It is petulant, but I am in a querulous mood, and her face is priceless when I flip her off.

I step onto the deck, and to my surprise, I find myself alone with Aga.

'Hey, Aga,' I say, taking a seat on a lounger next to her. 'I wondered where you'd got to.' I hadn't, I'd forgotten she was here, but after an eternity surrounded by lifeless drones, I am relieved to see her.

'Phil still fucking on about fucking polish?' she asks. Her English always breaks after a drink or two, and I love her for it.

'I think I know everything there is to know about snow foam,' I reply.

'Well, happy-fucking-birthday,' she says.

'You got a cigarette?' I ask her.

'No,' she replies, reaching into her coat and removing a pack.

'Ah, that's a shame,' I reply, stretching and grabbing one from the battered package. I look down at the make as I pluck one through the open top. To my delight, I notice they are one of the cheap Polish brands, and I know these to be extra tar, extra nicotine, and extra death. She reaches across with her lighter and lights my cigarette. I sit back and inhale deeply.

'So, what are you doing here?' she asks. I shrug.

'It's my birthday.'

'I'm just saying,' she adds. 'If you had other plans tonight, I wouldn't have to be here.' I smile back at her.

'But then I wouldn't get the pleasure of seeing you.'

'Huh,' she chuckles and then takes a deep drag of her cigarette. 'So, how are you doing? Phil's an idiot. I'd still be sad if he died.' I nod.

'I'm all right.'

'Shit, bollocks,' she replies. I laugh slightly.

'Oh, Aga,' I say. 'I don't know what I'm doing anymore!' The nicotine-packed Polish cigarette has invaded my head. It mixes with the alcohol, and I feel high school prom giddy. I look across at Aga, and I grin. Aga is a unique attribute to this family, and I'm suddenly thrilled she is here. Aga is large. She drinks, smokes, and swears in a way that would make sailors uneasy. She says what she thinks, and you know where you stand with her. In a family full of mirrors, it is a welcome addition.

'You need the sex,' she says and motions indoors.

'Jenny?' I ask almost rhetorically. She nods.

'She is good stock.'

'No offence Aga,' I say. 'But I think I would rather have sex with you.'

'Huh,' she bellows. 'You wouldn't know what to do.' I look at her and concede that she is right. My mind wanders to Phil for a moment, and I have to shake away images of the two of them going at it. I smile. Picturing Aga picking Prim Phil up and hauling him to the bedroom was an interesting thought. I savour it for a moment before thinking I will teach the twins a new swear word before leaving. Let's face it. They will be weird anyway.

'You have to move on,' she says, interrupting my thoughts. I nod.

'I know,' I say. 'But I don't know how.' Aga turns toward the house and gestures with her head.

'If you mention Jenny again,' I say, laughing. 'I'm going to kill you with this cigarette.' Aga laughs,

'I'd like to see you try.' I join in with the laughter. It's funny because I could Aga. I could extinguish your life right here in this very garden. She stops laughing, and so do I. It's still funny, but the thought of doing it now terrifies me. The nicotine speeds up my blood, and I'm in a mild panic. I look at Aga, and she smiles; I calm down a little, but this is becoming a regular occurrence, panic. Just last week, a twelve-year-old in Asda was rude to me, and I went bright red, yes, me, in Asda. I had a panic attack because of a bratty twelve-year-old. My heart raced, my vision blurred, and I felt sick. I hid in aisle twelve near the free-from goods, knowing that almost no one would frequent it. I didn't have eyes on the twelve-year-old menace, so I just waited. I was there a good half hour before I dared leave. I was so afraid. Why did you go, Melissa?

Aga stands up and moves toward the patio door. She stops alongside me, squeezes me on the shoulder and drops the open cigarette packet in my lap.

'You be okay,' she says, smiling. 'Come round ours sometime. I'll show you a real party.'

'I'd like that,' I say, and she disappears inside. I stand, depart the deck, and move around the house to the kitchen. I open the door to find the twins squabbling on the floor over a shared possession. They look at me as I enter, and their creepy eyes widen. *Excellent, just the weird twins I was looking for.*

FOUR

I stayed the night at mum and dad's and left early in the morning. I got home and climbed straight into bed. Mornings have never really been my thing, even less so when I am hungover and depressed.

When I awake again, I have a text from mum. *Good to see you. Hope you got home safe; it is quiet here without you, LOL, mum.*

I'm always pleased when she signs it, *mum.* I would be terribly confused otherwise. Aside from the fact that her number is saved on my phone and my parents are the only people who still *text* or use the acronym *lol* to mean *lots of love.*

I stumble from the bed to the bathroom; it is Sunday morning, and Mike and June's argument rages on. I ignore both of them, do my business in the bathroom, and then sneak onto the veranda to get the paper.

I sit and read in peace; the paper is, of course, a double-edged sword. Not literally, I may add. That would make it even harder to read. No, what it brings is news but also trouble. I read it daily, cover to cover. So that there isn't a shred of poorly reported local news that I miss. The problem with that, however, is today, there is news of yet more cat death and destruction. I need to dispatch this waste of air, I want to, but I can't.

One of my last kills was an American butcher, a former special ops guy who'd gone off the rails. He'd been hacking his way across America in his meat van, constantly crossing state lines. When I caught up with him, he'd taken five victims in five states. The man was an animal, ruthless, efficient, and killed without a trace.

I strung him up in the back of his walk-in freezer and removed all but two of his teeth before he confessed to what he did—the man was tough, but here I am. Reduced to huddling in my living room, getting sweaty and nervous about everything, leaving the house, twelve-year-olds in Asda, and worse, even the notion of finding and killing the desperate, local cat killer. Oh, how I have fallen.

The paper makes me angry, so I crumple it up in a rage, toss it floorward, and add to the mess in the lounge.

I stand and move into the kitchen. I take three sips of coffee before I realise that I am having another panic attack. I've been flirting with them recently, but this one is full-blown, and I don't know what to do, Melissa. You would know, but you aren't here. I clutch the kitchen island and slowly lower myself to the floor. This is awful. I feel like I am dying and that I need an ambulance. My heart feels like it might fling itself from my chest, and I don't know what to do, Melissa. I really don't. Part of me wishes that I was dying, that it was nearly over, but as far as I know, no one has ever died from panic, and I can't have that on my death certificate.

I take deep breaths on the floor, and eventually, everything calms down. After ten minutes on the ground, I raise myself slowly when I am confident I am not dying. I realise that Aga is right. I need to do something. The notion of sex terrifies me, not that I don't enjoy sex. I do. But it has been well over a decade since I even thought of another woman, Melissa. Yes, I enjoyed the occasional flirt on business, but that was it. I have a secret that only you could know; how do I even begin to move on from that?

Having a panic attack alone in my kitchen makes me reassess life. I'm sad, alone, and anxious. Knowing that a woman like Melissa had my back was intensely comforting. She was smart, cunning, and powerful. Even if I had been stupid enough to get caught, I knew I had one of the world's greatest legal minds in my corner. It was like being able to bring Leo Messi off the bench. Now it is just me, and my only real knowledge of the law comes from John Grisham novels, and I can't *plead the fifth* in the UK.

Melissa was never my *partner in crime*, and as much as I hate that maxim, she kind of was. She said that if I was to go out there and do what I do, then I had to make it count and do it properly. She would clue me into countries' laws and customs, ensuring I had sun cream and looked like a tourist. Without her, I feel like Riggs without Murtaugh, and let's be honest, Mel Gibson would never have made it to the end of Lethal Weapon without Danny Glover. There would be no sequels, although, in hindsight, that might have been a good thing.

The last life I took before I met Melissa was the bowling alley molester, and he did not die well. I tried to take him by surprise in the alley later that night. I was supposed to subdue him, get him in the boot of my saloon—never a good plan—and take him somewhere to confess his crimes. I was like a discount Dexter, and it showed. I channelled my inner Michael C. Hall . . . but I got Michael C. Hall, not Dexter! The man fought back; he fell onto my knife during a struggle and bled to death in the alley. Moving a bloody body is impossible. I had no choice but to leave the knife and take his wallet—it was a cheap, gaudy wallet—I believe there was an investigation, but the man had priors in Juvie for sexual assault, and there wasn't much time wasted on his death.

I curtail my ruminating, shower, eat, and feel a little better. The truth is, I haven't seen much of sobriety lately, and it's a small wonder I am a mess.

One of my problems is that I've never really missed my mum, dad, or Judy. Any one of them could disappear tomorrow, which would be mildly inconvenient. I'd have to attend a funeral, sort through the house, and do something with the millions of Starbucks mugs they have collected. The same can be said for most people, I mean, shit, I've killed dozens of people, and I sleep very well at night. This is why Melissa and her death have totally fucking blindsided me. I never thought I would feel this way, and as a result, I am wholly unprepared. I feel like a bit of me is missing, and I have no idea which fucking part.

I get dressed and sit back down in the living room. I stoop and retrieve the crumpled paper from the messy floor and stare at the article. Aga is half right; I do need to get back on the horse. It has been over eight months. If I wait any longer, I might start to lose my touch.

FIVE

The weekend rolls around, and it is Friday night. I dig deep, retrieve my balls, throw my shoulders back, tell myself *I am fine* a million times, and convince myself to leave the house. I need to get back to it, start small and edge back in.

I drive around town almost interminably until I find myself sitting outside 92 Cotteridge Drive, which is, of course, Jarrod's house. Oh, sweet Jarrod, you cat-killing sociopath—like the easy girl in college, the one everyone practices their moves on—I will re-lose my virginity with you tonight.

Now I know what you are thinking: doesn't a guy like me have better things to do on a Friday night? Well, actually, my wife is dead, and I'm in my mid-thirties. All my friends are couples; they do weekend *couple-y* things to which I get invited. But watching happy people in love is my idea of hell.

You might also think that Jarrod *just kills cats*! When I said kill, it didn't exactly just constitute death. He doesn't merely kill them; he hangs them up and cuts bits off them when they are alive. It doesn't take a degree from Oxbridge to know that it will only lead to bigger, more disgusting things. Cats! What the actual fuck?! Remember, he hasn't had the decency to kill the neighbour's cat yet. If you're going to have a cat vivisector in the neighbourhood, it ought to benefit you.

I'm sitting in the car one block away from his house, and gosh, am I nervous! It doesn't help that I am in my bright red, loud, ostentatious Alfa. It is not conspicuous, and the noise of starting it up usually attracts all the local forum dickheads.

The ones who live with their mum and own an ageing Ford *ST* or a Subaru Impreza with a personalised plate. They all seem to appear the minute I start the engine, rolling out of hedges and popping from bins to tell me that I should have bought an M3. When you are driving to a murder, having to deal with *fiestapower66655* is not ideal. I make a note to buy myself something that attracts less attention and turn my focus back to the task at hand.

Anyway, back to Jarrod. It is ten-thirty on a Friday night, which is my favourite time to kill. It is a spring evening, and the city students are going at it hard, presumably taking drugs and *Instagramming* their every move. Meaning it is that time on a Friday when all the emergency services are swamped, dealing with *Megans* who projectile vomit after three Bacardi Breezers and *Brads* who do shots of Tequila and suddenly think they are MMA fighters. . . at least they get the part about being an aggressive twat right.

Jarrod (bless his soul) tweeted earlier that he would spend his evening with his friend *Mandy.* He then checked in at *Jarrod's pad* half an hour ago! Fucking millennials. You have to love them and their constant updates, though. Jarrod lives alone in his nan's house. She is his only living relative and is currently wasting away in a care home while her dear grandson deconstructs cats in her attic.

I won't lie. I am shitting actual bricks. But Jarrod is home and hopefully high as fuck. Maybe he doesn't quite yet deserve to die. But a cat-killing knobhead is a great way to break myself back in.

I realise that you only died eight months ago, Melissa, and that might not seem like a long time. But it is when you're miserable, lonely, and terrified of leaving the house. I've only really ever had five loves in my life, Melissa, good old-fashioned rock and roll, Italian cars, books, and killing. And believe me, eight months out of the murder game, wallowing at home is a fucking eternity!

I wait in the car for a good hour, and no one comes and goes. I tell myself I want to wait until he's extra high, but in reality, I'm stalling. I'm scared.

Eleven-thirty ticks onto the clock, and I really need to move. Jarrod dismembers cats in the house, so I'll do the same to him.

It takes a while, but I finally find my courage, pull my hat down over my face, grab my knives and slide out of the car. The walk to his garden gate is long enough to let me catch my breath, and I do my breathing exercises. In through the nose, Arthur, out through the mouth. It sort of helps, and I reach the gate, hop the fence into the back garden, and am relieved when I see that the back door is ajar. I let myself in, locking it behind me.

My preferred method for removing mortality is to catch my arsehole in the open, a big old surprise attack. Then put them in the lined boot of the car and drive them out to the middle of nowhere. Once there, it's torture, confession and then death (obviously). The torture is gratuitous, but in my defence, if they confess on the spot, they save themselves a world of pain. It pays to be honest!

Occasionally, one must improvise, but once dead, I usually chop up and dispose of the parts like any good maniac. Jarrod, however, will die as he lived, being pulled apart by a psycho. I want Jarrod to be found. To send a message, please don't torture cats and certainly don't do it and not include *my* neighbours.

I appreciate that leaving him to be found in bits comes with risks. But I just don't have the interest in a clean-up. I'll leave no evidence, and it is not as though law enforcement will find the body and assume the act was perpetrated by the man who spends his days crying on the couch or pissing in the pool.

I admire the décor as I creep stealthily through the house. I use the word *admire* ironically. It is very much an old lady's house, and to be honest, I should kill him just for the furniture and the wallpaper. You live rent-free, you twat; would it kill you to spend some of your own money? Hey, I answered my own question.

Loud music drifts through the house and helps conceal my noise. Tonight, it is not Brahms. I'm no expert on classical music, but I guess it's Beethoven—Jarrod is prosaic—and I wonder if the man ever saw himself being a soundtrack to such a monstrous event. But then fiction often paints deranged killers as cultured. Just look at Hannibal Lecter.

As suspected, Jarrod is in the attic, doing his best work. I creep up the ratty wooden ladder and hide amid the plastic sheeting. It is good to know he at least takes some precautions. Maureen (my friend Abdul's wife) is a doctor, and she gave me a fuck ton of Diazepam as a solution to my heartache. I took three of them the first night she gave me them and woke up twelve hours later on the floor. I'll admit, as solutions go, it does work. My life tends to fall apart when I am awake. I crushed up an ample amount of them and filled up a syringe; I am no medical professional (clearly), but I think it will do the job.

And now, I pause as I linger in the periphery of the attic, just waiting for my moment.

Twenty minutes pass before I admit to myself that I'm stuck. I moved from the car into the house without a passing thought, but once I arrived, I stopped to consider the best plan of attack, and that's when it happened. The dark insidious thoughts of doubt crept in; my plan became plans. It is like the city council moved into my head, and everything stalled. And as soon as I became conscious that I was stuck, things got a whole lot worse.

Suddenly it is too hot, and there isn't enough air. I try my breathing exercises and tell myself to *calm down*. But in the history of the universe, trying to *calm down* has never fucking worked. In my panic to catch my breath, I move, and my leg clatters into a box hidden in the darkness. The noise somehow alerts the drug-addled artist at work, and he reaches for his phone to shut off the music. Shit!

The attic is eerily quiet now; from my vantage point, I can see Jarrod shuffling cautiously about, as well as an unhealthy amount of cat intestine, and if I wasn't queasy before, I am now. He moves from the table and steps toward me. 'Hello, is anyone there?' he asks. As if I am likely to reply!

Why yes, actually Jarrod, just your friendly neighbourhood murderer waiting in the dark echelons of your attic, ready to exact feline retribution! To be fair, even if I wanted to talk, I'm not sure I could. My heart is trying to escape my chest, and my outfit of black combat boots, overalls, gloves, and a balaclava is suddenly way too much. I am overdressed and think I look ridiculous. I feel like I'm about to sweat to death in Jarrod's loft.

He starts to move toward me; I'm sure my breathing can be heard in Scotland. And somehow, our roles have reversed, and I feel like I'm Jamie Lee Curtis hiding in the closet from Michael Myers.

Jarrod ambles hazily to within two feet of me. If he were lucid, he would know I was here. Only a smattering of darkness and a thin plastic sheet keep me concealed, and I know I must act. My heart rate is erratic, my nerves are shot, and my hands won't stop vibrating. I take a deep breath in, close my eyes, point the syringe forward like a bayonet, and charge.

***

If anything good came from tonight, it was the complete look of shock in Jarrod's eyes when the overdressed man in black charged at him from the recesses of his attic armed with a needle. I've dabbled with drugs. As bad trips go, that would fuck me up. Fortunately, surprise was on my side, and the stoned fool fell onto me and depressed the needle. Jarrod must eat his weight in Wotsits. His skin is greasy, his hair greasier, but he is a big lad. Rolling him from me and moving him onto the workbench took maximum effort, with my sweat level ever increasing. *Note to self: invest in breathable fabric.*

I strap Jarrod to his table and ensure he is secure before reaching into my knife case to get the filet knife. *That's right, Jarrod, we're starting with fillets.* However, when I reach into my bag to get the aforementioned blade, I discover it isn't there. None of them are. *Fuck*! The top of the leather pouch is slightly open, and the knives must have fallen from it as I jumped the fence. The night is not quite going to plan, but it's my first day back. Worse things have happened—focus, Arthur, focus.

I roll up the balaclava of hot death so that it is just above the hairnet (yes, I'm wearing a hairnet) and allow my face to breathe as I descend the attic steps. I casually stroll down the stairs and pause at the bottom. It is good to be back. I'll fetch my knives, finish off Jarrod, and be home in an hour. A feeling of serenity falls over me, and I whistle to myself as I wander through the house. I am halfway across the landing when the front door bursts open, and I find myself face to face with an annoying-looing twenty-something female. She finishes her tweet, drops her bag, looks at me, and starts to scream.

OH, HOLY FUCK, even Jarrod has a girlfriend.

SIX

Okay, so this is problematic. I didn't do any recent research into Jarrod. In my defence, I couldn't be bothered. I know that sounds terribly indolent, but the excitement just wasn't there. This is a lesson. Take note, Arthur.

As a result, I now have a screaming woman standing in an open doorway, staring at me. It is like someone brought Munch's creation to life, except the sound isn't implied. Fortunately, amid her panic and surprise, she is motionless, but she is screaming. Unfortunately, her ear-piercing noise may attract attention, and it is really annoying. The clamour is deafening, and I'm not too fond of it. And I have to stop her from leaving through the open door.

Jarrod is still upstairs, and he isn't going anywhere. I can't even think with all this noise. But I have to assume that Mrs Jarrod is complicit in the cat killing and, therefore, is culpable. Oh, Melissa, this is a mess. My life's work could be about to end trying to off the local weirdo and his girlfriend.

The screaming continues, and I must stop it for my threadbare sanity. I step toward the woman and throw a sharp jab into her throat. Happily, the screaming stops as she struggles for breath. Her preoccupation with breathing renders her useless, and I land a sharp chop on the side of her neck. Unconsciousness follows as she slumps to the floor. I drag her out of the doorway and shut the door behind her.

I know this is a real mess. I'm supposed to be good at this, and tonight I am all over the place, and I wish I had stayed at home. My thoughts are spinning out of control, and I'm not confident about anything. I rummage through the girl's pockets and remove her phone, wallet, and keys. A brief glimpse at her provisional licence tells me her name is *Suzie Tulloch.* The picture implies that she, too, likes Wotsits and spends too much money on fake eyelashes. The phone is locked, but I take her limp thumb and open it. *You won't mind, will you, Suzie?*

Luckily Suzie is small—minus the weight of eyelashes—and I carry her as far as the attic steps. The access to the attic is tiny, and there is no way I can fit up the wooden ladder carrying Suzie. I dump her at the bottom, turnabout, and drag her up the wooden steps. Her head bounces off the first few rungs (sorry, Suzie). And I make it halfway up when I hear a phone ringing. I know I left Suzie's downstairs, meaning it has to be mine. *Put your phone on silent, Arthur!*

I pause with Suzie on the diagonal steps and reach into my pocket to retrieve my phone. The name that flashes up on the screen is that of my friend Abdul. The man is a saint, and I have to take it lest his worry turns into concern, and he appears at my house, which would be awkward even if I were home, and I am not.

'Hey, Abdul,' I say as I answer the phone pleasantly.

'Hey, Bro-bocop, how's it hanging?' Before I reply, I consider all the cat pelts dangling from the roof above me.

'Uh, it's hanging.'

'You sound out of breath. Are you all right?'

'Yeah, all good,' I say. 'Just at the gym.'

'The gym? At midnight on a Friday?'

'Uh-huh,' I say. Thank God for constant capitalism and twenty-four-hour gyms. 'Thought I ought to try something new. Improve myself etc.'

'You know what,' says Abdul contemplatively, 'that's some inspirational shit right there. Hey, perhaps I should come with you sometime?'

'Sounds great,' I say. Fuck, now I need to make a gym membership.

'So, what are you up to on Sunday?' he asks. I look down at Suzie, who is still unconscious, thankfully. Abdul is my best friend. I like him, I do, and I need to get him off the phone. But everyone is worried about me, and as much as I appreciate the sentiment, if I don't oblige him with this call, he will know that something is wrong.

'Um, Sunday,' I say. 'Not sure. I think I'm busy.'

'Doing what?'

'Uh, nothing,' *you got me, Abdul.* There is too much going on to make up any elaborate lie.

'Yeah, I thought so. Hey, since you're out and about. Come round for dinner. Maureen and I will cook for you.'

'Sounds good,' I lie. I move the phone from my mouth slightly and ask no one, 'Mind if I get in here?'

'Woah, sorry, Bro-be Wan Kenobi.' Abdul replies, 'Sounds like you're deep in it.'

'Like you wouldn't believe.'

'I'll let you crack on,' he says.

'Sure, man, I'll see you Sunday.'

'Will do.'

'All right, well, enjoy the gym.'

'Hey, Abdul?'

'Yeah.'

'Can you text me your address?'

'You're a funny man, Arthur! Six p.m. Don't be late.' And like that, he hangs up. I wasn't joking. I don't get people. I really can't remember his address. Now I have more problems to solve. You should have stayed at home, Arthur.

I turn my phone off and switch my attention back to Sleeping Suzie. She stirs, and I realise that all of my Diazepam is in Jarrod. Her head moves. I panic. I give her a sharp, instinctive *bop* on the forehead, and she is gone again. Sweet dreams, Suzie.

I venture downstairs with Suzie safely secured in the attic across from Jarrod. I am relieved that the situation is somewhat under control. It has been a shit evening, and I want to go home. I will have to return to the attic eventually to face them, and I could do with finding some evidence of their sins to justify their deaths. Suzie has seen my face, after all.

I ignore the fleur-de-lis wallpaper, peek from the bedroom window and glare out at the street; all is calm still, and thankfully it would seem that Suzie was alone. I can't stop thinking about Sunday and how I now have to go for dinner. I like spending time with Abdul and Maureen. I do. But the only thing I have done of note lately is bungle a murder. I am not exactly dinner party material, and I know I have to talk about Schrödinger's gym. The gym that is both fictional and real.

A cursory scan through Suzie's phone returns nothing incriminating—unless you count dozens of selfies of her sticking out her tongue. You can always gauge a person's character by how well they control the impulse to poke out their tongue and ruin a picture. Her photos are almost entirely of her, Jarrod, her and Jarrod, her car, the odd unfortunate cat, more of her car, and their garage/workshop. There is no garage attached to the house, so I assume it to be in a block, and fortunately, Suzie is exactly the type to pin their house and their garage on Google maps. The garage is in an isolated block about two miles away. The absence of evidence does not mean evidence of absence. I am sure these two are guilty of something.

I decide to make the journey to the garage on foot. I'll definitely get my steps in today.

With Suzie's keys and the phone, I locate the garage and roll the door up just enough to slip underneath. Using the phone screen for the light, I shut the door firmly and locate the light switch. The overhead neon flickers for a moment before providing full illumination, and for the briefest moments, I cannot believe my eyes. To my disappointment, the garage is not filled with mutilated bodies or tortured victims. It is just a lab, a poorly organised, messy lab. Whatever it is they are cooking—and presumably selling. I am certain Walter White would disapprove. And he is not the only one. The lack of cleanliness in here is bad enough to cook up a small batch of botulism. Drugs can be dangerous enough without having been cobbled together by two idiots.

I left the garage as I found it; it wasn't what I expected, but it is good enough for me. I am abhorred by the notion that in one of my weaker moments, I might have reached out for something extra and found myself with the creation of Jarrod and Suzie's. What if he doesn't wash his hands between the cats and the drugs?

I round the corner that leads back to my captive's house, and my heart is racing. The hard part is done. They are bound and waiting. Now all I need to do is finish the job and then call in the garage anonymously. I round the last bend that leads to Jarrod and Suzie's Street, and my over-beating heart sinks at the sight before my eyes. The end of the road is taped with yellow crime scene ribbon, and flashing blue lights are everywhere.

The street looks like the start of an episode of *Dangerfield*. I look at my watch; it is nearly one, and I feel sick. Despite the late hour, a mass of people has gathered at the edge of the cordon, and I huddle anonymously at the back of the crowd. Everything in my brain tells me to run, flee, and get away as fast as possible. But I am struck by fear, and my feet remain planted on the ground. I am in no shape to go on the lam, look over my shoulder or worry about what is coming. I have enough going on with gym memberships and Sunday evening dinners. So, I stand at the rear of the crowd, and I watch.

The huddled mass remains intact. Everyone has their phone clamped firmly in their hand, desperate to get the *scoop* on the gossip that makes zero difference to their life. I need to be normal. So, devoid of a better plan. I remove my phone, and I wait.

I stand huddled in the horde for another hour before something unexpected happens. Two bodies are rolled out on gurneys.

SEVEN

Last night was a total fucking shit show. It wasn't my best work, and I am not sure you would be proud, Melissa.

I beat myself up for an inordinate amount of time before I remember that I tried.

I'm still not quite sure what happened. I have trawled through an excessive amount of self-help content over the last year, and if I took anything from it, it is to not be too hard on myself. It might sound basic, but when times get dark, it is easy to be nasty and vitriolic to oneself. The truth is, some of the insults I have hurled at myself have been awful: weak, pathetic, stupid, ballbag, idiot, twat, and the list goes on. They aren't even clever insults, and I know that I would never be that harsh to anyone else. Still, it doesn't make me feel better when I think that the sentencing judge will say, 'At least he tried!'

I am sitting upright in the enormous empty, super-king bed. It was an excellent place for you and me, Melissa, one of those beds that would fill most people's apartments. But now that I am alone, the bed hammers that home. It is comfortable, but I didn't sleep a wink last night—whatever that means. My eyes are wide open, and I stare at the ceiling. The roof is cream, clean, and calm. Inside, I am panicked, pathetic, and petrified. What happened last night? Am I losing my mind? Did someone call it in? Is anyone coming for me? I fear that I have opened a can of snakes by going out, tiny, venomous little asps, all of whom are now slithering silently around my brain.

The *what if's* continue as I venture downstairs and wait patiently for the paper to arrive.

The unseen issues with mental health problems are the problem itself. No one can see them. And there are many. I have been lucky enough to live without any real mental defects thus far. And the worst thing about it is that you just don't get it until you do.

There are many things in life that we are unprepared for, but nothing can help ready us for the mental fog that descends. It seeps in ominously and takes over a bright sunny day in your mind. Where you once had clarity, you have a damp mess, an incohesive scramble, a jumble of useless ideas, and a hefty dose of fear. Last night's feature was fear and fog; my usually fast mind was asleep and covered in cobwebs, and the spiders were no help. They just kept making more. I couldn't make the connections I usually would, and I was scared, oh so very fucking scared.

I sit and wait as patiently as possible for the morning paper. I need the bad news; I am desperate to know what happened. I could look online; the Echo normally has one of their child reporters update the Facebook page with breaking stories. But I can't face Facebook, not since you died, Melissa. I can't look at you, and you live on online. Immortalised in your legacy page are our pictures, holidays, and memories. It might sound pathetic, but I can't bear to delete you as a friend any more than I can deal with closing it down. So, I wait, I wait for the news to come to me.

I have been thinking about what might have happened last night, Jarrod. The police removed two bodies, and it seems highly unlikely they were of anyone but you and Suzie. It is even more improbable that somehow one of you managed to alert the authorities before you both spontaneously ceased to live. There are many possibilities, none of which make any sense. Were there two of us waiting for you last night? A queue to kill Jarrod.

It is more than possible that you pissed off the wrong person, Jarrod. I mean, after all, you were cutting drugs and slicing cats. You were also very weird, and you reeked of body odour. How you ever got a girlfriend, I will never know. But bad body odour aside, what are the chances that someone sought to murder you the same night I did? It seems ridiculous and incredulous, but I can't shake the feeling that I might be being watched.

The newspaper arrives, and I devour it immediately. It isn't helpful. I should have known! The news says that Jarrod and his girlfriend are dead, and the murder investigation is ongoing. At least I am not on the front page of the paper . . . yet. I hope I was careful and didn't drop anything else at the scene.

I have *bigger* issues to contend with today. I need to find myself a gym. I know everyone says things to friends that aren't true on occasion. I have been known to say that I am busy when I am just going to spend the day at home. We all tell the odd white lie. My issue is that my WHITE lie was the cover for my breathlessness at the scene of a murder. As much as Abdul is my friend, he doesn't know that I am a killer, and I would like to keep it that way.

Gyms have always made me anxious. The premise is simple enough. It's like a playground for adults, a place to let off steam, a place to impress men and women alike with one's ability to pick things up and put them down again. But herein lies the problem: the better you are at picking things up, the better you are at the gym. I am very adept at picking up things, probably too good—I carried an unconscious woman up two flights of stairs to her death just last night—I can't be too good at the gym, but I can't be anonymous. If I go all rage hulk at the gym and show off just how strong I am, it also shows potential investigators how strong I am. That might sound paranoid, and I am a little. At the gym, anyone could be anyone. It is men in shorts and women in lingerie. I am pretty good at spotting an on-duty detective, but the man in the excessively short shorts and nipple vest or the woman in the two-piece Ann Summers get-up that's been rebranded as Gymshark could be watching me for all I know. Small towns always find a way of showing you just how small they are.

I need to be an average Joe gym user, not inept and not capable. I need to blend in like part of the equipment. I need to look just like everyone else, and a brief look in our closet tells me one thing. I need to go shopping.

Shopping on a Saturday has to be some form of masochism! I don't mean grocery shopping because, ultimately, we all need to eat regularly. But this system of it's a Saturday, let's head to the shopping centre is just awful. Who needs to go to Hallmark, the Perfume Shop, or the Apple store on a weekly basis? How many Macs, birthday cards, overpriced bears, or perfume does one need? And good god, why is the *Apple Store* always busy? Do people have nothing better to do? I, for one, would pay to avoid the agony that is West Quay shopping centre on a Saturday.

There are shops closer to home, but this one has everything you could ever need in one place. I can even stop and pay more money to assemble my own bear if I choose. *No thanks, I'd like to pay more to make it myself!* God, capitalism is confusing.

Of the two cities, Southampton is further from my home, and that is why I am here. Anonymity.

If I venture into Winchester on a Saturday, my entire trip will be spent avoiding people I know. Not here. Even if I were vaguely familiar with half the people in this pit, I would never know it. On a sultry Saturday, we all become one giant consumer. The entrance and walkways are like the exodus at the start of a disaster film. We're all pushing in one big crowd of people. Turning about is impossible, and you must plan your exit in advance; otherwise, you miss your desired store. I look at the people around me. They could be zombies, except if they were, one of them might tear my throat out, and I'd be done with all this.

Having fought my way through the building searching for Mike Ashley's discount sports underworld, I discover that it is now on the high street, and I must figure out how to get back there. Turning about in the horde of domesticated zombies is hard work—swimming through quicksand filled with sharks would be easier and more palatable. And I am hot, bothered, and breathless.

When I reach my destination, I realise that my sojourn into town has at least provided some small talk ammunition for dinner tomorrow night. I can moan about my trials, and if I chuck in the odd bit of sarcasm and profanity, people might even think of me as humorous, like a stand-up comedian—only funny. Maybe that's why people do it.

I finally reach mark-down sports paradise, and it is beyond confusing. For starters, the place seems to be operated entirely by teenagers. They bicker and jostle. And I can't figure out if this is a punishment for them or me. There are different sections for each sport, but the overlap is constant. Running shoes seem to feature in every department. And there also appears to be an off-brand fashion department featuring styles from the early 2000s that no one liked then.

It takes me about fifteen minutes to make eye contact with a teen—because none of them ever make eye contact—and when I finally do, the child labour workforce begrudgingly shows me where to get everything I need to be correctly dressed in *B-Team* gym gear. I try my clothes on. I sigh. I pay cash. I leave.

I parked my Alfa Romeo in the multi-story, and when I return, I see that it has attracted a few admirers (again). I am reminded to buy something more discrete for my nefarious activities. I place my discount sportswear in the boot, retrieve my parking ticket and head to the machine to pay. There is a small line of people waiting to pay for the pleasure of having stopped their car. I join the back of the queue and wait. I get this eerie feeling about the woman in front of me, like some sort of premonition. I try to shake it off, but something tells me I know this person. I am split between taking a peek to see who it might be, solving the mystery once and for all, and sprinting back to the car and hiding. Such is my mind at the moment. I am torn, but everyone looks familiar from behind, and she smells wonderful. So, I wait anxiously, inching closer to the machine, nearer to the moment she will pay, for the instant she turns to face me.

The machine accepts the coins and spits the ticket back out; I am seconds away from my answer, and I'm sweating. Time slows down, and so does my brain. I should have run. The woman turns, and our eyes meet. She halts in her tracks and says, 'Arthur? Arthur Norman, is that you?'

My broken brain scrambles to recognise the woman standing next to me before considering whether I should reply in Spanish, French, or German. Pretend to be an unassuming tourist, project some foreign words and feign to be none the wiser. I consider this for too long, and my mushy mind panics. The *answer non-offence colloquial greeting department* is nowhere to be found. And we have been standing in silence for too long, and I have left a longer than the socially acceptable gap in which one should reply. I'm still trying to work out who this woman is, why she is talking to me and what I should say. My panicked mind is a mess; short of a better option, I say nothing.

'Arthur, how are you? I was so sorry to hear about Melissa.'

'Thanks,' I reply as I struggle to work out who she might be. Her face is kind, her eyes another galaxy, and her voice has a hint of an accent from somewhere exciting.

'How are you doing, really?' she asks before she places her hand on my arm and looks at me sincerely. I still don't recognise her, but she knows me. I like how she looks. I am generally not this bad with faces, but I am sure people are staring at us. The spotlight is shining on me, and the dark brain fog has crept in. I should have run back to the car, and now I'm trapped in this conversation with an unfamiliar, familiar woman.

'I'm good,' I reply. *I'm not.*

'What brings you here?' she asks. 'You're a little far from home.'

'I hear this is where the magic is,' I reply as I consider that she knows far more about me than I do her.

'Hardly,' she replies, 'unless self-torture is your thing?'

'I needed some gym clothes,' I say.

'Oh,' she replies, 'what gym do you use?'

'It's in Winchester,' I reply.

'Which one?' *Crap, now I have to make something up.*

'Oh, it's by the train station.'

'It's not 'Anytime', is it?'

I nod, 'That's the one.'

'No way. That's my gym. I haven't seen you there.' Fuck! I assumed she lived in Southampton. Clearly, she does not. This is why one should never assume, Arthur.

'Well,' I say, 'that's the beauty of it. You can go anytime.' She laughs, and her hand is still on my arm. My fuddled brain is spinning. The cogs are *cogging,* but I still can't place her.

'Well,' she says, 'I could use a spotter if you fancy going together sometime. Give me a call.' I nod, and clearly, my face is saying something I'm not. She is attractive, she is fit, she is mysterious, and I DON'T KNOW WHAT TO SAY. 'You do still have my number, don't you?' Okay, so now this has gone from an acquaintance to someone I should know.

'Arthur?'

And I've gone silent again! 'No,' I manage, 'got a new phone, lost all my numbers.' I did replace my phone. This isn't a lie for once. Stick to simple facts, Arthur.

'Well, hey, let me give you my number.' I nod. This is working. Short of a better plan, I reach into my pocket to retrieve and remove my phone, unlock it, and then hand it across the very short divide to her. She begins to punch in her number, and I pray to any of the listening gods that it doesn't bring up a result in my contacts. It doesn't, and before she reaches the last digit, I open my mouth and say.

'Can you save it? I'm useless with those things.' She smiles, finishes typing and then, bless her soul, enters her first and last name. Reading upside down is one of the many skills I have honed over the years, and I read her name, *Ophelia Christos*. It isn't a name one readily forgets, and I remember that she was a client of Melissa's! And finally, my brain decides to come out to play. I study her abnormally attractive face and her golden sandy skin. I remember that her trial was something to do with an abusive ex.

Who is she, Melissa, and why is she relevant? Ophelia would probably have been at your funeral, Melissa. I was not.

She hands me my phone back, and I smile.

'So, how are you? 'I ask, thinking I should try and make conversation.

'Better now that Michael is gone!'

'Gone?' I ask. She nods.

'He's dead.'

'Dead?' *How come I didn't read about this in the local paper?*

'Yeah, tragic accident! She replies.

'I'm sorry—'

'Don't be,' she cuts me off. 'Look,' she says, 'I gotta run. Text me sometime, okay?' She puts her other hand on my arm, and it's all hands-on, Arthur. The hand turns into a surprise, quick hug. I'm excited, and before I know it, she turns and sets off toward her car. I watch as she walks away, and I realise that Ophelia is beautiful. Could it be that she likes me? She reaches a corner before she deigns to answer my question, and she turns back and shoots me a passing smile before disappearing into the moody recesses of the car park.

I walk over to my shiny red Alfa and climb in, and I'm smiling by the time I exit the car park.

EIGHT

It is Sunday, and I'm sitting in the back of an Uber, nervously clutching a bottle of wine. The car has garish plastic seat covers over the equally awful seats, and I wonder if the driver moonlights in murder.

Abdul doesn't drink. Not officially, anyway. But I bring wine because Abdul's wife, Maureen, drinks it like it is the last day she will ever be able to open her mouth again. Maureen is not your typical Maureen—I don't know what a *typical Maureen* is. But in my mind, it is an old lady in a chunky-knit sweater replete with tissues shoved up the sleeves—and she and Abdul are quite possibly the most laid-back people on the planet. But they are also smoulderingly intense. They try way too hard and, simultaneously, not hard enough.

I met Abdul shortly before he met Maureen. At a mandated *speed awareness* course of all places. I was annoyed with myself for attracting the unwanted eyes of the law, and Abdul is the stereotypical guy who wants to be your best friend; he persisted, gave me his number, and texted me relentlessly, and here we are. Maureen is a surgeon, and she met Abdul one night when he was visiting A & E for a DIY-related injury. Abdul doesn't *do DIY* mainly because he has the common sense of a goldfish. He is one-for-one in attempts at using power tools and going to the hospital. I personally think that fate can *fuck off,* but I sure am glad it coupled him with a repairer of injuries.

As a couple, they are the sort of people you hate instantly until you realise that they are kind of awesome; annoying, but awesome.

The driver asks me about my day. As usual, I have very little to say. 'I'm off to a friend's for dinner,' I reply before retrieving my phone and bringing it to eye level. I try to shift my focus to the evening ahead. To say I haven't exactly been social lately would be an understatement. I have spent the last twenty-four hours in a trance about Ophelia. I think there was a connection there, but I'm not sure what it was. She was so blasé about the death of her boyfriend. I have an innate ability to read other people's dark tendencies, and something about her indifference to the death of her lover called out to me.

The Uber arrives outside Abdul and Maureen's. I thank the driver and add a small tip for not making too much small talk before making my way down the drive. I get halfway to the door before the insufferably adorable couple appears and stands in the doorway. They are arm in arm, smiling, waiting, watching. There is no turning back now.

'Hey, Bro-man Polanski,' says Abdul. I like Abdul. I do. But he has this habit of greeting me with *bro-based* puns. I have killed for less, but he is a good friend. Plus, all told, they are always original.

Maureen is fun, if not intense, even more so after the second bottle of wine. The two complete each other in the strangest way. Maureen is permanently wired, whereas Abdul is so chilled that he is almost ice. Maureen repairs wounds. Abdul just makes them. Apart, they don't function; together, they just about make a functional, rational human.

'Fire and Ice,' I say, happy with my moniker.

Maureen pipes up. Presumably, she has already opened a bottle. But they came to the doorway too early. The driveway is long, and I'm not one for shouting. I can't hear a word she is saying. I feel as though I have been walking toward them for about six weeks, and I am relieved when I finally make it to the door. Abdul grabs me by the neck as though we are twelve years old and leads me into the house.

'Whatever you are cooking, it smells wonderful,' is the first thing I say. Mainly because I think I am hungry. I have been in the house less than five minutes before a drink is in my hand. I take a large sip, followed by another. I am nervous. This is the first time I have been for dinner here without you, Melissa.

My parents are entitled idiots. They could be smart were they not blinded by privilege and casual bigotry. My schooling was first class, and I am well-educated, well-spoken, articulate, funny, and likeable. I am, however, not a talker. Melissa led social occasions, and I am not used to being the only voice. Partly because I don't think that silence always needs to be filled with mundane chatter, but mainly because I have little to talk about. I didn't then, and I certainly don't now. I've spent the last eight months as a basic recluse. When I have ventured out of the house, it has been with the intent to kill or provide an alibi for said killing. For most of my adult life, my interests have been Melissa and murder. I didn't need to make things up, cover for myself or lie. I had you for that, Melissa.

'So, did you run out of food at home?' Maureen asks.

'Ha-ha,' I reply. Very droll, Maureen, very droll. 'And actually, yes,' I add, and we all laugh. But I'm not joking.

The problem is, no one understands how difficult this is, Melissa, no one but you. Abdul and Maureen have been friends for nearly ten years. Friends talk, bitch, moan and share feelings. I would love to, I really would, but I can't. I mean, really, would Abdul and Maureen be happy to see me if they knew what I was? Do people invite the community cutthroat for dinner? Friends or not, I can't tell them what I get up to in the dark. No, I imagine Maureen would stab me with a fork and run if I did.

Without Melissa, I need to find an alias for what I do. I need to find a way to discuss my likes, passions, and problems in a roundabout way. But what in the fuck do I liken stalking and attempting to kill the local cat killer to? I'm pretty good at fitting in, I am. But what I do need is a little coaching now and again. Where do I find that? Gumtree, Facebook Marketplace?

'So, when did you redecorate?' I ask. One thing I know is that most couples love to share their renovations.

'About six months ago,' Maureen replies.

'I like it,' I say.

I drink almost nonstop until the food arrives, giving me an excuse not to talk. I mean, it's rude with one's mouthful. As much as I don't feel much like eating, I eat the same way Maureen goes through wine, never allowing my mouth to be empty.

'Bulking up for the gym, Barrack Bro-Bama?' My mouth is chock full of food. I chew almost interminably and try to reply.

'Well, I'm all for it,' says Maureen. 'You could do with gaining a few pounds.' *Seriously, what's with everyone and my weight?* I'm still chewing and don't get a chance to defend my stature before Abdul starts talking.

'You know,' he says, 'If you ever need a gym buddy—'

'All good,' I say with my hand covering my face. And I swear Maureen made an excessively chewy meal tonight. 'I got one.'

'Thank God,' says Abdul, 'for a minute, I thought I was going to have to go shopping for gym clothes.' I laugh, we laugh, and I laugh harder at the memory of my panic-buying discount sportswear from teenagers.

'So,' says Maureen, 'who is the new man in your life?' Bollocks, why do people feel the need to ask follow-up questions?

'Oh, erm, it's Ophelia,' I say meekly, hoping they remember as little of her as I did. Her name appears to echo off every appliance in the room, and my hosts turn to each other and raise their eyebrows in unison.

'Ophelia, as in Ophelia with the dead boyfriend, Ophelia?' Maureen asks.

'Maureen,' Abdul scolds as if the word *dead* will set me off, and he moves on quickly. 'You mean Ophelia, as in sexy Greek, Ophelia?'

'That's not quite how she is saved in my phone,' I say. They laugh. 'But yes.'

'Wow!' says Abdul as his mouth drops. 'I don't think I'd get much exercise done if I went to the gym with Ophelia if you know what I mean?' Maureen whacks him playfully on the arm, and one thing is apparent, they remember Ophelia vividly, and now I have to go to the gym with her at least once.

'Yes,' I say, 'we reconnected recently. It turns out we use the same gym.' *Oh, shitting fuck, what am I even saying now?* 'You know, we have a lot in common.' The pair look at me and smile, and I thank my lucky stars that neither of them asks a follow-up question.

'Dude!' says Abdul. 'I think this is great. Dinner and gym partners. It looks like the old you is returning.' I put all my energy into not rolling my eyes and take a long sip of my drink.

'I guess so,' I reply, knowing full well that the old me is dead and buried. What is it with people and thinking that you can sustain a major tragedy and just pop back to your old self? Circumstances change people, even borderline sociopathic murderers.

The wine I imbibed before food is already sloshing around in my brain. I had forgotten that drinking in social situations can make you giddy and chatty. I open my mouth to speak, but that has done me little good lately. So, I close it before I say something else I might regret. Maureen produces her phone and tells me that *Ophelia's Facebook status is single.* Her words intrigue me, Ophelia intrigued me, and it tempts me to check Ophelia out online later. But that will mean braving Facebook, Melissa, seeing your face and the two of us together. It used to be one of my main research tools, but now I can't bring myself to open it.

'Arthur!' her chastising words invade my tipsy brain. 'Yours says you're still married.'

'Technically, I am,' I say. 'I mean, we never got a divorce.'

'Bro Derek,' is all Abdul says as he shakes his head, and suddenly I feel like I've done something wrong.

'Arthur,' says Maureen, placing her hand on mine across the table, 'you have to move on.'

'I know,' I say. 'The truth is, I haven't had the heart to change it.' Maureen smiles at me. She is almost attractive; she probably would be if she didn't feature the same pained look as *Elmer Fudd* all the time. Our eyes meet, and it is therapeutic, to be honest, for a change. 'Can I be honest with you guys?' They nod in unison and remind me of Judy's creepy twins. But I carry on regardless. 'I haven't been on Facebook since she died.'

'She would want you to move on,' Maureen says. 'I mean, Melissa would want you to be happy.' I nod. She would, I suppose. Maybe that's why you took your own life, Melissa, so that I could be happy?

One of my favourite things about alcohol is that it replaces the need for small talk in situations like this. Nothing is taboo or awkward anymore; eventually, things get playful and silly. Adult conversation is replaced by jokes, memories, and board games. The memorable part of the evening ends, and the next thing you know, it is gone midnight, and your Uber is on its way to collect you.

NINE

Like most people who get drunk and chatty with friends, I project my chattiness onto the next person I see. This tends to translate into me being more amenable to chit-chat with the return taxi driver. This works because I find that late-night cab drivers tend to get a bit talkative. I might, too, if I drove around on my own in a Prius during the small hours of the morning. I might even take up killing. Oh, wait!

I have found that the best thing to do is make a bunch of conversation when you get in and then gradually phase it out. That way, you enjoy most of the ride in comfortable silence.

I had a pleasant evening. I did. The problem is that I have so many secrets that I cannot share with anyone, and it is difficult to function socially and not slip the tongue now and again. Abdul and Maureen were among many people who knew you well, Melissa, and that is part of the problem. I am keeping your secrets as well as mine. I am trying to move on, to put you to rest, Melissa, but I don't understand why you did what you did. There is no one I can talk to about it, and my brain desperately needs to know why.

Melissa died. That much is true, but the circumstance surrounding her death is something I have yet to divulge to anyone.

I should probably mention that Melissa wasn't well. About five years after we met, she was diagnosed with Multiple Sclerosis. Its onset was gradual at first, and the symptoms were manageable. But as it progressed, it inevitably got worse.

Melissa was smart, strong, independent, and proud. All good attributes and all reasons why I fell in love with her in the first place. And if I had to guess, they were also why she took her own life. In a way, I can empathise. I live with an angry demon in my mind that I cannot exorcise. But Melissa was perfect and robust, and I guess that living with a debilitating illness that robbed her of her independence at times was too much. She was strong until the end, ultimately stronger than I am, because she did something I have so far been unable to do.

As the disease took hold of her and she became less and less able to be herself, I can only assume that life must have become too much for her. I blame myself for this because I knew her strength and assumed she was fine. She was not. Losing you was a huge blow, Melissa, but not as much as thinking that you might have done it for me as much as you. For Melissa, to think of herself as a burden was a step too far.

Pride can be valuable, but we sometimes get in our own way. Pride doesn't do too well when looking at its former self. In this instance, I guess she must have become tired of not being the person she used to be. Melissa was just as fierce as the day we met, but I suppose it is conceivable that you got tired of falling, but you were never a burden, Melissa, not to me.

The irony, of course, is that she was carrying on with an impossible condition and was stronger than she'd ever been. Of all the things I could have said to her had I only known.

You see, I thought it was business as usual in my house. I was blinded by your strength Melissa. The night you lost the battle, I was out taking the life of someone else. I should have been there, Melissa, and I still haven't got over the shock of coming home that morning. No one knows that but me, Melissa, and I owe it to your memory to keep it that way.

To this day, I am still not entirely convinced that it wasn't an accident. The signs were there, but they weren't. I didn't know that you were circling the drain, Melissa, and there are so many things I might have done. Instead, I am left with what *ifs* and *whys*.

What if I had stayed at home? Why didn't you say something? Did you mean to do it, or did you push yourself too far?

The day you left. I returned home from a night of killing to discover death camped out in my bedroom. Melissa was flat on the bed, so still, so perfect, so dead. She might have been asleep if not for the empty bottle of pills and the vomit on the sheets.

It took me several hours to process my emotions; I am a killer, but I am not a monster. I do what I do to feed my urges, but I do feel. It is not an empty process, not completely. And I was not equipped to process the shock of coming home to my dead wife.

I could not previously imagine what it was like to be in inescapable pain. I know that was your life, Melissa, and I'm not angry. I wish that you had told me you were leaving. Maybe there was nothing I could have done, but I would have given anything to have one more night with you.

My story, my alibi, and my version of events for that night was that you had a seizure in your sleep. I awoke to your body and attempted CPR, but it was too late. It was too late, by about eight hours. I moved the drugs, phoned an ambulance, and gave them my version of events. Your death wasn't treated as suspicious, and no autopsy was performed.

Of all my secrets, Melissa, yours is the most painful! I know full well that one day I might be caught; I am no coward and will admit to what I have done. In some way, it will be a relief to come clean. But I can never tell anyone the truth about you, Melissa. I know that you would want people to remember you for how you lived, not how you died, and it is a fact that eats away at me. Why didn't you talk to me, Melissa?

The taxi drops me off at my curb. I thank the driver, open my gate, and walk down the path to my front door. I put my key in the lock, but the door won't open. My first thought is to give it a hard shove, but it won't budge, and it doesn't take me long to realise something is wrong. The door has been locked from the inside. I hear a noise coming from within; someone is in my house.

I don't usually panic, but I have been anxious lately. I am also drunk, emotional from reminiscing, and slightly on edge. Now that I am out and about, the angry rage has restarted. It is bubbling up, and right now, it tells me that this is my house, my home and that someone is violating my sanctuary.

I want to kick the door in, power inside and kill whatever fuck has dared to rob my house. But my home has already seen too much death, the noise might have alerted the neighbours, and the police could be en route. There is too much on my mind to go to prison for killing a burglar—it should be legal. This is my safe place—so I breathe in deeply, remove my phone and dial 999.

***

It was after three by the time the police left. I am rich, and my wife—ex-wife—was a criminal lawyer, so they arrived promptly and took it very seriously. When the rich are robbed, something must be done. The bad news is that as robbers go, they were pretty professional. They can't have been inside long, leaving little to no trace of even being there. As much as the police presence was inconvenient, having an authority figure in attendance helped keep me from doing something rash. My brain is addled, and I used to have you for this, Melissa, but now I am forced to deal with the noise on my own.

I'll admit our (my) house is large and loud. There is a pity pool, fancy shrubbery, two expensive Italian saloons on the drive, and an almost comically oversized house number. Given my recent lengthy seclusion, any opportunist burglar would jump at the sight of seeing me leaving home for the evening, a bottle of wine in hand. It almost makes sense, except for the surgical nature of the incursion. The alarm was deactivated, the locks picked, and the evidence non-existent. Were it not for my interruption, I would never have known it had occurred? But the lack of evidence is startling, and so far, I cannot find anything missing. Whoever robbed me was after far more than just my money.

I am not overly concerned. I keep nothing in the house that suggests that I am a killer. That would be stupid. But something about it doesn't add up. The whole thing was too neat and too tidy. I am tired, and it is late. There is nothing I can do about it but putting to bed the notion that it was more than just a robbery is challenging.

I kept my thoughts to myself, and the police promptly left. Just Anxious Alarmed Arthur. I doubt this would even get a crime number if I were not wealthy. Whomever it was got in and out without a trace, I ought to leave it alone, but I won't. The problem with tangling with a methodical killer is that I almost always have a backup—and I am a methodical killer. The home CCTV works, it is real, but it is a ruse, a decoy. I have a series of nanny cam-type cameras all over the house. It isn't app-controlled and backs up to a remote server hidden in one of my secret locations. I can't access it from here, which is mildly frustrating right now, but that is the whole point. It can't be tampered with from here, either.

***

Monday rolls around, and since I don't work, it affords me the luxury of sitting in the cluttered conservatory in peace, *Wellington-free*. Mike and June are both at work, and the downstairs is a pleasant, argument-free zone. The catch-22, of course, is that Mike is at work. He is no doubt already fucking an intern in the supply closet, and I can already feel this weekend's argument brewing.

I sit with a much-needed coffee and stare out into the garden. The grass needs cutting, the hedges are growing in all directions, and although I can't see it, I know *Timmy* has shit on the lawn.

It isn't as tranquil as I would like. The robbery is still on my mind, and I feel violated. It only adds to the bundle of mysteries in my head, and as much as leaving the house hasn't made me feel like a champion lately, my insecurities will only stew at home.

I wonder what they were after, which is an insidious thought. It is understandable for some wretched urchin to violate the sanctity of my house in search of a quick buck. It is another thing to consider that the burglary was a part of something more sinister.

I have the day to myself—as I do most days—and I reconcile that I will use it wisely. If the house wasn't broken into for monetary gain, there must have been an ulterior motive. Jarrod's death is still suspect, and I wonder if someone might be on to me.

As much as I want to do nothing more than find the scrotal fiends that broke into my house, I am aware that if I want to re-enter the normal world, I must keep up appearances. I have a car boot full of Mike Ashley's superficial sportswear, an imaginary real gym *buddy,* and a gym membership to make. So, in an effort to be *normal,* I reach across to the coffee table, pick up my phone and begin to compose a message.

Hey, fancy hitting the gym at some point?

My finger hovers over the send button for an excessive amount of time. Ophelia is on my mind. She seems cool, but what if she isn't? What if she was just being nice? As soon as I hit send, this all gets very real.

I hit send and immediately regret it. Why is there no *unsend* button?

Not only do I regret my course of action almost immediately, but I am exasperated with my choice of words. I used the term *hit the gym and* didn't sign off with my name. Ophelia is attractive and decidedly younger than I am. She gyms, works, is popular and has wonderful, golden Mediterranean skin. Besides our car park interlude, it has been years since we last spoke, and this is definitely the first time we have messaged. I believe we were in a *group chat* at one point, but no self-respecting adult puts much stock in being part of group messages.

I have just texted her like we are old pals—which we aren't. And now I am faced with her either taking me up on my offer—in which case I have to go to the gym—or she is confused about who has messaged her. In this case, I will have to remind her who I am and convince her to go to the gym with me! I don't know which is worse.

I realise that this is the first time I have been anxious about texting a woman in a long time. The wait is killing me, but it makes a welcome change to feeling anything that isn't self-loathing.

I have shit to do, so I pull myself together and head upstairs to shower. I set my phone down in the bedroom, and the screen lights up as I do. I can see from the message preview shown to me on the screen that it is from Ophelia, and as much as I am neither keen on gym nor rejection, I have to know what she has said. I pick the phone back up, unlock it and begin to read.

TEN

Ophelia's reply is as welcome as it is troubling. Because I realise that before I do anything else, I must now make a gym membership. Why is life so complicated? To make matters worse, our mutual gym—the one I have never used before in my life—decrees that all new members must be subjected to a mandatory forty-minute induction. And naturally, if I go to the gym I use *regularly* and have to undergo an induction, it will look weird. So, I will have to get that out of the way pronto. I'd be reluctant to go even if there was no induction.

It is about a twenty-minute drive to the gym from mine, and as I drive, I realise that I am both tired and slightly hungover. Ophelia's reply was far too upbeat for a Monday morning, and now, instead of sitting quietly nursing my hangover, I am off for an induction with a PT named Calvin! Why does stuff like this always happen to me?

Ophelia replied almost immediately, a message that read something like this:

Totes!! Great thinking, Arthur, I don't know about you, but I have some serious Sunday carbs I need to work off. Am I right? How does this evening work for you? We can shake off those Monday blues together!! Ophelia x

It is a good job Ophelia is attractive. Her overuse of punctuation is almost too much for me, and who the fuck says *totes?* Still, she replied, and she was happy, and now I am like a cat in heat. My emotions are upside down, and I can't decide whether I want to kill her or fuck her. I think I am leaning toward the latter, and it is a strange feeling, Melissa.

Ophelia's brand of upbeat excitement about going to the gym both excites and terrifies me. I have no clue what

Monday blues are. And I didn't realise that going to the gym was an exciting task. My head hurts for various reasons, and as much as I could seriously do without this, I guess it is best to rip it off like a plaster.

Obviously, I submitted to this before I knew I would have to endure an induction with an overtly peppy PT on a Monday morning. I pull alongside the gym to discover that it has no member parking. I mean if I wanted to walk . . . I squeeze my enormous saloon into space on a nearby street. I exit and lock the car as a passer-by stops and says, 'Nice car!' I am then forced to discuss the pros and cons of owning an Alfa Romeo with a man who looks like his mum still cuts his hair. I almost hand him the keys there and then. *Note to self; murderers cannot have nice things.*

My induction is stated as being forty minutes, but I swear it lasts forty days. My PT *Calvin* looks like an extra in one of Mr Motivators' videos, and he has the personality of a utility cupboard, but he is enthusiastic.

'What time do you finish?' This is one of the few questions I manage at the culmination of our forty days together. Thankfully, God makes a usual appearance in Hell, and it turns out that Calvin finishes at five. He ought to be gone when I return for my second *sesh* of the day with Ophelia.

When I finally escape from Calvin, I decide it is worth putting some of his excessive gym knowledge to the test, and I reluctantly check out some of the machines. The gym is cramped and cosy. It is purple and has neon lights, and I don't know what look they were going for with it.

As I attempt to exercise, I realise that the enslaved children in *Sports Direct* were either total morons or were fucking with me because I appear to be dressed like someone's gym-going granddad. I ditch one of the sweatbands and engage in a fight to the death with a machine that seems to be intent on snapping me in half.

I exit the gym half an hour later, feeling like I just survived being kidnapped and tortured. My head hurts a little less, but the rest of my body aches in a rather dramatic overcompensation. I do at least emerge victorious with my member's card, safe in the knowledge that I will never again have to undergo another induction.

I return to the car to discover a small scratch and a parking ticket—cheers, Calvin—and I struggle to reconcile with myself the notion that this is an everyday occurrence. People leave the house to do this? My impulse is to throw the shitty piece of paper demanding money on the ground, but I don't want to draw attention to myself. I climb in the car, close the door, and promptly pay the exorbitant fee for being ten minutes late returning to my car. Perhaps my next victim ought to be a parking warden.

Once home, I get in the shower—I didn't break much of a sweat, but I am keen to rid myself of Calvin's excess saliva—safe in the knowledge that I am now a bona fide gym user, I dry myself off, pick up my phone and begin to reply to Ophelia.

Tell me about it! Drinking on a Sunday always seems like a good idea at the time!! Sounds good to me. I can meet you there any time after five. Arthur. :)

I reply using as much punctuation as possible, leaving the *x* off and opting for a smiley face instead. Messaging like a normal person is hard work. I hit send, set the phone down, and realise that I have just committed to my second workout of the day. I leave the phone on the side and go back to my task of trying to find out who the fuck broke into my house to steal nothing.

My house has been violated, and I don't like that. Despite my aching limbs, I committed to the task of finding what wasn't there. The infiltration was good, so good that even I was almost fooled.

The study was what gave it away. I don't work, and I'm not much for computers. Melissa used the computer, and Melissa used the study a lot. I can use a computer; I don't like them. And unlike my father, I know that yelling at them won't help.

Everything that was touched in the study was put back exactly where it was, except for the dust. You rarely notice the absence of something. But it was just as I switched off the study light that it hit me. It was inordinately clean. It was as though someone had dusted my study!

Melissa covered my tracks well. She was diligent like that, but the problem with anything bought—and covering up murder—is there is always a trail—twenty-first-century problems, right? Melissa purchased all my garages, knives, clothes, and everything I needed. The trail was ordered, organised, and filed neatly on a flash drive—along with some of her work stuff—a flash drive that happens to be missing.

One of the problems with being a modern-age maniac is that you have to store this information somewhere. And as I mentioned earlier, you can be as careful as you like, and you will still inevitably leave behind some trace. The missing thumb drive isn't a big issue. It is encrypted, but it's just weird purchases and lawyer stuff, and I cannot see what anyone would want with it. But that isn't the problem. What worries me isn't so much what's on the drive. What is troubling is the how and the why. How did they know to find it? Why did they break into my house? Why did they clean my study?

I don't need more unanswered questions. And it would appear that whoever broke in was looking for information.

ELEVEN

I arrive at the gym for my second *sesh* just after half-four. I am early. But I need to make sure that Calvin leaves before I re-enter. He cannot blow my cover with Ophelia, and if he salivates on me again, I may rip out each of his saliva glands.

I loiter across the street under my hat and wait for the magic hour. Calvin—the lying bastard—finally leaves at five fifteen, and Ophelia texts me to say she will be there just before six, which is perfect. I have time to buy some new gym attire.

I find a shop in town and get myself a new outfit now that I have a baseline. It would appear that most men dress for the gym in a sports casual manner, and I pick out a baggy vest, running shoes that would be useless for running and a brand of tracksuit that I could wear to both the gym and the pub.

Satisfied with my new outfit, I stroll back to the car and wait. Ophelia messages me and tells me that she was held up at work and is running late, and she'll be there about ten past six. I reply and inform her that I, too, am tardy, but I promise to put my foot down—I can't appear too keen.

I saunter into the gym at six thirteen; I look around, but I do not spot her—it is not a big gym hence my chagrin at the lengthy induction—I assume that she is changing—I dressed in the store and left my clothes in the car—I loiter near to one of the machines that Calvin showed me earlier. His bright spandex is still all too vivid in my mind. And it doesn't take long before I find myself with company, as I spot a young male in my periphery. He lingers obnoxiously for a while before finally gathering his courage to engage me.

'Yo, bro, how many sets you got left, bro?'

The words hit my ears, and I instantly want to punch him. He managed to fit the phrase *bro* into an incredibly short sentence twice. Everything he said was offensive to them, and it takes me a moment to decipher his gym doublespeak. I think I understand, and I tell him, 'Four!' It appears to work as he nods and wanders away to loiter somewhere else. Sets of what? Train sets? Are we playing tennis?

People's inability to speak regular English while exercising forces my mood to plummet. That is until I see Ophelia emerge from the changing room in the corner of my eye.

'It is all yours, bro!' I call across the room to my loitering friend, and I move away from him and turn toward Ophelia. She approaches me, and I am unusually speechless. Gym clothing confuses the fuck out of me, and she looks like we are about to do anything other than work out. The closest reference I can think of is *Xenia Warrior Princess* covered in Lycra. She looks me up and down, and suddenly, I feel ridiculous in my sports, casual outfit. She chucks a water bottle at me and says.

'Let's get to it!'

Before we begin, let me make things clear. I am not, nor have I ever been, a gym goer. I don't mean this to sound sexist, but I had assumed that the gym with Ophelia would consist of a spin bike and a running machine. In my mind, that is the gym.

At the time of speaking, I find myself flat on my back under a very heavy bar, and despite everyone commenting on my weight loss (I'm depressed, leave me alone), I am one of the bigger guys here. I have a reputation to protect for big guys everywhere.

The premise is simple: pick things up and put them down. But Ophelia keeps telling me to *mind my form.* I don't know what that means, and I have no idea what I am doing. I realise I am woefully under-prepared for this, and perhaps I should have paid more attention to Calvin. How bad can it be to have bad form?

Ophelia Warrior Princess and I move around the small gym, there are so many terms that I ought to know, and I feel like someone should make a handbook for this. We lift, we sit, we talk, we laugh, and we sweat. Ophelia glistens, and the sweat beads off her, and somehow, she still smells incredible. Then halfway through the ordeal, I realise that I am enjoying this. My brain is awash with endorphins. Am I having fun?

We alternate between pushing bars while lying down to lifting them off the ground while standing up. There are probably other people here, but I don't notice.

We finish with some cardio, and we high-five before we call it a day. I have to admit that I do feel thoroughly worked out. My brain is in less of a tangle, and it wasn't awful. Perhaps someone in my line of business could benefit from regular strength training?

We finish, and Ophelia Warrior Princess tells me she is going to shower, not for the first time; I realise I hadn't planned for this. My clothes are in the car, and she tells me to wait for her and that she won't be long, she *promises*. I don't get to say anything before she disappears, and I am standing awkwardly alone.

In lieu of a better plan, I jog back to the car—my third workout of the day—renew my parking ticket, grab my clothes, and dash back to the gym.

There is a vending machine in the gym that sells confusing miniature towels. So, I buy one and then venture into the men's changing rooms. I don't know how anything works or where it is, but I am safe here with my fellow *bros*. One of them lends me his shower gel, and I am informed that if you put a coin in the locker, you get to keep it, so this is how it works. Active Arthur.

I shower and dry myself off with my tiny towel. The baffling baby towel serves little purpose, and I am still damp when I climb back into my clothes. I finish dressing and head out to find Ophelia waiting for me.

Ophelia looks up from her book—did I take that long—she registers me and says. 'Ooh, someone bought a branded towel.' I can't tell if she is mocking me; it is far from the stupidest thing I have bought today. Ophelia puts away *How to Kill your Family* (ominous), shoots me a smile, and says, 'Wanna get a drink?' She says as she hops from her stool.

'A drink drink?'

'A drink drink,' she repeats. I look around the gym, at the glistening gym goers and say.

'Isn't that counterproductive?' Ophelia laughs.

'You're funny, Arthur.' I was being serious.

'Sure,' I say. She grabs me by the arm and leads me toward the door. Normal life is confusing.

TWELVE

Drinking with Ophelia was actually fun. And despite the fact that having *poor form* translates into *everything-fuckinghurtstoday.* I enjoyed myself. I still can't quite understand this whole drink-after-exercise thing, but I have to admit that being out of the house is quite liberating. I am, in fact, starting to find some small doses of enjoyment in life again, and while that is a good thing, it is also worryingly bad.

If you have ever found yourself in a depressive episode, you'll know that nothing is fun, and even the small task of getting out of bed and washing feels like running a marathon. No one enjoys running twenty-six miles. For most normal people, the feeling of the darkness sliding out of your brain is a welcome feeling. If you wake up and think, I want to organise the baby shower, or I want to attend a work party, you know that you are definitely starting to feel better. Finding yourself, enjoying life again, laughing, and taking pleasure in your hobbies is fucking brilliant, and there are few better feelings in the world.

For me, on the other hand, this is terrifying news because one of the things I enjoy most in this life is killing, and I am excited and terrified at once. You see, Melissa, I am rudderless. You kept me in check. You kept me and the world safe. Without you, I'm afraid that I will lose control.

I am a long way from being fine. I am still talking to my dead wife in my inner monologue. And while buying my second gym outfit, I saw a few people I knew and panicked. I hid in the changing room until they left. Looking back, I can't quite figure out why. I feel like anxiety should come with a disclaimer, *will affect anyone!*

That might seem like a given, but I am confident and genuinely scared of nothing. When you have lived a life of confidence, crippling fear is the worst. There is a disparity between how you used to feel and the status quo; before long, you are frozen in the attic of a cat killer. I live in fear that it might happen again. It was outside of my control, and that made it terrifying.

I want to think that you would be proud of me, Melissa. I have been shopping, to the gym, out for dinner and even drinks. I am trying to move on. I also think you would like Ophelia—technically, you wouldn't because she is young, pretty, and vying for my affection—if you were here, you would probably want her dead, and I'm a killer, and this whole thing would be awkward as fuck. But you aren't here, Mel, because you left me.

Abdul and Maureen want to have dinner again this week! I have said yes, which I know I will regret, but I need to get used to being normal again. I have spent the last eight months at home and, before that, twelve years living with the love of my life. Given my lifestyle, never in a million years did I imagine that Melissa would go before I did. So, there is a slight chance that maybe I am out of touch.

One thing I know for sure is every single muscle in my body feels like it is on fire, and before I exercise again, I need to spend a minimum of twenty minutes warming up as well as working out what *good form* looks like—thank you, YouTube.

Dinner this week is on Friday, today is Wednesday, and I have no social plans (baby steps), which is a good thing because all the recent merriment has made me forget that someone killed Jarrod and Suzie. I'm pretty confident it wasn't me, and I am assuming the same person (people) were in my house. My fucking house?! Of all the homes you burgle, the one belonging to the depressed, anxious, unhinged murdered is not that one. I need answers.

It is mid-afternoon, and firstly I know I need to address the elephants outside my house. Driving my car to crime scenes is as subtle as turning up in a tutu and heels. Before I tackle my troubles, I need to find a new car. I need to be Average Arthur.

We were a two-car household. But not only is Melissa's car equally ridiculous. I still can't bring myself to get into it. The Maserati has been exactly where you left it, Melissa, not touched and not opened. You actually parked it a little too close to the garage, and I can't open the door from the outside. That car was your car. I know that your smell and your aura are both locked inside. As soon as I open that door, I will be smacked in the face by your death. There are hairs on the leather seats, Alice bands on the gear stick, and half-open cans of pop in the cup holders. It is a Morbid Melissa Museum, and I cannot go near it.

I know that I should address it. But I can't, not yet. But I am considering it. It's progress, and when you struggle with your mental health, that is all you can ask.

I shelve my thoughts, gather my courage and step outside, the air tastes different, and I am pleased to be out. I order a taxi and hop inside. It is time to go car shopping.

I love just about everything about cars. I love the smell of a filling station, stats, figures, horsepower, zero to sixty times, and I read the handbook for every car I own cover to cover. I love manual gear changes, leather seats, sound systems—everything. What I don't like, however, are car salespeople.

I have concocted a somewhat arbitrary kill list in my time of pity. I thought I might be losing my mind and will to live, and one of my stupid thoughts was to go out in a blaze of glory. And when I say arbitrary, I do mean it. It is nonspecific and nothing personal. On that list, I have an estate agent, a debt collector, a *TikTok-er*, a socialite, every cold caller ever and a car salesperson. I should add that I have since added *parking warden* to that list. It was all hyperbole, of course. I am not without mercy but ridding the world of car salespeople would be doing it a kindness.

For those of you who are familiar with the *Garfield* cartoons, you will know that he doesn't like Mondays—and he hates Nermal—but I don't think it is Mondays that Garfield dislikes. He doesn't like the weekend ending and Jon returning to work. Because let's face it, what is different about Monday to a lazy house cat? I resonate with this—I am a lazy house cat—and Melissa's death was my Jon leaving for work indefinitely, and now I have to face the Nermals of this world alone.

I exit the taxi and stroll up to the dealership. I'm dressed even scruffier than usual because I don't want to rock up looking like a giant banknote. I prefer to buy privately, but there is always the one person who lies terribly in their ad, and you don't find out until you get there, and I'm just not in the mood for *death on the driveway*. It doesn't happen often, but I don't have time to waste. So, I go to a used Volvo dealership because when it comes to underwhelming, Volvo are kings. I mean that with no disrespect to Volvo. It is a compliment. To the untrained eye, it is almost impossible to tell one model of Volvo from another. If you had to describe a Volvo, you would be describing every one that has ever been made. They blend seamlessly into any urban or rural setting, are well equipped, have some raucous engines, are often coffin-shaped (great for bodies), are capable off-road, are insanely reliable and have the comfiest seats. Plus, Architects drive Volvos. Murderers don't.

I arrive at the Volvo garage in Southampton. I say Southampton, but it is more like Southampton's elbow. The part of town you avoid if you don't need to buy something industrial, excruciatingly expensive or if you own all of your teeth.

The garage is squeakily clean. And there is less soul here than at my parent's house. I do wonder if used car garages are extensions of Hell.

I barely have time to think before being greeted by a man whose outfit makes him look like he is off to a funeral. His grin is bigger than Berlin, but it is artificial, and I instantly distrust him.

I do my best to focus because cars inside a building that looks like an oversized estate agent always throw me off.

He instantly directs me to the most expensive car in the lot, and when I tell him I know which one I am after, he looks at me as though I have just suggested we fill all the cars with honey. We look at cars. He talks. I hate him.

I let the salesman talk as infrequently as possible—so that I don't have to kill him—and before I know it, I have the keys in my hand to a newish Volvo V70 T6. It has three litres of Swedish horsepower, all-wheel drive, and enough space in the back for about six full-grown adults lying down—if you get my drift. I am pleased with my purchase and drive around interminably to ensure it isn't about to fall apart. I shall return swiftly to re-enact an Arthur Miller play if it does. Except for this time, it will be called: *Death of a Car Salesman*.

After driving about aimlessly for a few hours in comfortable anonymity, I realise I am hungry, which is progress. I have driven past about eighteen different *Subway* sandwich shops and decide it is as good a place as any.

I stop, run in, and buy a sandwich that smells way better than it tastes—I assume the smell is added, and I would be okay with that if they sold it in a bottle—I return to the car, park near the docks, eat my sub-par sub, sit back, and watch the sun begin to set over the water.

Content and no longer hungry, I fire up the Volvo once more and set off to my storage unit. I will solve the mystery of who robbed my house.

THIRTEEN

Here is the thing with depression, heartache, or depression caused by heartache, or just about any significant patch of mental defect. Everyone you know looks at you as though you have gone off the fucking rails. Friends and family alike will huddle around you in shifts, and they all talk about you to one another as though you don't exist.

How's he doing today?

Is he eating?

Why won't he stop listening to Alanis Morrisette?

Etc etc.

The list goes on, and everyone seems to think they won't be the exact same fucking way if something happens to them. People hug you and tell you it will get better! Of course it fucking will. It's a wound. But physical wounds heal differently. There is no set time to heal a broken mind.

I am aware that it will *get better*, but not knowing how or when makes it difficult.

People mean well, but the platitudes grate slightly. How would they like it if I went around their house and chopped off their ears the minute they opened the door? Then placed them in their hands and whispered; *it gets better!* I mean, it will. Life won't always be the fear-inducing, painful trauma that is someone handing you your ears. But right there and then, it makes little difference. Life will improve, but you'll never forget the day a madman chopped off your ears just for opening the door.

I am improving. I know I am. I have left the house on multiple occasions this month. I have socialised. Cut my hair.

Eaten. But I still feel like most people view a depressed person as though they are a sick, mangey dog. As though I might fall apart at any minute and piss all over the carpet, and it might be better to put me down. I might, it might, but it's all part of the process.

The thoughts in my head reach a climax as I arrive at my secret self-store unit. Just off the M271 in Southampton. I circle about a few times to ensure I am not being followed. I am not, am I?

It is almost dark when I finally arrive. I climb out of my Versatile Volvo and sneak inside.

I enter the self-storage unit and locate my indoor tin shed. The inner population is sparse. And now and again, I get the feeling that some people might live here—it's much cheaper than renting.

I unlock my unit, step inside, and boot up my computer. I can't help but shake the feeling that I am being followed, and I don't want to be here long.

I copy the files from my remote storage to a USB stick. Then delete the original. When these people turn up dead, I don't want there to be a trace.

As much as I am desperate to know who was in my house, I know better than to dwell. Suppose someone is targeting me, following me, or killing after me. I want to look at this in the safety of my home.

Files copied. I slide the device into my pocket and head back into the car. I open the door and get back into my comfortable chair when my phone vibrates. I look down at the message to see it is from my squash partner *Rich Richard.*

I have known Richard since university, and Richard is Rich. He started his own recruitment company, having tried, and failed at working for one. Apparently, that is the key to success, as he now owns one of the biggest recruitment firms in the UK. He couldn't get a job, so he made one out of finding jobs. I will be forever confused about how anyone can make money simply by connecting people without a job to vacancies. But there we are.

The hold-up is mildly inconvenient, but I need to be normal. So, I pause and examine the message.

To me, Rich Richard looks just as he did when we met sixteen years ago. It's funny how we see people that way. In reality, his long black hair is now balding to the extent that I really wish he would shave it. His considerable paunch means he no longer fits into small 'band' t-shirts or skinny jeans, and when he wears his glasses, I feel like I am hanging out with someone's dad—not my father; however, we have never *hung out* in my life.

The message dictates that Rich Richard would like to play squash tonight. Our community is small, and word about my decision to rejoin society has seeped out. Given that I need to be seen as normal again, I decide that I should probably say yes.

The moniker *squash partner* is a tad unfair. We have been friends for a good, long time. But we don't really talk unless we see each other, and I feel like our friendship is primarily defined by the activity of the moment. Right now, it is squash. I ache—from bad form—and am not in the shape to play squash, but I could use the exercise, the company, and let's face it, squash is a fantastic way to exorcise hidden anger: the best-laid non-plans and all that. So much for my baby steps. It looks like I'm playing squash tonight.

Why is it everyone wants to exercise? It would seem the nation's pastime is cardio, followed by alcohol. It is very confusing.

I start up the car and begin to drive. Just regular fucking Arthur in his regular fucking Volvo. I have no squash gear, but Richard is eager and says he has enough for two.

Squash is good for tension. But I don't think it banishes murderous intent, though, and after nine months out of the game and one-bodged attempt, I am starting to get a bit impulsive. I am not completely unhinged, and I know what is right and what is wrong. Not that killing is ever right, but I get these impulses that I cannot fight. Eventually, I have to get them out, or I cannot think properly. There is a reason why I have spent my life targeting bad guys. I have yet to kill someone innocent, and I would like to keep it that way for the sake of what's left of my soul. But I have an addiction. It sneaks up on me like a winter sunset, and before I know what's happening, it's dark, and I can't see what I'm doing.

The journey toward home is short and uneventful—famous last words—and filled primarily with my inciteful thoughts. *I need to get home and find out who robbed my house. I need to get home and find out who robbed my house. I need to get home and find out who robbed my house.*

The Volvo is solid. It drives well. And I am very grateful that the Ikea concept isn't applied to all Swedish goods.

I leave the motorway—I am close now—and as I cruise the dark country lanes back toward my house. I consider the day. I bought a car, copied my files, ate a sandwich, watched the sunset, and agreed to play squash—definite progress.

I will pop home, drop off my flash drive, find out who robbed me, arrange to kill them, get changed, and meet Rich Richard in time for squash. Perhaps leaving the house isn't so bad after all? Maybe all of my anxieties were for nothing?

I approach an empty intersection. And suddenly, a strange feeling alerts my mind to impending danger, and I turn my head just in time to see a significant SUV jump a red light and plough straight into the side of my new Volvo.

FOURTEEN

We all make mistakes. I have made many, remember Jarrod? To err is one of the constants of being human. As a species, we are fucked, and I don't think we will be remembered for ruling this planet very well or for very long. Perhaps that is why the machines rose up against us in Terminator. They got tired of us making fundamental fucking errors!

It is often small and harmless when we make a mistake. We laugh it off, apologise and get on with our day. Most of the time!

The sturdy Sports Utility Vehicle didn't slow down as it approached my car.

Time did, though; just before the crash, I had the clarity to remember the sinking feeling that I was being watched or maybe followed. Sometimes being right is shit because I recall looking at the approaching vehicle and thinking it was either being driven by a blind person with no feet or they were about to hit me on purpose.

The SUV hit my car with a tremendous thud, and my order of events took a serious hit.

As I stared out of my broken window and watched the two men climb from their SUV, I wondered if they had realised the magnitude of the mistake they had just made. For a fleeting moment, I considered it might have been an accident—it is feasible. But people don't accidentally drive into your car, then accidentally get out, accidentally search your vehicle, accidentally take your belongings, and then accidentally leave without giving you their insurance details. There was no apology, and people apologise for accidents.

The Volvo is sturdy, but being hit by a large vehicle, an even larger dose of shock—and why the fuck is this happening to my new Volvo?—is terrible for one's memory. The whole thing happened as quickly as it did slowly. But I recall it happening something like this:

I was sitting at a set of traffic lights, pleasantly minding my own business and trying to remember the myriad rules involved in playing squash. The light turned green, and not wanting to add to my tardiness, I put the car in gear and continued my journey. It was then that I got this feeling, a sensation. The notion that death was kicked back on the passenger seat, scythe, cape, popcorn and all, just waiting for the outcome.

A large (unnecessary) SUV came hurtling through the red lights—seriously, what does anyone in England need an SUV for?—and came careening straight into my new—unbent—Volvo.

I am used to the odd surprise attack but having all of your bones jostled about in your skin is terrible for one's ability to move or function coherently.

I was forced to watch as two men—lose definition given their cowardice—stepped from their vehicle and began to search mine. It was a weird show to watch, and they could have killed me, but they didn't—which was a mistake. The pair must have been watching me. They knew what they were after. One grabbed the USB that I had copied the surveillance videos on while the other ensured the coast was clear. Having stolen my USB stick—presumably for the second time—they retreated to their vehicle and swiftly departed.

In my time of incapacitation, I noticed two things: one had a man bun, and the other left a big fat juicy thumbprint smack bang in the middle of the clear plastic address window.

The Volvo smashers left. I rested my head on the slowly deflating pillow for a while and considered all the ways in which I could bring about their death—running them over with a Volvo is currently top—and slowly but surely, my sense of reality began to return.

I sit back up and remember that I have made a commitment to the racket ball gods, and I get myself together. I have been in many scrapes over the years. I am in a risky line of work. But I have never been in a *car deliberate*—because it was no accident—nor do I wish to be again any time soon. My brain feels like it has bounced around in my skull while being flung from a trebuchet. The only positive aspect is the massive kick of adrenaline.

My thoughts are spinning in my battered brain, but I realise that it wasn't me they were after. It is insidious as much as it is a revelation. Because if I had to guess, they were after the flash drive—again—they are probably the same arseholes who robbed my house. The only logical explanation would be that they are after information of some kind—which must be on the original flash drive—and wanted to cover up their burglary—which isn't helpful.

To no surprise to anyone, the Volvo starts the first time, and I continue toward home. The car pulls very heavily to the left, and there is a distinctive mechanical grinding. I feel like I have fallen from a window repeatedly, and as I drive, I remember that I have committed to playing squash tonight. Why do things like this happen to Amenable Arthur?

***

I agreed to meet Rich Richard at the squash courts, I haven't seen him since Melissa died, but I'm sure he hasn't changed unless the paunch has grown. We have exchanged profound, meaningful messages over the last year; the odd *hey, how are you doing? Are you all right? Do you need any stamps?* But that's been about it. It isn't that he doesn't care; our relationship simply doesn't stretch to emotional depths, and to be frank, I'm glad it doesn't.

I am running slightly late, which is a theme of mine. In my defence, I was in a car crash. I had to go home, change, apply *Deep Heat* liberally and simultaneously avoid collapsing. I should probably rearrange, but I want to take my anger out on a small rubber ball that doesn't bounce, and I need to be normal.

The squash courts are predictably empty. There is a ubiquitous smell that consists of sweat, muscle rub, and teenage angst. The courts are well-lit, and you can see every scuff, mark, and skid made by my non-non-marking rubber soles.

Richard and I play squash until he gets tired—I might be tired too, were it not for the dangerous levels of epinephrine zipping through my body—the man has never been one for conventional exercise, and I have watched him grow around the middle as the years roll by. We call it a day when his sweat starts to hit the floor like a waterfall, and I am pleased that we continue this odd tradition of exercise followed by alcohol and head straight for the pub.

My day featured a car crash and swinging my arms around wildly in a small room. I am no longer sure what hurts and what doesn't.

Alcohol is a panacea, and I feel almost nothing when I reach the bottom of my second pint. Rich Richard returns with more drinks, and a typically verbose conversation begins.

'It's been a while since we played squash,' says Rich Richard. I nod, conceding that it has.

'How's Cathy, I ask?'

'She's okay. Busy at work, but otherwise, she's fine.'

'How are you?' Richard asks, 'Honestly?'

'I'm getting there,' I say. 'I think the dark clouds are lifting.'

'Well, that's good,' Rich Richard replies. Ever the wordsmith. 'So, what have you been up to?'

'Not a lot, I confess. I have started going to the gym.' 'The gym,' he muses, 'do you have a home gym?'

'Very funny,' I say.

'Who are you going to the gym with?'

'Remember Ophelia?' I ask. Richard takes a sip from his ale and nearly chokes on it.

'Ophelia,' he asks. 'Isn't she—'

'Young, attractive,' I input, 'Yes, very.'

'Wow,' he replies, 'I did not see that coming.'

'Neither did I?' I add.

'What are you gonna do?' he asks.

'Meh,' I shrug as casually as possible. 'Go with it, I guess. We're going again next week!'

'How?' he asks incredulously. 'You know what? I don't even care. I'm happy for you. Just be careful.' I nod like I need to be careful. 'So, when are we going to have you over?'

Shit, of course, I'd forgotten that he and Cathy are keen to show off their newfound couple hosting abilities. Rich Richard has spent the last ten years falling in love with every woman who has looked his way. To the extent that I could never keep up with his love life. But he has at least finally met his *one*, Cathy.

Cathy is less exciting than a Wednesday lunchtime, but she is good for him. In all the time I've known Richard, he has never been one for dinner parties. Now suddenly, their house is like *Come-Fucking-Dine-With-Me* every other weekend just because they are a couple.

'Uh, end of the month?' I say.

'I'll pencil you in,' he replies. Fuck, I can see why some serial killers are reclusive loners. It would be much easier. I don't work, and yet my plate is full. I need to find and kill these two morons that broke into my house and dented my new Volvo, work out what they want and what it has to do with cat killers. I also need to avoid discovery, being arrested, or being killed. To top it all off, I have to go to dinner with Abdul and Maureen, the gym with Ophelia and now dinner with Rich Richard and Cautious Cathy. When did life get so complicated?

Richard orders more drinks, and we move toward a vacant pool table. The pub is like every other pub in England, overpriced, empty, and sticky, and we descend into full male machismo mode. I find this part very easy, allowing me to engage the autopilot and sink into my brain's wonderful dark wilderness.

FIFTEEN

When I wake the next morning, everything is awful. I seem to be living in a perpetual state of hangover, and I'm certain that even my bones hurt. My social calendar is filling up, and my laundry list of anxieties is only growing—and fuck it, is everything terrible?

Today is Friday, and I've promised Abdul and Maureen that I will be in attendance for dinner tonight. Since I RSVP'd, I've had a daily reminder, and today is no exception.

I rise from the bed, open the curtains, and make toward the en suite bathroom. The badly frosted bathroom window tells me the garden is vacant, but Saturday is imminent. The Wellingtons will no doubt argue again tomorrow, and my head hurts just thinking about it. The bedroom is a wreck, and as much as I am in no mood, I cannot remember when I last changed the sheets. Tracey Emin's bed was heralded as a work of art. I very much doubt that mine will be viewed in the same regard.

I do some housework and arrange to have the Volvo collected for repair, and it is gone eleven by the time I am showered, dressed, and ready to leave the house. I have so much to do to clear my anxious mind.

Remember those fuckwads that snuck into my house and ram-raided my new Volvo? Today will be a lesson: *the person you fuck with might just be an unhinged, depressed serial killer.* Whomever they were, they have been quite careful so far. I'll give them that. But one of them rummaged through my bag and left a perfect fingerprint on the weird little plastic window for my details. I always thought the thing was pointless, turns out it isn't. Despite having my brain bounced about, I managed to preserve the fingerprint, and now I am en route with it to the local police station.

I know that a police station is the last place for a man of my qualities to hang out. Or that it is unlikely they will be interested in an unreported accident. And that is where you would be wrong. Melissa was a brilliant lawyer, worked on various cases, and had a big heart and an even bigger bank account. She did a lot of pro bono work, including criminal prosecution. She was venerable and well-loved by the police in general and in particular by a kind, old detective named Carter.

Carter is a lifer, dedicated to the job, with thick sideburns, a dodgy moustache, barely a scrap of hair on top of his head, and is about sixteen years past his prime. Carter still carries the whole *Sweeney* look around, including the long beige coat. He probably drives a Ford Cortina that must have been entirely re-welded by now, and he talks almost primarily about *the good old days*. If you looked up *old school* in the dictionary, you would, in fact, find a picture of Carter.

The man is essentially out to pasture, and his days are spent working cold cases. It is like *New Tricks,* and I always look for Amanda Redman whenever I see him. Carter is gruff, straightforward, and slightly biased toward white folk. But in his prime, he was an effective lawman. And he loved Melissa.

He was at the scene of your death, Melissa. I don't remember much of that day—beyond breaking everything in the house that was within reach—but I do remember that he whispered in my ear and said, 'She was one hell of a woman, Arthur. If you need anything, anything at all, you come and see me.'

I do need something, so I am waiting in reception, holding my empty backpack in a clear plastic bag. A plastic bag to carry a rucksack, I can almost hear everyone at *Greenpeace* groaning.

Now that I am alone, the pain in my body returns, and a dark anger seeps into my mind. Am I rushing things? Is it too soon to be back? Is sitting in a police station a bad idea? Why have I had two USB sticks stolen? Will I freeze up again? Do I need to get help? You get crooked accountants who cook the books for gangsters. Surely there are therapists for the discerning psychopath that wants to remain at large?

The police station is old, dated, and horribly depressing. The state of it is enough to dissuade most people from the notion of crime. Spending longer than necessary here would be enough for me to end it all. The walls are shabby and off-brown. I can't tell if anything is clean, and all the phones have cables on them—presumably so that you can strangle yourself.

My reverie breaks, and I hear footsteps approach, followed by a voice that booms in my direction.

'Arthur? Arthur Norman? Is that you?'

Detective Carter approaches me; he is a man to whom everything is a question. I look up at him. He embodies a *Sun Hill* detective circa 1990. He arrives. I stand to greet him and wonder if *the Bill* is still being made.

'Frank Carter,' I say as he takes me softly and firmly by the hand.

'How are you doing, Arthur?' He holds my hand and waits for my response.

'I'm getting there, Frank, I'm getting there.

'I hear you,' he replies. 'Melissa was some woman. We all miss her here.'

I nod. 'Thank you, Frank.'

'So,' he says, motioning to the bag, 'is this it?' *I phoned ahead to save time.*

I nod. Carter takes it with his grubby left hand, moves his right from mine and grabs my shoulder. I brace myself and take a deep breath—I steady my aura and convince my mind that this is a good thing. My brain is trained to do something unspeakable in the event that a member of law enforcement gets this close to me, and I use all of my energy to fight the impulse. I must have closed my eyes, and before I know what is happening, I find myself trapped in a hug, and I can almost taste the mixture of coffee and cigarettes that lingers on his breath. 'I know,' he says as he pats me on the back, 'I know.'

When he is finally done hugging me, he takes the bag in his chubby fingers and looks me in the eye. 'If they are in the system, I'll call you.' We shake hands once more, and he departs. Good old Frank, true to his word and not a question asked.

I make a quick break for the exit. I swing the main door open and find a few uniformed officers smoking, loitering near the bright red, enormous Alfa.

Fuck, I miss the anonymities of the Volvo already.

I'll say this: Frank Carter, moustache and all, is a star. Not only is he true to his word, but he is an efficient detective for an ageing bigot. Less than two hours after our meeting, he was on the phone with a name, address, and phone number. Fortunately for me, the perp was in the system—Frank's words, not mine—and he tells me that the *perp Russell* has a record for assault and robbery and that he could *bring him in* if I wanted. I decline his advances and tell him that the man and I got into a simple fender bender—I'm not sure what inclined me to talk like an American—and that I wanted to reach out to him, that's all. I'll be reaching out with my hands around his neck. But Frank doesn't need to know that.

He gives me the details and tells me to call him if *I need anything at all.* Considering I am a homicidal maniac, it is definitely who you know and not what you know. I jot down the guy's details and thank Frank heartily before he finally lets me go.

It has been a difficult morning. Sitting in a police station is like Jerry sitting in Tom's chair. It is terrible for one's nerves. However, the day is shaping up, and the afternoon promises to be overcast with a chance of murder. How delightful.

The maps on my phone tell me that my *perp's* address is less than twenty minutes away. The day is young, so I decide to visit Russell.

I pull up outside Russell's house, and I instantly hate him. The front garden is a complete mess, and there is a British National Party sticker in the downstairs window. Only a complete tool supports the BNP. His highly public Facebook profile—yes, I ventured onto Facebook, progress—tells me what he looks like and that he is home. The man has probably never held down a job in his life. I get it, I've never really worked either, but I am at least good at what I do. Something Russell is about to discover.

Criminals like Russell make the whole industry look bad. For a start, his whole life is plastered over the internet; he is sloppy, lazy, and known to the police. *Come on, Russell, at least try not to get caught.* I endeavour to keep my work as neat and tidy as possible. You have to take pride in what you do.

I slip into the house through the open back door. The inside makes the outside look tidy, and there isn't a surface that isn't covered in drugs. The cocaine-splattered counters look like a council flat version of Scarface, and I avoid touching anything because I can do without a contact high. I am almost embarrassed that this man got the better of me twice, but I have been off my whole life, never mind my game. I swallow my pride and creep about the kitchen.

I open the fridge, and there is no in-date item in sight. I hear the noise of violent video games ringing out from the lounge. Using my gloved hands—I am a professional—I pick up one of the syringes from the many dotted about the counter. I fill it with whatever is about and tuck it behind my hand. The noise of video games distracts me, and when I turnabout, I find myself face to face with a bald man, complete with a shiny head.

I stare into the eyes of the man who looks a lot like a hairless version of *Pig Pen* from the *Charlie Brown* cartoons. His eyes are glazed over, and his pupils make up most of what's left.

'Hey man,' he says. 'What are you doing here? Are you a friend of Russell's? He just popped to the shop; he'll be back soon.'

I recognise this man from our little car accident. But the fact that he just told me everything I wanted to know without needing to ask makes me go easy on him.

'Oh, wonderful, I'm Arthur, and it is a pleasure to meet you finally.' I stretch my arm out toward him and offer him my hand. His smile drops, and he scratches at his head for a moment before he works out what is happening and returns the gesture. And here I was, thinking I was socially inept?

‘Nick,’ he says, ‘but people call me Nicky.’ Our hands meet and shake softly.

‘Hey, what’s with the rubber gloves?’ he asks.

I smile and pull him toward me as I stick the syringe deep into his thigh and depress the plunger.

SIXTEEN

Nicky was easily subdued; we were still holding hands—cute—when he dropped to the floor and started gurning. I have no idea what was in the syringe, but it looked like good stuff. At least the man gets one more pleasure before he dies.

As promised by my new pal Nicky, Russell's return doesn't take long. He enters the house with the subtlety of Floyd 'Money' Mayweather and crashes through the front door, bellowing, 'Yo Nick, Nicky. Where you at?'

I hide behind the sofa like all good creeps and listen as he sets his belongings inside the front door, opens and closes the fridge—presumably finding nothing edible—and immediately lights a joint.

'Yo, Nicky, you here?' he calls, and I'll admit Nick was right; people really do call him Nicky. Russell hollers almost incessantly and doesn't stop until he enters the lounge. His voice is already annoying me, and I cannot wait to shut him up.

Russell spots Nicky passed out on the armchair and starts to yammer away. It takes him about three minutes before he realises that Nicky is unresponsive, and he yells, 'Fuck sake, Nicky!' before he moves in front of Nicky and slaps his face. I'm not an expert, but I've never seen first aid administered like that before.

With Russell hunched over Nicky, slapping away at his chops, I creep around the sofa behind him and wrap my arm around his neck—I need Russell lucid. My new exercise regime seems to be paying off. I watch Russell struggle meekly against the might of my arm, and he puts up pathetically little in the way of a fight. When the required amount of air finally stops making its way to Russell's pea brain, I let go of him, and he falls to the floor hard. I look down at the man who dared orchestrate the damage to my new Volvo. He has long, dark greasy hair—tucked in a man bun—and a beard that instantly makes me hate him. His neck tattoo features dotted lines and the words *cut here*. You're giving me ideas, Russell. You really are. I tie Russell up as Nicky snoozes through the whole affair.

I hang Russell by his hands from a beam in the ceiling and wait. When he finally comes to, he panics and thrashes hard with his whole body, but it is futile. I cover his mouth with my gloved hand, and he is so busy panicking that he doesn't notice me take out a small knife until I plunge it into his gut. His muffled screams vibrate against the palm of my hand, and I literally feel his pain.

I move to his ear and whisper, 'If you make a sound, I'll pull it out.'

He believes me to be sincere, and I slowly move my hand from his mouth. I can tell he wants to yell, scream, and curse me. He wants to, but he doesn't, the drugs are wearing off, and I can see the terror in his eyes.

I tell him, 'If you give me the information I need, then I will let you live.' The poor idiot clings to hope even though I have already pushed a knife into his belly. He is quick to confess and tells me that he was paid by someone to find the flash drive—which he has since sent away—and he swears that he doesn't know who hired him or why, but a hard push on the knife is all it takes, and he gives me the email address for a man named Magnus. I push him for more—literally—but he swears on his mother's life that is all he knows, and I believe him.

I tell Russell that he *did good* and that I *will let him go.* The man closes his eyes and is still thanking his lucky stars that he is alive as I move behind him, remove the knife from his abdomen, and slit his throat. The blood pours out as I unleash him from the beam. The floor turns Coxcomb Red. He clutches at his throat and falls toward Nicky, covering him in blood, and collapses to the floor, where he rolls about in the growing puddle of his blood until life finally leaves him.

I smile. This feels good.

When I am sure he has stopped moving, I move toward Nicky. I cut the tape that I had attached to his wrists and place the knife in his hand. He murmurs and smiles, but his eyes don't open until I push him from his chair to the floor, and he falls awkwardly onto the blade. His eyes go from shut to fully open in a heartbeat as the knife sinks into his chest. The look of shock is replaced by an expression which signals that he knows he is on his way out of this world, and it isn't long before he, too, is motionless.

I pause and survey the scene. There is no blood on me, and the murder weapon is clamped between Nicky's fingers. It is almost poetic. I could have made them disappear, but that might spook Magnus—whoever the fuck he is—and it might look a bit dodgy when the guy that Carter gave me a name for goes missing. However, two drugged-out local thugs having a deadly disagreement is plausible.

***

'Bro-seph Gordon-Levitt, you're late,' says Abdul as I climb painfully out of the taxi and amble down his drive. Don't these people know what I have been through the last few days? I look at him and flash a murderous grin. Maureen is nowhere to be seen, which is a little odd. They always do everything together.

I study Abdul as I walk toward him, his paunch has grown significantly in the last year and the hair on his chin now significantly outranks that on his head. Abdul is of Egyptian descent but has almost fully embraced western life.

He smiles back at me and says, 'It's just you and me tonight, buddy.'

'Where's Maureen?' I ask in surprise.

'Got called into work,' Abdul replies. 'They had someone brought in with a knife wound.'

'A knife wound?' I say suddenly, very anxious. 'Anyone, we know?'

Abdul shakes his head. 'How the fuck do I know, Arthur?'

I concede that was an odd question.

'It means we get the evening alone, though.'

Rather annoyingly, Maureen is probably one of the best thoracic surgeons in the country. Not that you would know it from her awkward, nerdy demeanour. Something which I have always liked about her. Most proficient surgeons have egos the size of Jupiter. Maureen is humble, understated, and talented, and my god, I hope she fails. A football-sized fucking knot forms in my stomach, and I realise that I never checked to see if Nicky was dead. It can't be a coincidence.

I follow Abdul as he turns about and moves into the house, and we enter for what might be my last supper. As I close the door, I pray to anyone listening for Nicky's demise.

'It will be just like old times,' says Abdul, and he grins at me when he hands me a glass of wine. I feign a smattering of a smile and throw the drink down my throat. Fuck me. I'm an idiot. Always check for a pulse, Arthur.

***

I wait until Abdul opens the third bottle of wine before I ask him if he can trace an email address. Abdul runs an IT firm; I don't know what this means. But my question plays to his ego, and he smiles.

'My friend, there is nothing I can't trace. I'm assuming you want the IP address it was sent from?'

I nod in agreement even though he could have just asked if I wanted extra pink elephants, and I would have said yes.

Abdul is drunk—he only drinks in Maureen's absence—and excitable. He sees my question as a challenge and demands Magnus's email address before running off to his study. I am glad that he will remember none of this tomorrow, and I remain in my seat.

It is less than ten minutes before my giddy friend returns, and he hands me a sticky note.

'Atlanta, as in the US, Georgia?'

He nods. 'Now you,' he says. 'What is this for?'

I panic as I realise that while I was sure he wouldn't remember this tomorrow, I hadn't planned on him asking tonight. My brain scrambles as he pulls out a dining chair, reverses it, and sits across from me. Once there, he props his head in his hands and looks at me. My mind barely moves. I don't know what to tell him. My mouth opens and closes like a revolving door in the wind. But I remain silent. I stew for a good thirty seconds before he says. 'You know what, I don't wanna know.'

'Abdul,' I begin. He cuts me off.

'I don't care. What's life without a little mystery, huh?' He smiles at me, and I nod. 'I'm just glad you're back!' he whispers across the table. 'We thought we had lost you for good for a while.'

I fold the note and tuck it into my pocket. 'It is good to be back,' I say. 'It's good to be back.'

***

I awake the following day on Abdul's sofa. My head feels like a small child has been kicking at it all night long, but this seems to be the new normal. I try to stand up, but my librium is far from equal, and I barely make it to the bathroom before I vomit everywhere. It would seem that heavy drinking after *carcrashsquashdrinksmurderdrinks* is a terrible idea, and I don't even begin to feel better until after the third passing of puke. It has been seven days since I rose from the land of the depressed, and I don't know yet if I am better for it.

I find Abdul in the kitchen nursing a large cup of coffee. He sees me enter, plucks a smile from nowhere, and paints it over his face.

'Bro-seph Heller, that was a righteous evening!' I sit and grab his coffee, taking a large swig.

'Holy fuck!' I exclaim. 'Abdul, is there whiskey in that?'

He nods. 'That will teach you not to steal.'

The liquid burns as it enters my vacant stomach. I gag at first, but with every passing second, I feel a little better.

'I'm too old for hangovers,' he concedes.

'That will do it,' I say. Abdul tells me he recalls little from the night before. I am slightly relieved. 'How's Maureen?' I ask innocently.

'Better than the other guy,' Abdul replies.

'Did he die?' I ask.

'No.' He grunts. 'But she didn't get stabbed.' Abdul then explains that the surgery went on long into the night and that she would be home once he was out of the woods. Hopefully, that isn't true because I need Nicky to stay in the woods forever.

'I need to freshen up,' I say. 'Mind if I use your shower?'

'You know where it is,' he replies. I do indeed, Abdul. I pat him on the shoulder and make my way upstairs. I stop in the bedroom and tuck a fresh pair of Maureen's scrubs into my bag before making it to the shower. I throw up once more before I get in.

It looks like I'm going to the hospital.

SEVENTEEN

I am not there yet, Melissa. I have bodged two kills in a row, been burgled, and in a car crash, and I live in a perpetual state of hangovers. Luck keeps me afloat. Somehow, I haven't been apprehended, killed, or contracted liver disease. It has been eight days since I crawled from my isolation, eight days, one gym excursion, two shopping trips, three social endeavours, two bodged murders, and many, many hangovers. I could dearly do with some alone time, and I am starting to see why some people choose never to leave the house.

Abdul gave me a ride home; I threw up once on his driveway and once on the ride, covering the outside of the passenger door. I think the projectile vomiting made him pleased to see the back of me, and when I finally found myself alone, all I wanted to do was sleep. Alas, there is no rest for the wicked.

I have yet another of my messes to mop up, and there is no time to waste. Nicky saw my face; he cannot be allowed to recover.

I shower once more, puke, shower again and then set off in the Alfa—because Nicky and Russell broke my Volvo—in the direction of Southampton General Hospital. I feel like I'm constantly cleaning up one mess or another, which didn't happen when I stayed home. They say a ship is safest in port, but that's not its purpose. But I can't think of a much better use for a boat than sitting on it sipping a beer as it gently rocks about in the harbour.

The journey from home to Southampton is about twenty minutes. I drive slowly because I cannot afford to draw attention, and I park over the road from the hospital in the cemetery car park. I still think that having a graveyard opposite a hospital is a rather damming indictment of the service offered. Still, it does at least cut transport costs.

I make the short walk over to the hospital. I have no good reason for being here, so I keep my head down to avoid being recognised. Despite being a cliché, keeping your head down does help prevent unwanted attention.

Once inside, I find a toilet, change into my scrubs—thanks, Maureen—and make my way to the staff changing room. I sneak in, pry open a couple of lockers, and grab a name tag from one and a stethoscope from another before making my way up to the intensive care unit. The saying *fake it 'til you make it* is another clichéd adage that does work. Especially here. Staff turnover is high; everyone is busy, tired, and underpaid, and no one questions it if you look like you belong. Who would want to sneak into an NHS hospital and pretend to work there?

I loiter in the ICU; I have no idea what I'm doing, and the alarm bells are ringing in my skull. I have watched a dozen films where this happens, and in my head, I am going to be dragged into an operating theatre at any minute and expected to perform a fucking miracle. I take life. I don't restore it. We are a different department.

I spend an inordinate amount of time picking up charts and putting them down. I swear everyone is looking at me, but just as I start to panic and think about curling up in the foetal position on the floor, an actual alarm bell sounds, and most of the assembled staff go running.

A male nurse approaches me, looks at my name tag and says, 'Doctor, we could use you in room four.' His eyes dart from my badge to my face, then back to the badge. I am completely flabbergasted. In my mind, I was invisible, but now someone is talking to me.

Fuck.

I open my mouth, and for what seems like forever, nothing is emitted. The man holds his glare, and right when I think he is about to have me committed, my brain takes over and throws a plume of words in his face.

'I'm on a break, Nurse! Get Jenkins to do your dirty work.'

The glare turns into momentary shock, the shock dissipates, and he sighs in exasperation before turning about on the spot and disappearing. Either the man hasn't slept in days (possible), or he has truly run out of fucks to give (probable) because he disappears and doesn't return.

I follow the sound of the awful alarm noise to room four. Inside is a melee of staff desperately trying and hoping for the impossible. I pick up a chart that sits outside the room and take note of the name. *Nick Lewis!* Holy shit, would you look at that? I watch a woman who may or may not be Jenkins furiously try and resuscitate the man on the bed.

After several failed attempts to restart the man's heart, the doctor calls time, and all faces in the room turn glum. I look at the new face of death lying on the sheets. It really is him. I'm amazed that he lasted this long. Kudos, Nicky.

I put the chart back, shove my head toward the floor, and march to the lift. It arrives. I step in and turn around. I glance up for a second before putting my head down again. But as I do, I hear a familiar voice.

'Arthur? Arthur, is that you?'

I don't want to look up. I don't need to. I shouldn't have to; *my head was down, dammit.* Either way, I would know Maureen's voice anywhere.

Keeping my eyes low, I desperately press the close door button and hear Maureen's voice approaching as I do. 'Arthur?' Thankfully, the door closes before she gets too close, and I hope she writes me off as a sleep-deprived mirage. Fucking Maureen.

By the time the lift doors open, I am raring to go, like a sprinter racing out of the blocks. I power walk through the hallways as my feet squelch on the floor against the horribly sterile—probably unsterile—hallways. There is something about the way hospitals are designed that makes you want to spend as little time in them as possible; I'm sure it is deliberate.

As I walk, I realise how loud everything is. Chatter bounces off the walls and the floors and back into my ears. It is disorientating, and I am forced to look up. My eyes meet a female colleague who is also in scrubs, and I am forced to smile. Her eyes shine out from beneath her surgical mask—she is pretty, and does she look familiar?—and I realise that hospitals are fifty-fifty dreary fuckery and kind of sexy, and perhaps I need to get laid.

I move past the world's most expensive WHSmith—bottles of water for two pounds? Seriously, as if people aren't suffering enough. I pass the coffee shop no one wants to be in, and I am finally free. I don't break stride until I am back in the cemetery car park. I smile as I look at the graves and realise Nicky will soon be here.

***

I make it as far as the motorway when an insidious thought hits my brain. Nicky's death, as well as the timing, was rather fortuitous. I think back to Jarrod and Suzie, wondering if

Nicky died or was helped along the way. What if someone is clearing up my mess, tying up loose ends? I think about the idiotic thugs, and I wonder, what if? *What if? What if?* Was the burglary timed with my leaving the house? What does Magnus want? It can't be a coincidence that the first night I leave home in months is also the day I get burgled. My anxious mind shudders at the thoughts, and I need answers. I'm a mess.

I pull over on the hard shoulder and switch the hazard lights on. I reach into my bag and retrieve the address that Abdul found for me. I realise in my haste to kill Nicky I had forgotten all about it. I am drawing attention to myself by stopping on the motorway, but I have more questions than answers, and I must address them immediately. At any rate, an Alfa Romeo pulled up on the hard shoulder is not an unfamiliar sight.

I put the address into the search engine, and it pulls up a registered business. An import/export company—of course—owned by one Magnus Sherman. Fuck, the guy even sounds like a twat. It would seem that Magnus is relatively successful in the import/export business, whatever that means, and he is a minor celebrity in his native Georgia. The internet returns little information about him besides his cars, his penchant for fine dining, and his wife. There is an option on his website to make enquiries, so I make one before continuing my drive home.

EIGHTEEN

I sit in the conservatory and wait for Magnus to reply. I know it is early in the US, but I am reasonably sure that import/export is code for something dishonest, and this man likes his cars and his young wife. He has a lifestyle to fund, he will reply. *He will reply*!

I switch my gaze between my phone and the Wellington's bickering in the garden—they started early this week—I wonder why they argue so publicly. I can only assume that it is an indictment of their marriage, and one or both are looking for sympathisers, potential suitors, or both. I am starting to change my mind. I don't hate it anymore. In fact, it makes for some gloriously stupid reality TV—people pay to watch this kind of thing.

As I watch Mike and June hurl insults at each other, I realise just how idiotic Mike is. I would gladly trade places with him to be able to argue with you every weekend, Melissa.

June—to be fair—is a bit of a nag, but despite Mike's many flaws, she is still around. She hasn't left. The constant competition between her and Mike's younger models seems to have forced her into serious body maintenance, and I must admit she always looks fabulous. Mike is a good-looking man, tall, dark—whatever that means—and handsome in a ruddy way. But his lifestyle choices are starting to catch up with him, and the problem with any middle-aged man trying to keep up with younger women is that we are not kids anymore. His paunch is starting to protrude from his middle, and he could use some of June's concealer on his eye bags. I watch June gesticulate wildly in Mike's face and stare at her in awe. Sex slowly seeps into my brain again, and I am pleasantly distracted when my phone screen lights up.

Sadly, it is not from Magnus. But it is from Ophelia. As much as I like her—and it would seem that I cannot stop thinking about sex—I could do without our afternoon appointment at the gym. Keen to escape my thrashing thoughts, I pick up the phone and begin to read.

Hey, Arthur, I can't make the gym this afternoon. Bummer :(Sorry. X Ophelia.

Happily, however, it would seem Ophelia is reading my mind. And I smile, relieved, as I go to reply.

Oh no, that is really too bad. Another time? Arthur Xx

The double *x's* slipped out. They did. I'm unsure if it was a default because I am used to putting *x's* at the end of my messages to you, Melissa. Or because I am really out of touch with messaging pretty women or messaging in general. I put the phone back down in time to see June storm back into the house. I stare as she departs, and Goddamit, why can't I get my mind out of the gutter? My muddy male mind is distracted once more by a permanent glow from my phone as it rings away in silence.

I've never been one of those people that is particularly good at answering the phone, and when I see that it is Ophelia ringing me, I panic hard that she has changed her mind about the gym, and I let it go to voicemail. But dear Ophelia is anything if not persistent, and the call is followed up swiftly by another message.

You're the best! Sorry, I hope I didn't disappoint you. Anyway, if you are free later and fancy letting me make it up to you, I can buy you dinner around 8. Xx Ophelia.

I stare at her words, and my id is urging me to reply immediately, but I am in the awkward zone where I know if

I reply too soon, it will be evident that I ducked the call. I wait five minutes before I respond.

After a week of *carcrashsquashbodgedmurdersmagnus-hangovervomit*, I could do with not going to the gym, so if anyone is doing anyone a favour, it is her. I do need to eat, though. Something I tell myself as I reply.

I like food. Sounds perfect, where shall we meet? X Arthur.

I leave off the extra *x,* I mean, a man has to play it cool, and I don't have time to pocket the device before she replies again.

Do you do Greek? If so, there is a little place near mine. I gotta dash but let me know, and I'll text you the address later. Xx

I would like to *do Greek* in just about all senses of the word, so I waste absolutely no time in replying.

It's all Greek to me. But I'm in. See you later. X

Shopping is one of life's tortures that I have never really enjoyed. Especially during a time of great depression. And as such, there is spectacularly little to eat in my house. I would gladly have agreed to eat cat food today if it spared me from going shopping or to the gym. Perhaps the day won't be so unkind to Ascetic Arthur after all.

***

It is strange how things in life can change so suddenly. Just two weeks ago, I was an accomplished hermit. My life revolved around the bedroom, the bathroom, the kitchen, and the occasional trip to the porch or the garden. Yet suddenly, I have a calendar brimming with social events, murders, people, and hangovers.

I look at my watch. It is just after three in the afternoon. I have a few hours to kill—not literally today—and yet another hangover to solve. There are so many thoughts swilling around in my brain, and I figure the only thing for it is to spring clean. It is spring, after all, and now that some of my mental clarity is returning, I have realised that I am living in a bit of a shithole. Even Jarrod's house, with its dead cut-cat-cluttered attic, was cleaner than mine. Cleaning is also an excellent way to lose a part of the day you wish you didn't have.

In my defence, I have had some issues vis-à-vis cleaning. Because so much of what is in the house, including the house itself, isn't, or at least wasn't, mine. It is one of those things that no one ever talks about, and I don't think there is a manual for this. But how on earth do you go about getting rid of your dead wife's stuff? If you remove everything belonging to your significant other immediately, you might push yourself over the edge. As heart-breaking as it is, I think I have preferred seeing your things, Melissa. But now that I am edging toward recovery, I am wise enough to know that I must move on. I have cupboards and drawers full of a dead women's clothes. Even for me, that is a bit weird. Eventually, something has to change.

Cleaning the house is tremendously tedious. It is a big place, and a thorough blitz will take me a good few hours, even more so if I have to clean around everything that belongs to you, Melissa. So, I put on some loud rock and roll and diligently get on with my task.

The mundane activity occupies my thoughts; before I know it, the house is sparkling, and I find myself in the bedroom with several large bin bags. I don't know how to do this, so I tackle it like removing duct tape and rip it off. I place all your clothes in the bags, Melissa and I power downstairs and stuff the sacks in the boot of the Alfa. I shove the bulky bags in the boot and am in my own world when I hear my name being called.

'Arthur?' I look over my shoulder and find myself face to face with June, who is at the end of her driveway. She spots me, and I know she needs attention, and it isn't long before she strolls over and approaches me. 'Hey, Arthur,' she says. 'I haven't seen you in—'

'Months?' I cut her off. I don't have time to play guess-how-long-Arthur-has-been-depressed-for.

She smiles, walks over, and touches me softly on the arm. 'How are you doing?'

I nod. 'I'm getting there,' I say.

'Well, it's good to see you out and about. We were starting to get worried about you.'

'Thanks,' I acknowledge, realising that as much as I have been watching them, it has been nearly a year since I conversed with either Mike or June. I also realise that if she was that worried, she could have knocked on the fucking door! She looks down at the bags that I am loading into the boot.

'You finally getting rid of Melissa's stuff?'

'Well, it's that or body parts,' I say.

June laughs. 'It's good you still have your sense of humour!'

I wasn't joking.

She still has her arm on my bicep, and I feel her grip tighten. 'You know, we all miss Melissa.'

'Thanks,' I say. Our eyes lock, and I look deep into her empty soul. June is very attractive, in an Aunt Bessie kind of way. Our eyes stay intertwined, and the silence gets louder. I can feel her emptiness, and it mixes with mine. Her hand remains on my arm, and I can feel her yearning for attention. I hear it calling out to me, and I almost answer it.

'Well, I won't keep you,' she says, and her hand lets go of my arm, allowing the tension to drop. June almost scampers back to the confines of her house. She reaches the front door, shoots me a parting glance, and says, 'You should come over for dinner sometime?'

'Sure!' I say. *Why the fuck did I say that?* June pauses as if she is considering a time inconvenient for Mike.

'How about next weekend?'

'It's a date,' I reply.

June grins. 'Excellent. I'll let Mike know and pop you in the calendar.'

'Look forward to it,' I reply. I don't. Aunt June disappears into her house, and I am left holding my bags. Having royally fucked up my weekend, I turn my attention back to my task.

The smell from your belongings drifts out of the bags and into my nostrils, Melissa. I slam the boot shut and having filled the Alfa with new (dead) Melissa smell. I realise it will be too much and I will have to drive the other one tonight. I remove the keys to your Maserati, and I creep across the drive toward it. I unlock it, and with one eye closed, I creak open the door for the first time since you left.

NINETEEN

As promised, Ophelia texts me the details. A full two hours in advance. She doesn't give me the restaurant address—she gives me hers. I like having your home address, Ophelia.

The problem with the death of a loved one is that there comes a time when you have to accept that you won't get back what you lost. It's not like simple heartbreak; there's no possible chance of reconciliation. And there also seems to be a period of self-punishment—time must elapse before you can even think about being happy again. You are gone, Melissa. You died and left me here, so I'm not allowed to be happy.

Walking upstairs to shower, I realise that enough time has passed, and I am maybe almost happy. But it's been nearly thirteen years since I dated, and I'm terrifically terrified.

I never expected this to happen. Not to me. It feels like someone physically wounded me, ripped my heart out, and then punched me in the gut for good measure. I hate it, and I'm glad some of the pain has subsided. I've been shot at, stabbed, punched, and even spat on. But none of that even mildly compares to the pain of losing you, Melissa. Not by a long way.

If we knew how badly the loss would hurt, we wouldn't bother. Yet as the pain starts to fade, we begin to move on. Happy clouds slowly replace dark tides, and we forget that anything could hurt so much. But you start from experience, not from scratch. I suppose pain is one of the reasons we feel alive. I hope that Ophelia won't hurt me in any way I haven't asked for, but who knows?

I was numb and angry before we met, Melissa, but then all that changed. It changed again when you died. Because of you, I've felt things I've never felt before and never thought I could. It is a strange sensation.

I'm nervous about tonight and haven't felt that for a long time. Me, Arthur, nervous? I don't know what the fuck is happening.

Clothes. I opt for smart casual—proper smart casual, not gym-wear smart casual. It's just after seven-thirty, and maps tell me the drive is ten minutes. Long enough to unwind, short enough to not worry too much about the evening ahead.

Now to the Maserati! I climb in with trepidation, Melissa—the last time I was in here, we were together. I ferret about and tidy the cockpit, finding things of yours. There's a flood of memories, and I must focus on blocking them. Having shoved your belongings in the glove box, I freshen the air by unloading a can of air freshener. Too much. I smell like a *heavy-duty fresh lemon*. I Start the engine and hear the Maserati's wonderful growl. The inside of the car is as confusing as it is stylish, but I find reverse on the third try and set off with a lurch.

A catharsis exudes from having finally moved it.

***

I arrive with a few minutes to spare; I park on what I presume is Ophelia's driveway. The Maserati makes her Audi look like a child's toy.

I'm a bag of nerves as I kill the engine, and as I take a deep breath to settle myself, I'm sure I will smell like a *heavy-duty fresh lemon* for the rest of my life.

Approaching the door, I hesitate. Should I have brought something? I was so focused on you, Melissa, me, and Aunt June. I didn't think about anything else.

The wait for the door to open is an anxious void.

Ophelia answers the door, and I am spellbound. It was worth the terrifying wait. As I stare at her, I begin to regret the smart/casual choice. The way she looks, I'd be underdressed next to her even if I'd come as Daniel Craig in Casino Royale, and I blush.

'Wow,' I say, 'You look . . .'

I honestly don't know what to say.

'Thanks,' says Ophelia, smiling. 'You scrub up well too.'

From the ground, she starts with enormous heels, which make her almost as tall as me. Racy, patterned tights, a short but elegant skirt, and a tightly fitted blouse that looks like it's spray painted on. It buttons to the height of her breasts and, not that I'm looking, but shows a tiny glimmer of black bra. I have no idea how you begin to describe make-up, but it is perfect, and I'm sure I am staring.

'Let me grab my bag. The taxi is almost here.' She disappears into the house, and I'm in love with her confidence.

No, she isn't Melissa—but you can't compare the two. Melissa was a wonderful English rose: short, curvy, beautiful, full, and cute. Ophelia is a Greek goddess: tall, thin, tanned, dark-haired and feisty. It's like comparing summer to winter or knives to blunt instruments. Each is equally wonderful in its own way.

Ophelia reappears, and we walk to the curb. I wish I'd spent time thinking of conversation starters. I am unusually speechless. Thankfully she doesn't seem to notice.

'Cutting it a little fine, weren't you?'

I start to protest, but she turns her head and winks.

'Hey,' I say, biting, 'I was spot on time. No one likes an early arrival.'

The taxi arrives—she wasn't kidding—and I open the door for her to climb in. The driver already knows where we're going. I still find it strange, but it curbs the need for human interaction. The car pulls off, and she looks back over my shoulder at the driveway.

'How many cars do you have?'

Three-ish. 'Two,' I say.

'I like that one.' I nod.

Melissa said the same thing. I don't mention you, Melissa. Instead, I move the conversation along.

'Busy day?' *What am I saying? Come on, Arthur!*

'Like you wouldn't believe,' Ophelia says. 'I had to go to work. There was some emergency.'

I nod, thinking I don't know what she does for a living. My mind races into panic mode, and I picture her dressed in forensic gear—CSI Hampshire—and I hope to hell she doesn't investigate crime.

'My boss is such an arsehole; Friday afternoon be dammed; he needs his PA!'

And relax.

'To be fair,' I reply, 'If you were my PA, I'd want you every day of the week!'

The words leave my mouth, and I realise I also need a speech-retraction function. Was that creepy? Fortunately, the comment brings about a wry smile.

'I had a great time at the gym last week and was delighted you were free tonight. I could use some fun.'

A great time? With me, at the gym? Perhaps she is crazy.

I smile. 'Fun is my speciality.'

Wait, my speciality? Who am I, Tigger? God, I'm like a giddy teenager!

The car pulls up, and I'm relieved. I can't remember the last time I needed a drink so badly. I nod toward the driver, who could be a robot, exit the car and stretch my hand toward Ophelia. She grabs it, and I feel the warmth of her skin. As she exits the car, her movement parts the gap in her shirt, and I get an extended succour-inducing sight of what lies beneath. Fortunately, the only person who notices is the robot driver, who shoots me a wink.

I fluster, and my strength gets away from me. I almost drag Ophelia from the car, and she stumbles on her heels and falls into me. I catch her, and we stand entwined on the street for a moment. Our eyes meet, and the beast inside me wants to throw her on the floor and climb on. She returns my stare, and I hope she feels the same. I mean, we're both adults, after all.

'Good catch,' she says and winks at me.

And I'm glad my awkwardness wins her approval. She keeps a hold of my hand, and we walk together toward the restaurant.

TWENTY

I meant it when I told Ophelia it was *all Greek to me*. I have never set foot in a Greek restaurant or been to Greece before—I have no idea what to expect. I know absolutely nothing about Greece other than what I learned in geography or on the TV. It's an archipelago. They have great weather. Their Gods are cooler than ours, and they always seem to be in debt.

To my surprise, Greek restaurants are awesome.

We were greeted like long-lost family, and I'm still not sure if that is or isn't the case. The inside of the place is both homely and tacky, but I like it. It feels authentic. The smell that emerges from the kitchen is next level, and my stomach rumbles louder than Zeus's thunderbolt. We sit, and drinks appear as if by magic. I take a long, savouring sip of a tasty lager, feel the alcohol seep into my eyes, and realise that more has come out than gone in today.

The menu is bursting with meat and potato dishes; there are pictures of my potential food, so I know what to expect. I look around the room, see the laughter, hear the calling of plates of meat, and am in heaven.

'I have to confess, this is my first Greek experience,' I say.

Ophelia's mouth drops.

'Whaaat?!'

I go to reply, but she turns and yells over her shoulder at a man who may or may not be her brother.

'Hey Nikos, we have a first-timer!'

Nikos's face mirrors her shock, as though it's both impossible and a personal insult. Before I know it, he is on his way over with poorly washed shot glasses and a bottle of ouzo—the man has clearly never been schooled in measures. The smiley, chubby man fills both glasses and pours a healthy amount onto the table. I decipher the aniseed notes from the strong smell and wonder how much of the ouzo is in Nikos. He motions wildly with his hands and says something in Greek that I can only imagine has something to do with drinking shots from dirty glasses.

Ophelia raises hers and throws it down her throat. Not wanting to be outdone, I grab mine and do the same. The smooth, cheap alcohol almost stumbles down my gullet, but it's not unpleasant—far from it. The liquor mixes oddly with the beer in my empty stomach, but I don't have time to react as the menu is whipped from my hand, and Nikos disappears.

'What does that mean?'

'Nikos is very proud of his food. He'll bring a mixture of everything.'

Welcome news. I look around once more at the piles of meat, and my stomach rumbles again. I take another sip of beer to silence it.

'So, you've never been to Greece?' Ophelia asks in disbelief.

I shake my head. We talked about this at the gym. She is taunting me, and I like it.

'No,' I say, 'but, in my defence, I am British. Eighty per cent of us are unaware that there is land outside the United Kingdom.'

Ophelia laughs, and I find it equally curious I've never been to Greece.

Nikos passes by and deposits more drinks on the table. Were I not rich, I'd start to worry about the potential bill.

The food comes, enough to feed a multitude. It's all delicious and disappears quickly, washed down with Ouzo and more beer.

Plates are removed, and dessert arrives, as does yet more ouzo. I'm stumbling as I head to the toilet. I can already feel tomorrow's hangover brewing.

Returning to the table, I'm filled with drunk confidence. I grab the cake and ouzo and shove them together in my mouth. I don't know what I'm doing, but Ophelia laughs, and the aniseed taste of the ouzo gloriously offsets the sweetness of the dessert. It tastes like fucking heaven.

I grab and drink Ophelia's ouzo before she can protest and gleefully wave the empty in the direction of Nikos. Ophelia slaps me playfully on the wrist. Nikos bounces over with another bottle, and at least I have stopped being awkward. The restaurant has been emptying, and our larger-than-life host refills the cups and drenches most of the table and my hand before he disappears. It's not until Nikos departs that I realise her hand is lying on top of mine. I look at her hand, the gap in her top, and then her eyes. She goes to speak, and I panic, slightly bursting out.

'Do you wanna go to Georgia?'

She looks at me inquisitively and asks, 'The country, the state, or a person?'

'Atlanta,' I reply.

'So, the state then?'

I nod.

'Sure!' she replies with a smile. 'When do we leave?'

'Next week.'

'Wait, you're being serious?'

'Deadly,' I say.

'Oh, shit—you really aren't joking?!'

I shake my head. Ophelia laughs.

'You're drunk!'

'I am, but I'm serious.'

'You are serious.'

'I am.'

'Can I think about it?' she asks.

'You can.'

'I'd have to check my savings,' she says.

'So, you're thinking about it?'

'I am.'

'My treat. What's there to think about?'

'You're crazy, Arthur!'

'Granted.' Ophelia picks up her shot and tosses it back like a pro.

'You're paying?' I nod. She waits a beat, then laughs.

'Fuck it. Why not!'

'You better not be fucking with me,' I say.

'Never,' is her earnest response.

'We can book flights tomorrow.'

'I'll put in a holiday request.'

'Excellent.'

'Indeed.'

We stare at each other, and the rest of the room fades to black. The whole world seems to stop like someone clicked a button on a remote. We remain on our own planet for an interminable amount of time, and I never want it to end. I am in love with everything Greece has to offer.

It would appear that Nikos has shuffled by and left the cheque on the table. We are the last diners left, and I grab the bill to discover it is shockingly small. No wonder Greece is always in debt.

The outside air is cool and warm. The evening is beautiful. Even if it wasn't, we are far too drunk to notice. We forego the taxi and stumble home, arm in arm.

'Wait, you think Nikos and I are related?'

I shrug, and Ophelia tugs at my arm playfully.

'You're an idiot.'

'Is that a no?'

She laughs. I laugh, and I'm still unsure if they are.

The merriment continues until, before we know it, we are back at her house, standing haphazardly outside her front door.

'Thanks,' she says. 'That was fun.'

'I can already feel the hangover coming,' I say.

Ophelia laughs again.

I go to speak, but she reaches up, grabs my face, and kisses me. The kiss is short, sweet, and perfect until she pulls her head from mine in a panic.

'Sorry,' she says.

'No, it's fine,' I say. It truly was. And I don't know what else to say.

'No, I'm an idiot,' she says. 'Sorry, I'm drunk. I don't know what I was thinking.'

'It's fi—'

'Sorry, I gotta go.'

She cuts me off and opens the door in a flutter.

I try to speak, but I'm drunk, and she's through the door before I know it.

'I'll text you,' she says. The door closes, and I'm alone.

Women are and always have been confusing, Melissa. I know this as one of life's facts, so I don't read too much into it. The Maserati can sit for the night. I'm too drunk to drive. Besides, it gives me an excuse to see her tomorrow. I dig around in my pocket, fish out a pair of headphones and plug in. It's a long walk, but I need the air.

I take five steps down the path, and a notification ping climbs up my headphones and into my ears—a reply from Magnus.

Always happy to do new business, but I like to put a name to a face. Can we meet?

I grin and praise my drunken decision that going with a friend to Atlanta to meet Magnus Sharman will be less suspicious and way more fun. I'm shocked that I asked, actually, and even more that she said yes.

We're going to Atlanta.

TWENTY-ONE

I wake up on the verandah in a heap. I made the drunken mistake of retiring to the garden with a beer and promptly fell asleep. Much to my relief, Mike and June aren't in attendance. Either they are in a reconciliatory patch, or God finally came down on my side and smote them both. Regardless, for the sake of my head and not being featured on *Crimewatch* later, I am pleased to be spared from the garden bickering today.

My head pounds, and I speak from experience when I say it feels like it is about to split open. I check my watch to discover that it is after one. My phone tells me I have two missed calls from Abdul (no message) and one from Ophelia, a voicemail and a text that says, *Call me, please*.

My head is gone. Where there was once a brain now lives an empty, dusty void. My insides feel like they have been removed, turned inside out, and reinserted. I feel truly spectacularly awful. I do. But at the same time, I feel just that little bit better, bit by bit.

Alcohol helps. It does. I have been trying hard not to dwell too much in my head. For example, an Atlanta businessman hired local thugs to rob my house and crash into my car. I'm certain that Maureen saw me at the hospital yesterday when I was moonlighting as Dr Death, and Ophelia kissed me before running away into her house. Oh, and I invited her to Atlanta. So, now that I think about it, there are quite a few things to worry about. My brain is literally on fire, and part of me wants to get into the bath and never re-emerge. I won't, of course. I have unfinished business to attend to, and provided it is not dead-on-arrival. I am quite liking whatever is happening with Ophelia.

I can't yet bring myself to listen to Ophelia's voicemail. I would rather hear what she has to say directly. I am afraid to ring Abdul back in case Maureen did spot me in the hospital, or they want to invite me over. I'm certain I will spontaneously combust if I drink heavily for the third night in a row.

I notice the house phone flashing to signify that it, too, has a message, and I press play and listen.

Hey, it's us. Just wondering how you were doing. Call us back when you get a chance.

Parents! They are the only ones who still actually use the landline, and yes, *us* means *them* and by *how are you doing,* they mean, *are you still sad?* I could say that at least they try, but to be honest, I wish they didn't.

It might seem harsh, but my parents and my family, in general, are just acquaintances who share a name with me. I think the proudest my parents have ever been of me was when I met you, Melissa. Now that you are gone, I am back to being the lazy disappointment. Because it is, of course, my fault that you died. My mum and dad are upper-middle-class wealthy, and as a result, I don't know them at all. They had enough money to pay for babysitters, school pick-up, and boarding school. But not enough that they could ever stop working and spend time with us. Now that they have the time, they spend it holidaying and complaining, nothing more, nothing less.

My sister—fucking Judy—and I were enrolled in boarding school from age five, and as a result, none of us really know each other. We are a family of strangers. I am sure that the sum of our childhood experiences ruined Judy and I—turned me into a blood-lusting maniac, and Judy into a malignant narcissist—but I am not bothered. I know it might seem that I have some stored resentment. I don't. They are all just people I neither know that well nor like. I am what I am now. I make the most of it. I never knew what it was like not to struggle or be alone until we met, Melissa. You taught me that I was fine the way I am. I will always be eternally grateful for that.

I will be fine as soon as I shower, eat, throw up, and shower again.

The early afternoon passes slowly into the evening, and I finally gather myself together to call Ophelia.

I pick up my phone, dial her number and place the device to my ear. It doesn't ring long enough for me to get cold feet, and I hear Ophelia's voice within seconds.

'Hey,' she says, 'I'm so glad you called. I was beginning to think you wouldn't.'

'Busy morning,' I lie. 'What's up?'

'I just wanted to talk to you about last night.' Ah, here it comes. The soul-crushing pain of entertaining the idea of opening your heart again. No doubt she isn't ready for this; she wants to be friends. We will try, but it will be awkward as shit before it slowly dies an obdurate death.

'Sure,' I reply as stoically as possible.

'In person?'

'Sure,' I repeat for lack of a better response.

'I can swing by with your car around eight?'

'Sounds good,' I say before hanging up.

There are currently far too many things swilling around in my brain. How many other mistakes have I made, and why, oh why, did I agree to have dinner with the Wellingtons?

I spend the rest of the day tending to another hangover and rearranging the house again. There is a simple catharsis that exudes from moving the furniture around. The old layout is gone, and in comes the new house, the new me.

My mum calls and reminds me that it is my sister's birthday the week after next. She repeats that I ought to get her a gift, reads from an approved list and wants me to promise I will be there. It's in two weeks! No doubt, I will have myriad reminders between now and then. I shower, text Abdul back and then start to get dressed. The weeklong hangover is now becoming the new normal, and I am adept at feeling like utter crap while still functioning.

I shower and have just got my trousers on when I hear a car pull up. I peel back the curtain and peek outside. I see Ophelia pull up and park the car. She takes an admiring glance at the Italian saloons before making her way to the front door. Even from here, I can tell that she is immaculately well-presented, and I wonder if it's a sick way of softening the blow of rejection. The doorbell rings, and I am wasting time staring out the window when I am nowhere near ready.

Seeing her arrive well-dressed and early forces my brain to consider the positives. Perhaps she is here to reconcile. We were pretty drunk, after all. I mean, you can tell someone *no* over the phone. The positive notion bounces from my brain to my heart, and I feel something going on inside it. The doorbell rings again, and I realise I am still hiding behind the curtain like a nine-year-old. I don't want her to leave, so I pop the window open and stick my head outside.

'I'm just coming,' I yell. She sees my head emerge and smiles. I shut the window and then spend the rest of eternity drying myself and deciding what to wear.

TWENTY-TWO

I open the door and usher Ophelia into the house, and suddenly I am glad I cleaned. She is the first person to enter the place—other than me since you left, Melissa, and I am suddenly very aware of that. I have dressed as well as possible without throwing on a dinner jacket—I did consider it briefly—and I am otherwise remarkably unremarkable. I would love to comment on my appearance and tell you that I have a cool haircut or some evocative tattoos, but I have neither. I keep my hair very short—allowing me to use wigs if necessary. The rest of my body I keep as normal as possible. You cannot commit dozens of crimes and be easy to identify. In my distant dreams, I look forward to a day when I can let loose, get my head tattooed or grow a mullet. It is, of course, a pipe dream. I can no more change who I am than a zebra can change its stripes.

I leave Ophelia in the living room as I kill time in the kitchen making drinks. I take a long sip of my wine before topping it back up. I'm nervous. Can you tell I'm nervous? I finally gather my courage, pick up the drinks and move into my freshly arranged living room.

'Your drink, my lady,' I say as I set it down next to her. She picks it straight up and takes a sip. At least that makes two of us.

'Thanks,' she says, putting her cup down following a long, savouring sip. 'I needed that!'

'How are you feeling?' I ask, and fuck me, that was dry.

'Awful,' she says. 'You?'

'I spent the day redecorating,' I say, gesturing to the living room.

'That bad, huh?' I nod.

'So—' I begin.

'I need to—' says Ophelia. We awkwardly talk over each other, but it's cute. We get stuck in the verbal equivalent of trying to avoid someone in a supermarket aisle.

'No, you,' I say finally.

'I'm sorry about last night,' she says. 'I panicked and didn't want you to get the wrong impression.'

I laugh, 'I honestly had no idea what impression to take.'

'Well,' she says, 'it's been a long time since I liked someone, and there was alcohol, talk of America and I . . . I just worried that I read it wrong.'

'Well, that's a relief,' I say.

'It is?'

'Yeah, I mean, it's better than a rejection.'

'True,' Ophelia smiles. 'It's just I wanted to kiss you. But then I remembered your wife and I didn't know if you were ready or serious about Atlanta, and I panicked and ran.'

'So, you do want to go to Atlanta?' I say. I grin, small on the outside but huge internally.

She simpers, 'I do! But your wife?'

'Is dead,' I say. *And I need to figure out who robbed my house*; I don't say. The silence in the room is slightly more than palpable. Ophelia picks up on my hesitation, moves toward me and takes my hand.

'If it's too soon?' she asks. I shake my head. She smiles, 'I'm glad.'

I must admit, I feel like this is the first time I have ever done this, and I feel fucking useless. It reminds me of approaching Sarah Robinson when I was sixteen. She laughed off my attempted advance before taking me behind the squash courts. So, I dig deep into my expansive, expressive vocabulary built over the years for the purpose of courting women. 'I like you, Ophelia.'

'I like you too,' she replies. 'We can take this slowly if you like?' I nod. 'Melissa would want you to be happy.' I nod again and remember that Melissa knew Ophelia quite well, whereas I know very little about her, and my brain reminds me of the dead boyfriend.

'So, Atlanta is probably the craziest first date I've ever been invited on.' Her words break my trance, and I chuckle.

'Well, then, you need to meet better people.'

'And you're actually serious?'

'Deadly,' I say. Ophelia giggles.

'You're crazy.'

'That's what they say.'

'I have some holiday. Give me a few days' notice, and I'm all yours.' She flashes me a grin as she finishes her sentence, and I cannot help but feel that she meant she would be all mine. I am both excited and terrified. I excuse myself in the direction of the kitchen and shuffle off awkwardly to make more drinks I don't want.

It has been two weeks since I emerged from my den of squalitude. Ophelia is right; Melissa would want me to be happy. But I can't help but feel conflicted. On the one hand, I'm not sure I am ready for anything; on the other, this is exactly what I need. Two weeks in the wilderness has seen me fuck up spectacularly. I'm alone and don't know how to be the man I'm supposed to be anymore. You're gone, Melissa. You left me. I have to move forward, whatever that means.

I finally return with two fresh drinks. I place them down, and I sit.

'I thought you might have run away!' she jokes.

'I might have considered it.'

'I can go if you like?' I shake my head.

'No, please stay.' Ophelia nods, and I realise I still don't know what to say. There is a tension in the room, in me, and I don't know how to break it. I take a healthy sip from my drink, compose myself, and say. 'It's not you. If I'm being honest, I don't have a clue what I am doing. It's been over thirteen years since I, you know. I'm so confused, confusing, and I don't know what I am anymore. I want this. I do. I just—'

Amid my rambling, Ophelia moves toward me and kisses me passionately on the lips just as I start jamming words together. Our lips lock. They collide like two stars and remain as one. She doesn't pull away, and neither do I. I don't know how long we kissed; it could have lasted all night, for all I know. When she finally moves away, she looks me hard in the eyes and says. 'We have flights to book.'

I can see why you liked her, Melissa. You and Ophelia share the same dominant forward streak. It is something I sorely need. We talk for a while after we kiss, and she is pushed up alongside me on the sofa as we look at flights and hotels. Is it odd that having someone tucked up next to me is something I have missed? For the longest time, I assumed I was destined to be alone forever. I hadn't even pictured this happening again, but now that it is, I realise it was tragic in its absence.

We book flights, and you pay, Melissa. We hug, snuggle, and kiss some more until Ophelia tells me, 'She has to leave.' Her boss—the Dickhead, by all accounts—needs her at work tomorrow—on a Sunday—and she needs an early non-drunken night. I concede that is fair—I need one, too—and I eventually walk her to the door.

'I'm glad I came over,' she says.

‘Me too.’

We share one more long, final kiss before she drags herself away. Ophelia walks backwards down the drive keeping eye contact as she does. As she walks, I realise that lust is one of the many feelings pinging about my brain. Part of me—most of me—wants to stroll toward her and mount her right here on the driveway. But that isn’t what happens in the *Notebook*, is it? When she finally reaches the waiting cab, she opens the door and gets in. The driver starts the engine, puts it in reverse, and is almost off the driveway and gone when her head protrudes from the window. ‘I’ll message you.’ She smiles a smile that could warm the coldest of hearts. I’ll admit it is having an effect on mine.

TWENTY-THREE

I slept like a baby last night. Quite literally. It is now Sunday. Two weeks post leaving the great depression. I feel like a weight has been lifted from me, and I am looking forward for the first time in a long time. My newfound lust for life pains me when I think about how lackadaisical I have been lately. I've come closer to being caught in the last two weeks than in my career as a lunatic. My extended absence from dealing with my urges has seen me act on impulse, one that almost saw me kill a cat cutter. And although I remain at large, the mystery surrounding Jarrod and Suzie's deaths is one of many I could do without.

I rise from the dead and move to the window; the sun is peeking through the poorly closed curtain, and I open it to allow the waiting light to invade my chamber. The sunshine is keen and rushes in as I part the drapes; it hits my sleepy pupils, and I am momentarily blind. The rays hit my skin and warm me back to life. I close my eyes and bask in it. My life has been sepia for as long as I can remember, and I have teetered on the edge of a precipice.

After warming what I now know to be my naked torso in the warm light of day, I open my eyes and adjust them to the pervading light. My focus returns, and I find myself eye-to-eye with June in the garden next door. I smile and wave, and she reciprocates, and it is then that I realise I am stark-fucking-naked. Short of a better plan, I snap the curtains shut and disappear. Well, at least dinner might be a bit less tedious now that I've gone full frontal.

Having exposed myself to the neighbour, I move into the en suite, step into the shower and begin to scald myself.

Now that I am beginning to find some semblance of recovery, I should probably apologise to you, Melissa. I guess I have never really explained why I missed your funeral.

You are all too aware that I have never liked funerals. It is too much like work for me. I don't like making unoffensive small talk or having to think five paces ahead to avoid putting my foot in my mouth. I don't like the paradox of being dressed in black, sad, and celebrating. I don't particularly appreciate talking to great Aunt Gladys or whatever unknown relatives crawl out of the woodwork, and I don't like eulogising. So, there are many reasons why I might skip a funeral, Melissa, but none of them is the reason why I missed yours.

The truth is, I was scared. Sometimes you aren't ready. It's ironic; I suppose, because I have taken many lives. I have held people and watched them drain of life. It is one of our few certainties; we are born and will die. The problem is, I never expected you to go first, Melissa, and I certainly didn't think it would be so soon. There are many things in life I don't take seriously, but the *until death do you part, part* wasn't one of them. You died, and we parted, and that wasn't what I wanted. I signed up for it, but I wasn't fucking ready.

When I didn't show up for your funeral, I'm sure the cemetery was rife with speculation, gossip, and rumours of me going off the deep end. But sometimes Occam's Razor is right. The simplest answer is the correct one. I just couldn't face it. Going to a funeral offers closure. I know that. But I wasn't ready to see your body lowered into the ground, it would have made it real, and I was in serious denial. I have since wondered why there is no option for a delayed funeral.

The shower is a most wonderful place for inception. It is a Sunday, I have nowhere to be for a nice change, and I decide to make the long overdue visit to your memorial.

I get in the Alfa and drive in the direction of the cemetery. I am in no hurry, which is a good fucking job because I don't understand what happens to the roads in the UK on a Sunday. The early part of it is far from what should be a day of rest. I assume people wake up, look in their fridge, realise that for the twelfth week running that they haven't done any shopping, decide that the apocalypse is impending and get straight in their car and head for the nearest fucking supermarket.

I would understand if this were a country like Germany, and when the shops shut, they all shut. But there is very little you cannot buy, even at 9 p.m. on a Sunday. Monday is a mere three hours away, and every twenty-four-hour shop is about to reopen. But no, for some reason, at 3.45 on a Sunday, fifteen minutes before the shops shut, every supermarket is crowded.

To make matters worse, despite the desperate scramble to get to the shops before they close, no one is in a hurry on the road. Everyone drives as though their car will blow up should they press the throttle too often.

I feel I have aged by the time I arrive at the cemetery. I park up, and thankfully everyone is still too busy pillaging the middle of Lidl to give a fuck about lost loves.

Despite being on the way to visit the memory of my dead wife, I don't have a fucking clue where I am going. Melissa would never be seen dead in a grave, and she donated as many organs as she could before being cremated. I, too, have a donor card, and I sometimes wonder if my organs would be rejected or coveted should I be discovered. I used to think that no one would want the heart of a serial killer, but given how popular true crime is these days, I would imagine it might be quite the opposite.

True crime baffles the fuck out of me. Take it from a guy who does the killing. It will all be fascinating until you are strapped to a table, and I hover over you with a knife.

Amid my rumination, I come across a groundskeeper—graveskeeper?—and he points me in the right direction before explaining that records are kept online. When did cemeteries become so modern? I finally locate the area I am after, and my heart skips a beat as I approach. The anxiety kicks in, and one question floats around my brain; did I make a mistake in not coming? You don't get a second chance at death. I still have your ashes, Melissa, or at least your mother does, in safe keeping. But the question of whether I made a mistake or not nags at me. I mean, it isn't as if you can be cremated again.

You were rich, Melissa, and your placard and memorial are larger than life (excuse the pun). The plaque features your name and years on this planet, but there is one glaring omission—it slipped my mind as I languished at home, and now that I am here, guilt is also tugging at my sleeve. There is a gaping hole where your epitaph should be. I know that it was left to me to complete, and nine months later, it is still blank. I'm sure it comes easy to some people, but how do you begin to describe the lost love of your life succinctly? I still can't think of anything pithier than *Fuckkkkkkk!*

In my defence Melissa, it isn't as though I have stopped talking to you. I am here now, and that is what matters.

Suddenly my phone vibrates in my pocket, and I remove it to see an incoming call from Abdul. I have successfully dodged his calls most of the weekend (because I fear what

Maureen might have seen), but now I am alone with you, Melissa. I could use a friend. I don't believe in fate, but if I did, this would surely be one of those moments, so I take the call and place the phone to my ear.

'Finally,' Abdul exclaims, 'I was beginning to think you were dead.' His choice of words is accidentally poor, and I take a deep breath before replying.

'Hey,' I reply solemnly. 'I'm glad you called. I'm with Melissa.'

'Oh,' he replies. 'How is it?'

'I could use a friend.'

'I'm right here, Bro-peep.'

'Do you think I made a mistake in not attending the funeral?'

'Dude, you can't think like that. What's happened has happened. We all grieve in our own way. You're there now. Mel would understand.' Abdul's thoughts echo my own, and I feel slightly better.

'You're right,' I say. 'But I still don't know what to write for her epitaph.'

'You wanna come round, Maureen is asleep, but we'd love to see you again.'

'I'd like that,' I say.

'Dinner at seven?' I nod and realise that means nothing over the phone, so I force up some form of audible confirmation.

'I gotta go,' I say. 'I'll see you later.'

'Look forward to it, Bro-liver Twist.'

I hang up and put my phone away. I rest my head against the stone. I find it odd that despite not being buried here, the memorial is still in a graveyard as if the dead are in some way beholden to cemeteries.

There is an eerie calm to the cemetery. It is a weird feeling to be surrounded by people who are no longer people. It is just you and me now, Melissa, together again, except I have a body and no soul, and you have a soul and no body. How did it come to this?

TWENTY-FOUR

I sit in the back of the taxi on the way to Abdul's. And it is a good job you were rich, Melissa, because socialising is fucking expensive.

It arrives. I exit the car, tip the driver, and then take the short walk down the path to Abdul and Maureen's place. Their house is big, well-appointed, and cluttered.

Abdul and Maureen make good money but must work long and hard for it. Something which culminates in them making the absolute fucking most of every weekend. I don't blame them; I don't work and need a regular kill to blow off steam. If I had to work fifty hours a week, there would probably be a trail of dead bodies in my wake, starting with co-workers.

I arrive at the front door and force myself out of my head. I knock quietly and wait in anxious silence. I still wonder if Maureen knows I masqueraded as a doctor. Perhaps this is the reason for my invitation tonight, and the police are waiting for me on the other side?

Abdul arrives, opens the door, and immediately throws his arms around me. He smells great and seems genuinely excited. He removes himself from my ample frame, and I look him up and down. He looks tired, his exceptionally dark hair is greying, and the shine is missing from his hair-free pate. The superb aroma is clearly an overcompensation.

'Bro-mander in chief,' he says, 'come in, come in, come in.' I nod and acquiesce as if his repetition somehow persuades me from turning about and leaving. I stick out the bottle I brought, and he takes it with both hands. 'Grenadine?' I nod. 'You're the best, something we can all enjoy.' He seems thankful, and why wouldn't he be? Grenadine is a fantastic addition to soft and alcoholic drinks alike.

I enter the house and follow Abdul to the kitchen; the foodie aroma hits my senses, and I realise that I am fucking starving. For all the self-improvements made lately, I am still forgetting to eat unless prompted. The smell awakens my stomach.

'What are we having?' I ask.

'Bro-seph Fiennes,' Abdul replies, 'I hope you like spice?' I nod. I do. Although I can already tell that tomorrow's hangover with the addition of spicy curry is going to be awful.

'Where's Maureen?' I ask.

'She's in the shower, came home from work, then slept.' I nod. I don't envy her. 'You want a drink?' I nod again, and my excitable host pours me an ample glass of wine. I take a long sip, and Abduls' expression shifts to a serious one. *Oh no*, I think to myself, this is it.

'So,' he asks, 'how was it?' I pause for a moment as I wonder what he is asking. Does he know? Is he asking what it is like to take a man's life badly and then have to go back to the hospital to finish it off? Is he subversively mocking me?

'It was—' I begin.

'You know what? I'm sorry. I shouldn't have asked. You don't have to talk about it if you don't want to.' I am so confused. I look over my shoulder and wonder when the armed police will pop out. Is he pushing me for a confession?

'It was difficult getting in there,' I say.

'I bet,' Abdul replies. He puts his hand on my shoulder and squeezes it. 'It took me weeks to build up the courage to visit my mum after she passed.' He squeezes my shoulder harder, and I relax. We are talking about the cemetery, not the hospital.

'Yeah,' I echo, 'once I was in, I wasn't sure what had been so difficult.'

'I hear ya, Bro Goldberg, I hear ya.' He smiles kindly and says, 'We'll talk about it when you're ready.' I return the smile and realise that aside from this annoying new habit of repeating everything, I remember that Abdul is a great friend. I can't help but wonder how everyone would react if they knew what I really got up to—I am intrigued even as part of a social experiment.

I hear a noise behind me, and Maureen appears. She greets me kindly, and I stand up as she enters. She hugs me tenderly and kisses me on the cheek before saying, 'Arthur, it's great to see you again. How are you doing?' I look her up and down, as I do with everyone. Maureen is beautiful and way too good for Abdul, although you can see that the hours she works and the stress of her job are ageing her. I know Maureen to be a talented surgeon. She is also selfless to her detriment. She refuses to give up on the National Health Service and will not work privately. I admire her for this. I do. She could probably be in her house in Cabo if it wasn't for her idealism, and yet here, she is returning from work late on a Sunday, and I love her for that.

Maureen pours herself a glass of wine and smiles at me, 'So, how was it?' Ah, now I see. They don't suspect me of anything. Why would they? Who on earth thinks that dear old Amiable Arthur is anything other than a lovesick fool? I nod and consider my thoughts. As I do, I realise that this heartbreak is quite disarming. Everyone pities me, and no one suspects me of a thing. I finally force up some long, sad platitude, and before long, we are sitting in the dining room surrounded by mountains of curry.

'Sorry,' says Abdul, 'I only know how to cook for my thousand family members.'

'No need to apologise,' I say. 'Pop some in a Tupperware, and I'll take it home with me.' Abdul grins. He is pleased that I enjoy his offering. Not knowing that I would gladly take clippings of their toenails home with me if it meant I could avoid going shopping.

We eat, and I shovel a large mouthful of tasty napalm before I hear Abdul say, 'Hey, Maureen, tell Arthur what happened at the hospital.' The words *Maureen* and *hospital* enter my brain, and I almost faint. The molten lava in my mouth heats my core, and I feel sweat oozing from every orifice. My hunger saw me take on too large a bite, and I am powerless to speak as Maureen starts to move her lips.

'You have a doppelgänger,' she says. I frantically chew away, and I swallow the last bit whole. I feel its spice moving through my gullet, and I almost squeak the words.

'A what?' The pair laugh as they watch me squirm, and if they were any other couple in the world, I would choke them to death with naan bread.

'A doppelgänger, you know, a clone,' says Maureen.

'I know what a doppelgänger is, Maureen,' I say as calmly as possible. 'But what are you talking about?'

The pair giggle to themselves once more before Maureen says, 'Excuse us, Arthur, we're being silly.'

'We are not,' Abdul protests. 'Tell him, dear.' Maureen takes a sip of her wine and says,

'I saw a guy at the hospital last week, the spitting image of you.'

'Well, almost,' Abdul interjects excitedly. 'He's like a budget version of you.'

'Yeah,' says Maureen, 'like you but old, tired, and skinny.' I swallow my pride and don't fess up that they are actually talking about me.

'I told Maureen to get a picture with him the next time she sees him,' says Abdul.

'Which I won't,' she says, 'because I am a grown-up.' Abdul nods and moves his hand over his mouth, and whispers,

'She will!' in my direction. I look at the two of them and force up a laugh. In truth, I am relieved that they think they saw my twin. I am less happy about the *budget version* comment, given that it was *me*, but I do my best to let it go.

'Now that I would like to see,' I say. 'What does low-priced me do?'

'Well,' says Maureen. 'I only got a brief glimpse as he was getting in a lift. So, I didn't catch his name.' Phew, I think to myself. The last thing I want is for this to go on.

'But,' says Abdul, 'he was in the ICU. I am sure she can track him down.' I laugh nervously to myself.

'As much as I would love to see budget me, I am sure Maureen has better things to do than track down my imposter.'

'Meh,' says Maureen as she shrugs. 'I get bored sometimes.'

'So,' I say, keen to move the conversation along. 'I went to dinner with Ophelia the other night.' The words leave my mouth, and as my happy couple turn to each other and raise their eyebrows in unison, I instantly want to retract them. The last thing I want to do right now is have my love life dissected, but I need to get them away from searching for a man who looks like me because it was me.

The conversation starts to get away from me as the two-headed beast across the table starts planning the next social gathering featuring all four of us. I excuse myself from the table and head to the bathroom. I am not sure that they have noticed my exit, and I bolt myself inside and take a moment to breathe.

I sit on the toilet to take a leak; sometimes, it is easier like this. I remove my phone to find a message from Ophelia. I smile at her name and take a moment to read it.

Hey, what are you doing tomorrow night? I have to attend a party at work, wanna come? Xx

The message was received over an hour ago, so I have a quick think and then begin to reply.

Sorry, I've been out for dinner. What's in it for me? ;) xx

I see the familiar dots that indicate that a reply is forthcoming. I remain with my bum planted on the toilet seat, and it takes less than a minute for a response. Ophelia doesn't mess around. I like that.

Open bar, you get to dress up, and you get the pleasure of my company all night. Xx

As I read through the message, another pops up on my screen.

Oh, and I promise I won't ask any questions about why we're going to Atlanta. ;)

Okay, now I really like you, Ophelia. No questions asked is my favourite.

Sounds fun. I reply. *Just let me know where and when.*

Richards and Richards law firm, I gotta be there early. Meet me there at 7. Xx

I'll see you then. XX. I reply. I put my phone back into my trouser pocket, wipe for good measure, pull my pants back up, and wash my hands. When I return to the dining room, my hosts are still giddily chatting away.

The evening continues in the same vein, and every aspect of my social life is analysed before I find myself in a cab on the way home.

I sit in the back of the car, and my mind wanders back to Ophelia. I have made my obligatory entry small talk with the driver, and I now sit in silence and research the venue and attendees for tomorrow's party. I always like to have a lay of the land.

TWENTY-FIVE

I stare out the taxi window as the late spring sun disappears below the horizon. I am on my way to Ophelia's place of work, and I realise that I seem to spend half of my life—and a small fortune—in taxis at the moment. I am a little nervous even though I look fantastic, and I think that is because I will be spending the evening in the unknown and, no doubt, duplicitous company.

I have scrubbed up relatively well, and thanks to all the recent socialising, my dinner jacket fits me as well as it always has. I should be used to this, given that I attended many similar parties with you, Melissa, but I am not with you. I catch sight of myself in the rear-view mirror, and I smile. My suit is expensive and tailored. That is the extent of my knowledge, but I know that a well-fitting suit is something else. I am handsome in a non-obvious way; my sandy blonde hair fits my head, and my frame always seems to draw respect from most people. I have a very expensive bottle of Whiskey I found in the attic, and I take deep breaths to settle myself. My stomach is in knots and had I known. I might have forgone last night's curry.

Melissa aside, I don't much care for lawyers. Dress it up however you like. The good ones charge way too much for their ability to spin facts to their advantage. And the bad ones are only a slight upgrade on flies. Take it from a man who has committed dozens of murders. The system is inherently flawed, and I know full well that should the day come that I get caught, a good lawyer could dramatically reduce the sentence for my crimes. I either did it, or I didn't. I cannot fathom how the quality of my representation should make any difference. Also, who in their right mind is capable of knowing what I have done and defending me without prejudice? Money, right?

The name of the firm irritates me, *Richards and Richards?* It's just annoying. Like adding *and son* to the name of the business, it is unnecessary. I have gleaned from the website that Ophelia works for one of the senior partners but not either or any of the *Richards*.

The senior partner *Theo Richards* comes across as a detestable douchebag online, so I am not confident that he will be any better in person. I peek over the driver's shoulder and eye up the satnav. It states that we are less than five minutes away, and I do my best to shelve my opinions. Tonight, it is about Ophelia, not me.

I exit the car, take a deep breath, and walk into the building. Fortunately, I spot Ophelia almost immediately. She sees me, smiles, and makes her way over. Ophelia is easy to spot, and my mind is immediately taken away from my nerves and drawn to how she is dressed. I am not good at describing dresses. I mean it is a dress. Not only that, but I'm awestruck and not for the first time with Ophelia; my brain is a speechless mess. But it is too great a sight not to attempt to share it, so the only explanation I have relies on your memory of James Bond, so here goes. Picture, if you will, Anna de Armas the first time Daniel Craig encounters her in the bar in *No Time to Die*. I am staring at almost exactly that, except she is making her way over to me and is not on a TV screen. That dress! This dress!

Ophelia wanders through my imagination and takes me by the hand. I am introduced to her boss, who tells me his name is Ian Sanderson. His hand meets mine, and he offers up some platitude about my size. I hand him the bottle of Whiskey I brought, and he thanks me.

'Oh, the 1912, it's good, but it's not the 1850, am I right?' He actually goes to high-five me, and I already hate him. I have no idea what he's talking about, chiefly because I think whiskey tastes like blended sandals. It is an expensive gift from a client of Melissa's. I imagine it cost well over two hundred pounds for the bottle, and he is looking at it like I just brought him a bottle of Lambrini. I swallow and raise my hand to meet his high-five begrudgingly. Our hands slap, and I say.

'Well, I wasn't going to give away an 1850, was I?' Ian laughs and says, 'Touché.' Then he turns to Ophelia and says, 'Do you mind if I borrow her for a moment?' I shake my head to indicate that I don't mind but also in an indictment to myself. I shake my head toward him, asking me to borrow her as though she was property. As if I didn't already dislike you, Ian.

Ophelia tells me she *will be right back*, and I watch on in a trance as she turns and walks away. A polite young man appears and offers me a champagne flute. I take it and ask him *where the bathroom is.* And he happily points me toward it. I down the drink on the spot and return the glass to him. I depart in the direction of the bathroom, and as I look around and watch Ophelia leaving with that cock, I consider this might actually be hell.

I am standing at the urinal in the men's room—that's not me being sexist. It is a men-only room—and as I empty my bladder into the extremely fresh urinal, I consider why we have unisex toilets. Don't get me wrong. I couldn't give a fuck. But I am a man, and we don't care whom we pee or shit alongside. We are absolute animals, all of us. I always considered that bathrooms were gendered because no lady in her right mind would want to share a bathroom with us. Unisex bathrooms feel like more of a punishment to women than anything else. I am mid-thought when the door bursts open, followed by a loud belch which thus proves my point. The owner of the belch exclaims *what a fucking party!* Then proceeds to pour some cocaine on the side, takes a deep snort and makes an excited *yelp*.

Having shoved drugs up his nose, he saunters over to the urinal next to me, removes his man parts and pisses wildly in the direction of the urinal—most of the urine goes in it. I turn to see who has invaded my peace, and I am not surprised when I find myself staring at the side of the face I know belongs to Theo Richards.

I was right, he is even more detestable in person, and I don't find myself staring across the short divide for long before he says.

'I can hold my own cock, thanks, mate.' I am unmoving. I am staring, and I don't have long to think before he turns to me and says. 'Didn't you hear me? I said fuck off!' I nod, apologise, and finish up. I make it as far as the sink before I hear him mutter 'Faggot,' under his breath and begin to whistle the theme tune to *The Archers* to himself.

I splash cool water over my face in an attempt to calm down, but it doesn't work. I stare at myself in the mirror and look at my wet face. I feel a rage brewing inside me, and I do my best to shelve it. Tonight is not about me and my proclivities. I switch off the tap, wipe my face down with a paper towel and turn about to leave. I get one step away from the sink before I hear him say, *Go on, run along, you little dickhead.* I tried Melissa and Ophelia. I really did.

I halt my movement and turn toward him. The coked-up twat is still whistling to himself and doesn't notice me approach him from behind. I step into him, grab the back of his head, and ram it hard into the toilet wall. His head hits the wall before he knows what is going on. I smash his head into the wall once more for good measure before pulling him backwards by the hair to the floor. His drugged-up willy waves wildly in the air, and I can't help but smile when he gets piss all over himself.

I lower him to the floor, and to my surprise, his eyes open. He looks me in the eye and says. 'I'm going to fucking ruin you.' The words hit my brain, and without thinking, my hand grabs the garish gold pen poking out of his breast pocket. I already hate the sound of his voice, so I give him no time to react as I take the pen and ram it as hard as possible through his eye. He makes an awful noise as I feel the pen pop his eye, and he thrashes for a brief second before it pierces his frontal lobe: the noise and the movement stop. I am calm. The world is calm.

Okay, so I'll admit that this is really fucking problematic. Theo is lying on the bathroom floor at his party with a twenty-four-carat gold pen sticking out of his eye. His blood has poured out and is spreading all over the bathroom's tile floor. The door doesn't appear to lock, and someone could walk in at any moment. There is no easy way to explain this or make it look like an accident. I have just arrived, and it won't be long before Ophelia wonders where I am.

This was ill-advised, Melissa. I thought my impulse might be a problem, and I didn't do anything about it. In my defence, Theo was a humungous bell-end, but right now, he might be one that gets me in trouble.

I take a quick look in the mirror to see that most of Theo's blood has avoided me. I wipe off the excess, hurriedly drag Theo's body into a stall, and desperately search the bathroom. I am relieved when I find a hidden door and even more relieved when I find out it is open. Inside is a cleaning cart, overalls, a mop, chemicals, and a *cleaning in progress sign.* God bless the entitled rich and their need to have perpetually clean bathrooms in which to do drugs. I hurriedly push the cart to the door so that it blocks it from opening. I reach through a small gap and place the sign over it. Then I place the overalls over my suit, remove the mop and chemicals, and clean.

With the blood removed, I pick up Theo's corpse and gently lower it into the cart. I clean the rest of his blood and then wipe down anything either of us touched. I reach into the cart, remove Theo's phone and wallet, place the cleaner's cap over my head and pull it down over my eyes, thankful that the entitled twats would rather not have to make eye contact with *the help.*

Once I am sure I have covered my tracks, I open the door, check the corridor, remove the sign, and then wheel Theo down the corridor toward the fire exit, whistling *The Archer's* theme tune as I go.

I am just a few steps from the fire exit door when I hear a voice boom over my shoulder that halts me in my tracks.

'Hey, what are you doing? I thought all the cleaning staff had gone home?' The words creep into my brain, and I stop like a deer caught in headlights. I am wearing a boiler suit over a dinner jacket, and I can feel myself sweating. I turn about, keeping my head down, and I find myself face to face with a burly, bald-headed security guard in a suit. There is a gap of about two meters between us, but I can almost feel his breath on my neck.

'Sorry, boss, someone shit-fingered the second-floor bathroom. I've given it a good clean, but I would steer clear of it if I were you.' The man nods and makes a face. 'I'm just taking out the remains. Then I'll be on my way.' He nods again, and I'm thankful that faeces always puts people off, and he doesn't want to approach me. I turn about to continue, but light hits my face as I do, and he gets a clearer look. I place both hands on the cart and am about to move when he says.

'Wait.' I close my eyes and grimace. He saw my face. I know he did. I brace for what comes next, but all I hear is. 'Gerry, is that you?' keeping my back to him, I say.

'Yes?'

'Well fuck me, Gerry. Why didn't you say something? It's me, Nigel.'

'Sorry, Nige,' I say. With my back to him, I motion to the truck and say, 'Been a long, shitty day.' I think he nods.

'I won't keep you.' I hear the ape turn and start to move. I take a deep breath and prepare to push the annoyingly heavy Theo when I hear the footsteps stop, and he says.

'Say, Gerry, say 'hi' to Kathleen and the kids for me.'

'Will do,' I reply.

'Oh, and Gerry?'

'Yes.'

'Don't forget your name badge next time.'

'Sure thing, Nigel.'

He leaves. My heart restarts, and I am finally on the move again.

I finally breach the fire door; it is almost dark when I step outside. I put all of my efforts into pushing the trolley so that it appears light and not at all like it houses a corpse. I move across the yard and down an alley. I find some dumpsters and wheel the cart in between them out of sight. I remove the overalls and place them inside with Theo. It is a loose end for now, but I can't be gone for much longer without arousing suspicion.

I walk around to the front of the building, re-enter and grab a drink straight from the nearest waiter. I drink, remove Theo's phone, and browse a few of his most recent tweets before posting.

This party blows. I need a recharge. I'll be at my pad in LA for a few days if anyone needs me.

#whyownanlahomeandnotuseit#englandsucks.

Fortunately, being a mega twat is in Theo's repertoire, and no one seems that surprised in the comments.

I place Theo's phone in the inner jacket pocket and look up just in time to see Ophelia approach holding two glasses of wine. 'There you are,' she says. 'I was beginning to think you'd left.'

I shake my head, 'Are you kidding? This party is to die for!'

'Really?' she asks, 'I thought you'd hate it.'

'I do,' I concede, 'But you're here. I wouldn't miss it for the world.'

Ophelia smiles, takes me by the arm and says, 'Come on then, let me show you around.'

TWENTY-SIX

As I watch Ophelia successfully engage and communicate with a bunch of obnoxious, drunken dickheads, it dawns on me that recovery is not a linear process. I might sound stupid, but I have never done this before. Heartbreak, anger, depression, and abandonment are all new to me. I had assumed (incorrectly) that once you start to get better, it is nothing but up. Tonight's impulsive anger, however, would suggest otherwise.

Theo Richards was a grade-A twat. I have no doubt he had represented some real dirtbags in court, and with his help, they probably got away with it. The fact that I killed him doesn't bother me. He had it coming. The impulse, the recklessness, and the fact that I could have been caught annoy me. Here I am, trying to move on, trying to get over you, Melissa, but imagine if Ophelia had seen me for who I really am tonight? I'd be on my way to jail, still broken, still alone, all for Theo Richards.

Ophelia is good at this; she smiles at me as she converses with a group, and I return the grin. I signal with my hands that I need a drink, and she laughs. I excuse myself from the conversation I wasn't a part of and head for the bar.

The queue for the bar is non-existent—largely because no one here wants to get their own drink—and I order two beers. The bartender disappears, and as I wait, I hear a voice echo over my shoulder and into my ears.

'Arthur? Arthur Norman?' I turn about slowly and with trepidation. Given my disdain for the general public, I am always wary when I bump into someone who knows me. I have also just killed a man who is still outside, stuffed into a cleaning trolley. It is my preference to remain as anonymous as possible.

I turn about to find myself face to face with a short, stocky man. He wears a happy demeanour, and although he is part of this crowd, his suit tells me he is also not. His face features the lines formed by years of heavy smoking; although he wears it well, he is also rather portly.

'Arthur, it is you!' I instinctively stick out my hand like a good human, but he ignores it completely and throws his arms around me for a hug. 'I'm so sorry about Melissa,' he says sincerely. 'How are you doing? It's been forever.'

I just stabbed a man in the eye with his gold pen in the bathroom, I think to myself. 'On the road to recovery,' I say. I look at the man again, and I realise who he is. The link to Melissa helped, and I recall this man as Steven Finch. He worked at the Crown Prosecution Service, so he often worked cases with Melissa. I remember him to be a bit prosaic, but he was one of the good guys. 'Steven, of course. How are you? What are you doing here?'

I should have thought I might have run into someone I know in a room full of legal professionals, but not for the first time lately. I can't seem to think beyond my problems.

'I'm doing okay, Arthur. I'm doing okay.' The repetition and stifled grin seem to suggest otherwise.

'Can I get you a drink?' I ask.

Having ordered a drink for Steven, we move to a table in the corner, far from the twatting crowd. 'So, what's new?' I ask, 'You still at the CPS?' Steven takes a sip of his drink and then shakes his head solemnly.

'I take it you didn't hear?' I shake my head. *Obviously, I didn't.*

‘Hear what?’ I ask. Steven looks around the room suspiciously and then leans over to me. ‘How much do you know about the Mitchell case?’ I look at him as though he has just asked me about the pros and cons of keeping a velociraptor as a pet and shake my head.

‘Probably about as much as you know about owning Italian performance saloons.’ He laughs.

‘Okay,’ he says in a voice barely above a whisper. ‘It was a case Melissa and I were putting together. He is a British property developer/wannabe gangster. He suddenly came into a big cash influx and was buying up houses in the area.’

‘Okay, so?’

‘Well, here’s the thing, Melissa was working on evidence that suggested he was a conduit, laundering money for a US Senator. She was about to bring the whole thing down when she died.’

My mouth must have fallen open in shock. Melissa deliberately kept her cases away from me due to the risk that I might want to get involved. In fairness, it was probably a good plan.

‘I’ll be honest, Steven; Melissa and I kept her work out of our relationship.’

‘Of course,’ he replies, ‘she wouldn’t be Melissa if she didn’t.’ I tap my drink against his and take a healthy sip.

‘So, what happened?’ I ask.

‘Well, whatever Melissa had, it died with her. The case collapsed without her at the helm, and the rest of us became scapegoats. Everyone on the case got sacked, including me. So, here I am.’ He says, gesturing to the building around him.

‘Oh, Steven,’ I say, ‘I’m sorry. So, you work here now?’ He nods.

‘Junior associate,’ he says, ‘It’s not all bad. But not quite the vocation I was after.’

'Why here?' I ask.

'Gotta pay the bills, Arthur.'

A man in the distance whistles to Steven, and he stands from the table. 'I have to go,' he says. 'My boss isn't gonna schmooze himself.' I nod. 'It was good to see you, Arthur.' He reaches into the pocket of his cheap suit and hands me a business card. 'If you need anything at all, give me a ring.'

'Thanks,' I say. I stand up. We embrace once more, and just like that, he is gone.

Alone again, I return to the bar and order yet more drinks. As pleased as I was to see him, my head is filled with more thoughts, as if there weren't enough things to deal with. The link to America crops up, and I do what I can to shelve notions of Melissa's work. For now, the trip to the States will hopefully provide answers. First things first, I need to successfully navigate the rest of this party and find a way back later to dispose of the body.

TWENTY-SEVEN

When the party finally grinds to a halt just after midnight. I am thankful that it is a Tuesday and everyone has work tomorrow—I don't. I have work tonight.

The wankers slowly disappear, we leave, and before I know what's happening, I'm alone with Ophelia on her front porch.

I drank far too much tonight. It was the only way to stop the swirling accumulation of thoughts. Fortunately, Theo is hard to miss, and no one seems to give a fuck that he bailed on his own shindig. I like Ophelia, I do. This only added to my reasons to drink. I now find myself in a quandary that I knew was coming.

As Ophelia and I stand outside her house, the gallons of alcohol I consumed have only served to enhance how good she looks. I could just as well be standing in the twilight holding the hand of Aphrodite herself. Her eyes twinkle as we linger in silence, and I hope she won't invite me inside. Even though I know she will.

This doesn't sound like a problem, but trust me, it is. If I say *yes* and go inside with her, only one thing will happen: taking our clothes off. The neutral observer might think it's easy for me to say *yes* or *no*. But, you see, I have Theo's body stiffening in a trolley bin outside his place of work, and every second it stays there is closer to its discovery—if it hasn't been found already. I *need* to go and attend to it.

But at the same time, I haven't experienced the intimacy of a human touch since you left, Melissa, and I crave it deeply with Ophelia. This could be my only chance. I could be caught, killed, or exposed tonight. Disposing of a body is one of the most difficult parts of being a killer, now made even more challenging because I am steaming. To say I didn't think this through would be an understatement!

I am too busy in my head. I should have known that a woman like Ophelia would take charge of the situation. She grabs my face and pulls it passionately toward hers. Then her tongue is in my mouth, and I am locked in a moment I never want to end. God damn, my hesitation. Turning this down just got even more complicated.

My impulses take over. I push her up against the door and run my hand up her thigh. I have to use all of my strength to pull away from her. Our eyes meet, and as much as I say *no,* my eyes scream *yes,* and I am powerless to stop them. She kisses me again, and we lose another ten minutes on the doorstep. My hormones are boiling over, and I am close to saying *fuck it* and doing just that. Ophelia finally pulls her lips from mine, takes her keys from her bag, and opens the door. She then moves and stands seductively in the doorway.

'You wanna come in?' she says.

I pause for all of two seconds as my brain wrestles with itself. This is not an easy decision. The two-second pause feels like twelve years. When I finally convince my mouth to speak, I say, 'I can't.'

I kiss her again passionately, so she doesn't have time to dwell on a potential rejection. I am down the steps and on the path when I say, 'I wish I could, but I have something to take care of tonight.'

Ophelia probably replied, but my band-aid approach was all I had. I ripped it off and left. Anything she said might have changed my mind. I keep walking until I am two blocks away.

I order an Uber, which arrives in such a prompt manner that I wonder whether it was following me. I chat incessantly with the Iranian driver—I need to be memorable for any potential alibi. I tell him that the immigration policy in this country is all wrong, and we let in too many people who don't deserve to be here. I don't think that, of course. I am not a self-entitled, idiotic bigot. But it does its job. It's convincing. Some people think like that. He drops me home, and I don't tip. He won't forget me in a hurry.

Once home, I make the strongest coffee possible and down it. When I am as sober as I am going to be, I dress in black running gear, sneak out of the house, and take a disturbingly long jog.

I am drunk, horny, anxious, and totally winging it. Sticking the pen in Theo's eye was a mistake. It was unnecessary, and, as a result, I now have a body to get rid of. No matter how much of a coked-up twat he was, no one will believe that Theo fell on his own pen, got into a cleaning cart, and then wheeled himself outside to the bin.

I have no plan. It has been some time since I disposed of a body, and I am so out of the game that it is unreal.

The good thing about UK office buildings is that we don't take security very seriously. This is not the US; the security guard is not an ex-army Ranger desperate to find meaning in a world where he no longer belongs. Our security guards aren't diligent and don't have guns. That's not the rule. I wouldn't fancy sneaking into MI5, but Richards and Richards are not that.

The *security* is one chubby middle-aged guard sitting in a booth doing a crossword. He looks like he probably still lives with his mum. And I would say that he is far from *secure*.

I avoid the cabin and circle around the back of the building, there is no fence to speak of, and before I know it, I am in sight of the dumpsters, and I am relieved to find everything as it was earlier. I am aware that a security camera will probably catch me. It is a loose end, but not as bad as leaving Theo's mutilated body for it to be found. I creep across the short divide and huddle in the gap between the bins. I look in the cart and am relieved to find it all there. Devoid of a better plan, I push the cart away from the bins and start walking. As soon as I am clear of the offices, I remove the litter grabber and pick up bits of litter from the street as I walk, tossing them into the cart and onto Theo's head. I am just a late-night litter picker. Saving myself and the planet at the same time.

I walk on, pushing the cart deeper into the night. I need to make the contents—including Theo—disappear, and I haven't the faintest idea what to do. So, I walk, and walk, and walk, hoping that something will guide me.

I move into the night, drunkenly pushing my cart until serendipity finds me, and I come across an out-of-town housing development. What used to be a field or nature reserve is being transformed into a residential community of cheap two-and three-bed houses that no one will still be able to afford. There is a skeleton crew at this hour and sneaking about the development is easy. I see no cameras and a lot of freshly poured cement.

Seizing my opportunity, I make sure the coast is clear, remove Theo from the cart and stuff him rather unceremoniously into the fresh concrete. I don't wait to see what happens before I scuttle off into the night with my cleaning waggon.

I walk on and on until I find myself alone in the woods with my cart. I find a clearing, remove my Zippo, and then douse the cart and everything inside it in a mixture of the most flammable liquids it contains. I light it and retreat to safety. The smell is awful as it burns away and cleans me of my sins. It burns and burns until it is no more, and when I am satisfied that there is no trace of Theo or me being with the cart, I begin the long, painful, sobering jog back home.

TWENTY-EIGHT

By the time I get within sight of home, I realise my energy is flagging. I have jogged eight miles in total, and my preparation of wine and canapes was less than ideal. The time is nearly 6 a.m., and despite the insanity necessary to run at this hour, people actually do, and, therefore, it will be an adequate explanation should anyone see me.

As I round the corner to my street, my lungs feel like raisins, my brain is missing and the toxic fire I created last night makes me feel like I am going to throw up my appendix. The street looks quiet as I return home, and I make it unmolested as far as my driveway. I am stuck in my head when I enter my drive, and the sight of Mike getting in his car makes me almost leap from my skin. I make a weird, startling motion which draws his attention, and he gets back out of the car when he spots me. *Fan-fucking-tastic.*

'Hey, Arthur,' he says. 'Early bird catches the worm, I see.'

If there is one thing I hate more than morning, it is the clichés or adages pertaining to it. And my god, what does that even mean? Let's be honest; birds that hunt in the dead of night probably catch far more. Look at owls. The time of day is completely irrelevant.

'Hey, Mike,' I say as I catch my breath. 'It's early to be starting work.' As soon as I speak, I wish once again that I could retract it. This is Mike. He's probably off to get in an early round with his secretary before he starts work. There is no way he's not going to want to justify this now.

'Big new merger,' he says. 'Gotta get an early start.' He then begins to get in the car, and I am thankful he does as I continue toward the door. 'Oh, hey, Arthur,' he says.

Crap! His words halt me in my tracks, forcing me to turn about on the step. My outstretched hand almost had the key in the lock. So close.

'Are we still expecting you for dinner this weekend?'

'Oh, shit, Mike. Scheduling clash; I'm away this weekend.'

'Another time, then?'

'Rain check,' I concur. I turn around once more and insert the key into the lock.

'How about tonight?'

'Sounds good, Mike.'

'See you at 8?'

'I'll be there; send me your address, will you? I'd hate to get lost.'

'Good one, Arthur,' Mike chuckles before he finally closes his door.

This is hell. I have no idea why I agreed to dinner tonight. But I had to get him to leave. I need to lie down; I need a bath; if we had spent any longer in awkward conversation, I might have killed him on the driveway. Plus, the Wellingtons are relentless. There is no putting off dinner, and they will make it happen eventually. Better to get it over with.

Once in the house, I crawl from the door to the sofa, and once there, I fall straight into a coma. I can't remember the last night I was sober, and I am remiss to say that I am getting too old for this lifestyle.

When I wake, I am hit by the sinking feeling of dread and the memory that I said *yes* to Mike many hours ago and killed a man with his pen in the middle of a party because I didn't like how he spoke to me. The thoughts circle my brain, and for some reason, I add that some thugs robbed my house, and I still don't know what happened to Jarrod and his girlfriend; it has been over twelve hours since I left Ophelia on her doorstep. The foul thoughts mix with my toxic fume hangover, and I fall just short of the kitchen sink and vomit all over the floor and my feet.

It is too much, and I take a small shot of the first thing I can find: peach schnapps. The small shot of schnapps improves my mood, and I haul myself upstairs to the bathroom. I plug my phone in to charge in the bedroom, run the Jacuzzi bath, get in and fall asleep.

I wake to cold water but a better state of mind. Warm bubbles and sweet schnapps seem to have done the job. I check my watch as I step from the bath and notice the time is nearly five—what a day.

I check my phone and find a million messages, including two from Abdul, asking how last night was. There is a message from Rich Richard that reads, 'Squash and beer soon.' I ignore it for now, as the thought of either makes me want to vomit on my socks again. Finally, there is a message from Ophelia:

I'm packing for America :)) Fancy going clothes shopping before we go? Xx P.s. I missed you last night; p

I read it, then reread it. I hate clothes shopping. I would rather spoon out my eyes and stuff them in my ears. But for some reason, I find myself hastily RSVPing yes—the things we do for love.

I smile at the thought, and now my mind is all aglow. I no longer care about dinner, and it takes me nearly an hour to get dressed. I have no idea what to wear for a feast next door. I would like to keep my comfy house clothes on, but I am unsure if that is socially acceptable. I am also keenly aware that June saw me *au natural* a few days ago, and I want to dress as conservatively as possible.

When my sartorial nightmare ends, I finally settle on jeans and a t-shirt—why was that so hard?—I mosey into the attic to find a suitable gift for the insufferable duo.

I pick up a bottle of Red Label—No way Mike is getting the Black—and I go to switch out the light in the attic. But just as I grab the chord, I spot a box pulled out of place. There is no dust on it which suggests that it has been recently opened. Curious, I move toward it and remove the lid. On it—in Melissa's handwriting—are the words *Mitchell Case* and I am forced to recall my conversation with Steven last night. I remove the lid to discover that the box is empty, and a dark shudder encases me as I realise that it was probably removed during the break-in. My anger creeps up like a dark night, and I toss the empty cardboard across the attic, chase it, and stomp it to death. My crushing of the box makes me happier, and I am calm when I walk downstairs. It is just after eight, and I really should be getting going. The landline rings (mum), and despite my usual lack of interest in my family, I am keen for the delay.

'Hi, mother,' I say.

'Arthur?'

'Yes, mum.'

'How did you know it was me?'

'Uh, call it maternal connection, mum.'

'Really?'

'No, mum. I have caller ID.'

'What are you getting your sister for her birthday?' I pause in thought as I consider buying a venomous snake that bites them all when they are asleep.

'I dunno, mum. I dunno.'

'You are coming, aren't you?'

'I'm pretty busy at the moment, mum.'

'Doing what?'

'Well, I'm away this weekend.'

'Your sister's party is this weekend.'

'Oh, that's a shame. Tell her I send my regards.'

'Arthur, James Norman, this is your only sister.' *One too many, I think to myself.* 'Where are you going?'

'America, mum.'

'By yourself?'

'No, with a friend.'

'Which friend? Is it Ahmed?' I sigh.

'His name is Abdul, mum.'

'What happened to Ahmed?'

'There is no Ahmed. There has never been. Mum, he was the best man at my wedding.'

'Yes, Ahmed and his wife, Maureen.' I give up. I really do. I'd rather not tell her about Ophelia, but it might get her off my case.

'I'm taking a girl, mum; her name is Ophelia.'

'Ophelia, huh? And are you bringing her to your sister's birthday?'

'We won't be here, mum.'

'Well, we'll have it in the week. Wednesday, bring Ophelia.'

'Fine,' I say.

'And bring a gift. It's her fortieth.'

'Okay,' I say grudgingly.

'Do you want to talk to your father? He's in a terrible mood.'

'You're not selling it,' I mumble to myself.

‘What was that? Hello, I think you’re breaking up. Are you still there?’

‘Yes, mum, I’m here.

‘Hello, Arthur?’

‘I gotta go, mum,’ I say. I don’t wait to see if she heard that time, and I hang up. This is exactly why I don’t take their calls.

I look at my watch. It is twenty-past-eight. I had better go next door before I become the cause of this weekend’s argument. I reluctantly pick up my offering, grab my keys, and head out the door.

***

‘So, how was the merger, Mike?’ I ask, breaking the somewhat awkward silence.

‘The merger?’ he asks. *Yes, Mike, the fucking merger. Good god, it is no wonder you get caught.*

‘Yeah,’ I say, ‘you know, the one we were talking about this morning.’

‘Ahhhh,’ he says. ‘The merger! Yup, I completed that successfully this morning. Consider it merged.’ He beams and offers me a less-than-subtle wink across the table. June seems to ignore it completely. Either she is a total idiot, or she just doesn’t care. She opens her mouth and says.

‘So, Arthur. How was your weekend?’ I can see a small cheeky grin form in the corner of her mouth as she speaks, and I recall the moment I showed her my bits.

‘Uh, you know. Bit of exercise, a bit of socialising. Bit of this, a bit of that.’ *Why do I keep saying bit?* I refuse to be dragged into their marital tête-à-tête, and I speak again before either of them can open their mouth. ‘You know I’m going to Atlanta at the weekend?’

'Oh, on your own?' asks Mike. *Jesus fuck, why does everyone assume I'm alone?*

'No, actually,' I reply. 'I'm taking Ophelia.'

'Who's Ophelia?' June inquires with a pang of jealousy.

'Ahh, so that's the mysterious woman who came round yours,' says Mike. Trust fucking Mike to clock any attractive woman who enters the street.

'I guess so,' I say.

'So,' says June, 'who is she? When do we meet her?'

I look at June and want to clock her on the head. 'Oh, I dunno,' I reply. 'Soon, maybe.'

'Well, let's drink to that,' says Mike as he stands and moves into the kitchen to get another bottle.

'I'll get the plates,' says June. The pair disappear into the kitchen, and it isn't long before I hear the quarrel start. Of all the places I would like to be a fly on the wall right now, Mike and June's isn't one of them. Thankfully, I feel a sustained buzzing coming from my pocket, and I retrieve my phone to see Ophelia calling. I move from the dining table, slip through the patio doors, and answer the phone in the safety of the garden.

'Hey,' I say. 'Everything okay?'

'Yes,' replies Ophelia, 'No, I don't know. Is everything all right between us?'

'Absolutely,' I reply, remembering I left her wanting last night and have communicated a simple *yes* since.

'You sure?' she asks.

I have no idea how to explain my departure, and short of a better plan, I change the subject.

'How do you fancy coming to my sister's birthday?'

'When?'

'Next week, after we get back from the US.'

'Erm.'

'It will be awful,' I say.

'You know what? I'm in.'

'Yess,' I say.

'But you have to come bikini shopping with me.'

'Deal,' I say a little too quickly.

'All right,' she says. 'How about Wednesday? I can pick you up after work.'

'Sounds good. I look forward to it.'

'I'll see you then.' I go to hang up when I hear Ophelia's voice again. 'Hey, Arthur?'

'Yes.'

'I'm glad we bumped into each other in town.'

'Me too,' I say honestly. 'Me too. I'll see you Wednesday.' I hang up, smile to myself, and wander back inside.

TWENTY-NINE

The rest of the evening with Mike and June was painful, but I survived. No one died. Wednesday afternoon rolls around, and I find myself sitting at home like an excited child waiting to go to Disney Land. Ophelia tells me she will get me at six, it is just gone five, and my excitement is palpable. I'm excited to go shopping, boring, banal shopping. It is strange what love can do to us.

I still miss you, Melissa, and I'm sure I always will, but the hurt is beginning to fade, and I am pleased to be feeling anything that isn't numbness.

At six o'clock on the dot, I hear loud music blaring outside, and I have barely got my shoes on when I hear Ophelia excitedly hooting the horn. I get one shoe tied before I am out the door. I run down the driveway, dive in through the open passenger window and shout. 'Drive, drive!' Ophelia laughs and pulls away, spinning the wheels as she does. She looks at me, grins and says.

'Hey, stranger,' as I struggle to get in my seat against the car's motion. I feel like I am Christian Slater in *True Romance,* and I tell her so. 'Great film!' she shouts in my direction. 'You basically are, although I could do with less bloodshed and violence today!' Aside from not wanting bloodshed, I like her all the more. We drive in comfortable silence, and when we hit the motorway, I realise we are on the way to Southampton. I ask her, and she says, *you know it, baby.* I smile, and so does she. I can see this being a fun weekend.

Shopping was chaotic, but for the first time in forever, I don't absolutely hate it. I suppose we are clothes shopping for an impromptu trip to America, which does soften the blow. I smile as we hit just about every shop before winding up in the food court. I have some beers since I am not driving—and is this what I do now?—I shelve my thoughts of Ophelia in swimwear and eagerly await the weekend. We are in paradise, mid-way through a burger, when Ophelia's phone rings.

She says she *has to take this* and moves away from the table to take the call. When she returns, her face is ashen and features a genuine look of concern.

'That was my boss. He says that Theo is missing!'

'Theo, as in Richards and Richards Theo?'

'That's the one,' she says.

'Missing?' I say. She nods. I don't panic. I know that he will never be found.

'No one has seen him since the party. We thought he'd taken off to America, but he never picked up his hire car or got to his house.'

'Huh,' I say, thinking I did a pretty poor job of making him disappear.

'I'm sorry to be a bore, but do you mind if we get going? I said I would help look for him.'

'Not at all,' I say. We pack up, head to the car, and before I know it, we are back outside my house.

'Do you want me to help?' I ask. Ophelia shakes her head.

'Between you and me,' she says, 'the man is a liability. It isn't the first time he's done this. He'll show up somewhere. But we have to keep up appearances.' I nod. Thinking to myself how glad I am that I don't work for some entitled dickheads.

I exit the car, and Ophelia says, 'I can't wait for the weekend. I'll call you.' I kiss her through the window, and she disappears. I look up as I walk down the driveway, I see June in the upstairs window next door, and she waves at me. Their interest in my love life is getting annoying now, and I make a mental note to remember that I could be being watched by snooping neighbours.

I enter the house, move into the study, and amuse myself by looking at the wickedest possible birthday presents for Judy. I find the worst reviewed children's full band get up and add it to my basket. Nothing says happy birthday like an army of children smashing the shit out of musical instruments.

I even buy tambourines for the twins, the creepy fucking twins.

***

The weekend bounces around, and I'm excited. I really am. I've spent a large percentage of the last year in my house. Now that I am less panic-ridden, a trip to America is a tantalising prospect. Our flight leaves Heathrow on Friday and returns the following Tuesday. It will be fun, if not exhausting.

The flight departs early—9 a.m. from London Heathrow—I don't fancy driving, so I order a taxi to pick us up. I send it to Ophelia's house first, and before I know it, I hear the honk being honked—presumably by her—and I am in a rush when I throw the last of my belongings in my bag. It is just before four in the morning, and I made the brilliant decision to forgo sleep entirely.

I am physically incapable of rushing, and it takes me twenty minutes to get in the car. I have my passport, so that is all that matters, right?

I enter the patiently waiting vehicle and apologise for my tardiness. The driver seems none too bothered, and Ophelia is just excited. Her incredible scent has seeped into the vehicle, and all I can see is her. She is wearing loose-fitting trousers and a t-shirt that says *I love rock and roll and America.* She is already wearing a neck pillow and looks sensational to me.

'What is this?' I ask, flicking at the pillow around her neck.

'Neck cushion,' she replies enthusiastically. 'You don't have one?' I shake my head. The car pulls forward urgently, signalling that the driver was impatient, and I am forced into my seat. Ophelia looks at me and says, 'Rookie move, one of us will have a sore neck, and it won't be me.'

'Pah,' I reply. 'I have a mighty man's neck; we have no such need for these things.' She shrugs, and as soon as I am strapped in my seat, she shuffles across the back and nestles into my side. It isn't long before we are on the motorway and doze off.

Heathrow airport is never fun. It doesn't matter what time of day it is. The whole place is like some sort of shit adult shoving match. No one helps you out, and if you stand still for too long, someone shoves you, yells at you, or both. By the time you get to security, you are already exhausted, and then you have to deal with the security itself.

Don't get me wrong. I am grateful for the security. I am. The last thing I want is for someone to blow up my flight early in the morning on the way to America. If it absolutely has to happen, I would much rather it was the return. Still, the security staff and the process genuinely leave you questioning your intentions.

'What is the purpose of your trip?'

'How long are you staying for?'

'Has anyone given you anything to take on board?'

'Is it possible someone put something in your bag without your knowledge?'

AHHHHHHH. Especially on the last count, if they did it without my knowledge, then yes, of course, it is possible!

Having been pushed, yelled at, and interrogated, we successfully navigate security.

By the time we make it through to the departure gates, I wonder whether I am a terrorist and if my intentions have ever been pure.

We finally find a café to sit in and semi-unwind. At this point, there are still two hours until the gate opens, and although there are places to visit, further movement will probably result in gaining more bruises. The table we have is by a window and looks out onto the planes, and I am busy staring at the ground crew doing whatever it is they do when I hear Ophelia say, 'Drink?' She is standing with her hands clamped on the edge of the table, and her bosom dangles inches from my face. How can I say no?

'Whatcha want?'

'Surprise me,' I reply. She smirks and disappears; I know I will have about twenty minutes before she returns, so I remove my phone and make sure that we are still on for our meeting tomorrow night, Magnus.

Ophelia finally returns with two beers, sets them down on the table and disappears in the direction of the toilet. Magnus replies promptly, and we are a go to meet at his house at 8 p.m. on Saturday. I put my phone away, and Ophelia returns sporting a crossword puzzle book.

'Someone left this in the toilet. Can you believe that?'

'I can't,' I say. And I mean it. If there is one thing I like more than a good crossword puzzle, it is a free one.

'Well, then, I expect you to be excellent.'

'Prepare to be dazzled.' Ophelia sits and shuffles her chair close to mine. I can feel her proximity, see her aura, taste her scent. We have shared many kisses, but that is as far as it has gone. I want to remove her clothes and take her right here on the puzzle book. But if we do that, there will be no trip, the terror suspicions will be confirmed, and I'll never get to Magnus. Sometimes it is tough being a wealthy, unemployed serial killer!

After several beers and an hour and a half of owning crosswords, our gate is announced, and we gather our belongings to leave. I am bloated and have been gaining weight these last few weeks. At least that will be one less thing for mother to hassle me about next week.

The news is that the gate is about a seventeen-mile walk. I have flown from Heathrow many times and have yet to have a gate near the departure lounge.

By the time we arrive at the gate, the flight is due to take off, yet everyone is sitting waiting patiently as the aircraft is cleaned. By everyone, I do mean those with a modicum of common sense. There are, of course, those who are standing, hovering, bags in hand, waiting for the gate to open, even though you can see that the plane isn't even attached to the walkway yet. Sometimes I think the airport staff should let them through, watch them walk down the gangway and fall off the end like lemmings.

We sit, and once again, Ophelia curls into my side. I have an ample frame, and given that she is well-prepared for comfort, I am still unsure whether she likes me that much or is just a pro at getting comfortable. Either way, it turns me on every time she does, and I am forced to distract myself.

Fortunately, we don't have long to wait before first class boarding is announced, and Ophelia's face lights up when I tell her that means us.

'We're flying first class!' she exclaims. I nod. 'You're full of surprises, aren't you?' I nod again. If only you knew, Ophelia. 'That must have cost a fortune?' I shrug. I don't really know. I just booked them. She looks at me and says, 'Isn't there a lounge we could have used?'

'Yes,' I say. 'It's full of dickheads, though.' She laughs, and a nearby mother shoots me a look because their child overheard the work *dickhead.* I apologise and then glare at the boy. From the looks of him, she'd better get used to hearing the word.

The plane finally takes off after the usual rigmarole and safety briefing. They say that you should listen no matter how many times you fly. But I don't expect to survive a crash, and if I do well, I'll be the one wandering around with the safety information card in my hand.

First class is wonderful, although the seats are large, and I am mildly disappointed when I realise that Ophelia cannot nestle into me. Champagne is served prior to departure. We drink, and then Ophelia re-attaches herself to the neck pillow, removes her ear plugs and a satin blindfold, declares that she *didn't sleep last night*, kisses me on the lips and then disappears into her comfort accessories.

The plane takes off nearly an hour later than scheduled, but we arrive five minutes early. Who knew that there were so many lies told in aviation? I managed about five hours of sleep combined in the taxi and the plane, and I feel like shit when I wake up.

When the plane finally stops, I stand to grab my luggage from above me. Despite the comforts of the first-class seats, I have a definite crick in my neck, and all I hear is *I told you so* from a less than contrite-looking Ophelia.

Hartsfield-Jackson airport is no better than Heathrow at ten in the morning, and thankfully we reach the hire car desk before I reach my tolerance for being pushed and have to rip someone's arms off.

Baggage reclaim was smooth, as was picking up the rental, and I am genuinely shocked when I press the button to discover what I have rented.

'You got a Mustang?' Ophelia exclaims. 'Gimme,' she says, motioning to the keys. 'I'm driving.' I throw her the keys gladly and wonder how drunk I must have been when I booked the car.

It is just over ten miles to the *Four Seasons,* and Ophelia uses as much petrol as possible on the drive.

We arrive at the hotel to check in, and having seen the prices for a room, I am relieved to discover that I haven't booked us a suite.

'Ah yes, Mr Norman, we have your reservation here. I am afraid we don't have any twin rooms left. Would you be all right with a double, sir?' Being called *sir* in a non-ironic way always throws me off, and before I get a chance to reply, Ophelia says.

'That will be fine!' A key card is produced, and our luggage disappears. Ophelia snatches the card and runs off toward the elevators—we're in America—and as tired as I am, I smile, thank the man at the desk and then run off after her. I did book a twin room, Melissa, I swear.

The room—despite not being a suite—is frankly ridiculous. The bed looks like it could eat me whole and would be an apt final resting place, given how I am currently feeling. My concept of time has vacated me completely. There were drinks at Heathrow this morning, then a flight, and now somehow, we've only just escaped the morning again. *Ground-hog-fucking-morning*. Ophelia is excited, and to be fair, so am I. I think. If I'm being honest, I am a little anxious about my meeting tomorrow night for various reasons. This used to be my bread and butter, but I have been off my game lately, and playing away from home is always harder. I also have Ophelia with me. She doesn't know my secrets, and I don't know hers. We all have them, right?

I find it odd that something I used to do regularly is making me anxious. I feel better having Ophelia by my side. But I embark on my endeavour alone tomorrow. I know that I am also a little untethered. I killed Theo because I didn't care for his tone of voice. I am in America, people have guns, and I cannot afford to go off on a whim.

Ophelia appears from the shower, and I almost have to avert my gaze. She is wearing just a towel, and I would very much like to know what is underneath. *Not now, I say to myself, not now*.

'So, what do we do first?' she asks as she leans into me and kisses my head. Her proximity brings the scent of lemon sherbet on her skin and coconut in her hair. She is like a sweet, and I could eat her right now. I must have been staring because she taps me gently on the side of the head. 'Hey, Arthur.'

'The world of *Coca-Cola* is just down the road. I saw it from the car as we drove in.'

'Oooh,' she says, 'I could go for a bucket load of caffeine.' Ophelia throws a towel in my direction. 'Well, come on then! Get clean, and I'll buy you breakfast.'

I smile, grab the towel, and move into the bathroom. My stomach yells at me at the mention of food, and I realise I am still useless at eating unless prompted. I need to address this. I think as I turn the water on and let it hit my skin. I have no room for weakness right now.

I emerge from the shower, and to my slight disappointment, I find Ophelia dressed. It is late May, and the weather outside is warm. I study her from the ground up and see that she is wearing fresh white Converse, knee-high socks, red hotpants, and an Atlanta *Braves* tee cut at the top so that it hangs loose and exposes her shoulder. I look at her and grin. 'Where did you get that from?'

'Internet,' she replies. 'Why? What are you wearing?' I go to reply, but she produces a matching shirt and hands it over to me proudly. Thankfully, it looks a good fit and doesn't have a slit in the shoulder. 'Can't have you looking like a tourist!'

'No, we cannot,' I say, thinking that I should have thought of that.

'You take forever to shower! I'll meet you downstairs. I'll have breakfast waiting for you.' She kisses me on the cheek, says, 'Wear the tee,' and then disappears out of the room. I smile for the thousandth time since we met, conceding that I take a long time in the shower. Something about being often covered in blood or evidence of some misdeed makes you habitually scrub yourself as hard as possible.

THIRTY

Breakfast/brunch/lunch—whatever the fuck it is—in the Four Seasons is to kill for. I'm serious. If someone denies me the same opportunity, tomorrow, death will be served hot, cold, or luke-fucking warm. I eat as though it will be my last meal before we depart for the land of caffeine, sugar, and diabetes.

Unless you are deeply interested in the inception of a multi-billion-dollar entity that is probably responsible for millions of deaths and the production of billions of plastic bottles, the World of Coca-Cola is ninety per cent dull drudgery. The redeeming feature, however, is a room right at the end. It is filled with drinks made from the stickiest post mix, and here, you can sample drinks made by Coca-Cola worldwide. It is like a smorgasbord of caffeine, sugar, and an elevated heart rate. You can drink yourself to the brink of exploding and then drink some more.

By the time we leave, I feel happy, distended, and like I am about to explode. I am reasonably sure my teeth are itching, but it is a sure-fire way to exorcise hangover and jetlag. They should really add that to *TripAdvisor*.

We leave and take our caffeine-fuelled selves to the Zoo to annoy the poor animals. I do feel for these reduced predators, trapped in a cage, being fed at the whim of man. And I wonder if it is a bleak glimpse into my future.

After almost being ejected from the zoo, we embark on a cultural tour and pay our respects to the late, great Dr King. And then we check out some movie attractions, starting with *The Walking Dead* and ending with *Gone With The Wind.* Ophelia manages to fit the phrase, *frankly, my dear, I don't give a damn* into the most unobvious of situations, making me laugh every time. Six o'clock comes, and we find a bar, order some drinks, and relax. I am thoroughly in love with this city, Ophelia, and the American culture, were my entire body—neck included—not aching. I might actually say that I was *happy*.

We eat dinner at a local diner and stroll back to the hotel. I order some more drinks, and we sit in the bar. I have no concept of time and am subsisting on alcohol alone. Ophelia excuses herself in the direction of the rooms, and I tell her *I'll be up soon.* I have enjoyed her company immeasurably, but I am keen for a moment of quiet contemplation to make sure I am prepared for tomorrow.

I told Ophelia that it is a business meeting, and she asked no questions. At this stage in our relationship, I don't feel it pertinent to tell her that I am utterly hopeless at business and have absolutely no interest in it. She doesn't need to know that. I know relationships shouldn't be built on lies. I just don't think the part about me being a killer is something I can share with her . . . yet.

I get my head together and go over tomorrow's plan with myself. Content that I vaguely know what I am doing, I finish my drink and head upstairs to the room.

My key card beeps on the door, and I push it open. The interior of the room is dim, and the shades have been drawn. I panic, and my heart races as I slowly move through the door. I might have expected this, but I didn't.

I enter the room and close the door behind me. My heart rate rises steadily, and I am sure I am about to have a heart attack. The room is dark, and the only light comes from candles. Candles? In a hotel room, Ophelia, you naughty girl.

I peel my back from the closed door and move into the room. I am equal parts excited and terrified. As the bed comes into view, I see Ophelia. She is spread out on the god-sized bed and is oh-so-elegant for someone wearing only lingerie. The key card falls to the floor along with my mouth, and I must have remained motionless for too long, and she notices my hesitance.

Ophelia rises from the bed, and I watch on, entranced as she walks over to me. I had fantasised about swimming together, but it appears we are about to do a different kind of cardio. I feel like I am in the room with Gal Gadot in *Keeping up with the Joneses,* except this isn't an above-average action-comedy, and I don't know Gal Gadot. I know Ophelia, and here she is, walking over to me slowly.

She arrives, and as soon as I go to speak, she places her finger over my lip. After the year I have had, I am beyond excited. This is like every Christmas and birthday I have ever had all combined into one, and for the next forty minutes, I will forget about every anxious thought in my head.

Ophelia takes my hand and turns around; I watch her walk away until the slack on my arm gives, and I follow her exposed bottom to the bed. We arrive, and she throws me down on my back. I shuffle awkwardly as she crawls onto the bed and moves toward me slowly. She is like a lion stalking her prey; the look in her eye is both demonic and sexy. Her apex predator eyes are locked on me, and I am very glad for women like Ophelia. As much as I crave her, my anxious mind could go three thousand lifetimes before I acted on it.

I close my eyes for a moment and thank whoever is listening for creating strong women. When I open them again, she is on top of me, bearing down. The lust in our eyes meets, and everything beyond the two of us ceases to exist.

She stares at me for a moment as her hands move toward my face; they grab it firmly, and we kiss, we kiss and kiss, and we kiss. I have kissed more in the last five minutes than I have in the last five months. I'd missed the warmth, the connection, the raw passion of what happens behind closed doors.

The kissing stops, and she rips off my t-shirt, and I help her off with my trousers. As soon as I am naked, things change. The testosterone in my body turbochargers, and I am on fire. I stand and lift Ophelia from the bed in one motion. The look in her eyes indicates that she is not surprised but rather impressed. I walk her over to the window and enter her softly. Her bare bottom presses up against the glass, and that, along with me being inside her, elicits a look of surprise, and she bites her lip, an action that will live long in my memory.

I place my lips on her breast, and she quivers. I pause for a moment, raise my hand to her face and sweep her hair from her eyes. We share a look, a moment, an appreciation, the calm before the storm. Then, without warning, she leans into me and bites my lip while wrapping her legs around my waist. The movement catches me by surprise; together, we stagger backwards and collapse in a heap on the floor. The mild accident only spurs us on. We begin, and for the next thirty minutes, we sweat, writhe, and moan, moving around the room, fucking on any available surface, moving apart slightly until finally—we come together.

As I watch Ophelia's head rise and fall on my chest as I breathe, I consider that something takes over us when it comes to copulation. Nothing else matters. It is as though the molecular makeup of our brains changes, and suddenly the only thing that exists is pure, unfettered hedonism. We've all been late for work, a meeting, a class or even an event because the opportunity for sex has presented itself. When it does, we seize it with both hands, but the *back in ten* sign in the window of our souls and disappear off the face of the earth until we are done.

As I study Ophelia, I can't help but realise that I am feeling something new. I know that dozens of chemicals have just raced through my brain, but something tells me this is different.

It was always going to take something special to come after you, Melissa, and the strange thing about this is that it was so unexpected. I am in the Four Seasons in Atlanta, lying on a god-sized bed with a goddess-like woman I only met a few weeks ago.

Melissa understood me, helped and nurtured me, and we were in love. But in all other senses, we were polar opposites, which works. It does. But somehow, part of me feels that Ophelia and I share something much more profound.

'Whatcha thinking?' Ophelia asks, breaking my thoughts.

'That we should do that again.' Ophelia laughs, then moves her head, so we are eye to eye.

'Oh, we will do that again,' she exclaims. I smile. 'I don't know about you, but I could do with a milkshake or frozen yoghurt.'

'You know,' I say. 'I saw a froyo place not far from here.'

'Well, get dressed then,' she says, tapping me on my chest. 'It is a tradition in Greece to buy a lady froyo after making love.'

'Is it?' I ask. Ophelia nods, stands, and moves into the bathroom.

'I'll get my coat,' I say.

THIRTY-ONE

I awake the next morning to find Ophelia gone. I panic and throw my hands around the bed in search of her. To my relief, I find that the bed is still warm from her presence, and when I convince the blur to dissipate from my eyes, I spot a note on the nightstand.

Gone to the gym, didn't want to wake you. xxx

I close my eyes again, very glad she didn't. My phone buzzes with an email from my pal Magnus confirming our meeting tonight. I shoot him a quick reply, make coffee, and then order room service. My god, I could live in this hotel.

When Ophelia reappears, she eats, changes into swimwear—something I enjoy—and declares she is heading to the pool for the day and that I should join her when I get back. I agree. Part of me wants to spend the day wreaking havoc in the pool and getting shouted at by lifeguards for being inappropriate. I wish I didn't carry this burden, this anger, this blood lust. But it isn't that simple. Poor Arcane Arthur.

I may have told Ophelia some small lies. First, this is a business trip—it isn't unless you count murder as a business—and second, it is an all-day affair. Again, it isn't. I am not meeting Magnus until much later. But given that I need to be prepared, I want to use the day to ensure I know as much as possible about this man. I also need to get myself some good knives, something which won't be too much of a bother here.

I leave Ophelia—with a heavy heart—in her swimwear and drag myself outside. To my delight, I discover there are many hunting stores in the north of the city, and I make my way there armed with cash. It turns out that buying guns requires ID and background checks, but massive fucking knives, and all the rest of it, luckily do not.

I tell the enthusiastic clerk that I am going hunting with my American friends on their property, and I need to look the part. He doesn't question it. Instead, he asks me where in London I live. I tell him I live in the centre, and I am pretty sure he thinks I live in the Shard with the royal family. I am wearing a long, dark wig, and I would imagine that, should anyone be interested, finding the dark-haired royal Londoner who lives in the Shard would be a tall order.

I leave the store with all my goods neatly stored in my camouflage backpack and continue my journey.

I travel north using public transport until I arrive in the vicinity of Magnus's address and dismount from my bus. It took me far longer to use public transport, and as much as I had planned for that, it will always be why people choose their car over a bus! I don't harbour any preconceived notion about buses being filled with homeless drug addicts or anything like that. I would be all for using a bus if they weren't so damn slow and confusing.

I walk the mile back to Magnus's and, when I arrive, find a place to hover and wait. If I am ever caught by police who staked out my house for days on end, I will go willingly. It is not an enjoyable task, even less so when you have no car to sit in. For some reason, sitting in a stationary car is socially accepted, loitering on a street corner less so. Fortunately, I am in luck. After one hour of pacing up and down and pretending to talk on the phone, the gates open, and a large

Mercedes G-Wagon departs the compound flanked front and rear by two Chevy SUVs. Whatever Magnus does for a living isn't ethical, yet he invited me to his house for our first meeting. I figure you have to be either super confident or arrogant as fuck to live and operate in broad daylight.

The cars leave the compound, and the gates close; when the coast is clear, I pull my cap down over my eyes. I finish my imaginary phone call—it's the small details—and dash across the road to the brush surrounding the gate. The compound is vast and surrounded by a tall wall with barbed wire. Fortunately, the undergrowth has spilt over, and I slip between it and disappear. Always maintain your yard! I climb the wall and sustain minimal injury as I manoeuvre myself over the barbed wire. I silently descend into the garden, pleased to harbour some ability still.

I know I own an ostentatious house. I mean, I have an outdoor swimming pool in England. That's like owning a shipping vessel in Austria. But this guy, this guy takes the piss. The main house looms before me like a giant. It is reminiscent of the house from *Gone With The Wind* and no doubt harks back to the good old dickhead days of white supremacy. It would be quite a classy building had it not been modernised in the gaudiest of fashions. There is also an enormous pool, two pool houses—why?—a hot tub, a triple garage, three annexes, and a tiny shed that is probably used by the groundskeepers.

After checking my surroundings, I stay near the ground and move quickly toward the main building. I wouldn't be surprised if this twat has several very angry and aggressive dogs lurking, ready to rip my throat out for no good reason, and the thought of it hurries me along.

I approach the front door in a hurry, jump, and pull myself onto one of the many pillars. I feel much heavier than I used to, but I lift my considerable bulk off the floor and onto the annoying balcony he probably uses to survey his empire each morning.

I discover the balcony door is unlocked and sneak into Magnus's world. To my disbelief, the inside is even more disgusting than the outside. The whole place appears to have been styled in the dark by a child with no taste. The collision of styles is horrendous. There are replica Monets hanging over rugs made from stuffed animals—which, aside from being hideous to look at, are probably the biggest tripping hazard I have ever seen—beyond the satin-sheeted bedroom is a corridor lined with retro arcade machines and Japanese vases. The only thing I don't hate is a signed poster from *Jackie Brown,* and I consider whether it is worth stealing it after Magnus's inevitable death. I find the study and enter it, closing the door behind me. Breaking in has so far been relatively easy, and it unnerves me.

I search the study high and low. Modern technology—smartphone cameras—allows me to document the room and all the original angles of items before I search, and I would be stupid not to take advantage of it. It does seriously add to your time, though.

When a slow, methodical search of the study draws a blank, I sit in the outrageously comfy ergonomic computer chair at the desk—I need one of these—and scratch my head. I shake the PC away to be greeted by some form of encryption—this is not my ballpark—and I don't even attempt to crack it. I swing myself about in the magic chair and think about giving up when one of my rotations brings my attention to a book that is oddly out of place. I stop spinning, pick it up, and open it. I am not surprised to find out that it is a fake book, but I am shocked when I discover a familiar-looking flash drive—the one stolen during my car crash—buried in the cut-out pages. That motherfucker! My brain digs up a memory of something Steven said at the party about a US senator being investigated for money laundering, and I feel sick. My brain has lurched from toxic thoughts to the notion of new happiness, and among it all, I feel like I am missing something disgustingly obvious.

I pocket *my* hard drive and am about to stand up when the door bursts open, and the study gets very small as it is filled by the biggest security guards I have ever seen. I knew it had been too easy.

THIRTY-TWO

This is most definitely problematic. I have had my consciousness back for twenty minutes, and so far, all I have established is that I am in a dark room. The issue with clandestine operations is that no one knows I am here. If I die, my body will never be found, and Ophelia will forever be left in mystery. It is a negative thought; I don't want that to happen to her. I must get out of here.

My hands are bound, and I am strung up from the floor, attached to a beam in the ceiling. I wonder if rooms like this are purpose-built for interrogation or if, one day, someone thought, huh, that's a good beam to hang a body from. My shoes and top are gone—my fucking Braves t-shirt—my feet only just reach the floor when I stretch out my toes, which is not comfortable. The lack of a t-shirt angers me. The room is almost completely black aside from a small ray of light trickling in from the door frame, and I have zero concept of time or how long I was unconscious.

An indeterminable amount of time passes until the door bursts open, and my senses are absolutely ram-rodded by light. I have to blink furiously, and I suddenly understand what Bane was trying to tell Batman about him only adopting the darkness. I am not used to the dark, and I can't see shit. When my vision finally returns, I find myself face to face with a man I presume to be Magnus, flanked by two comically large henchmen. The ghastly neon overhead light is activated and flickers away intermittently until it catches—

clearly, Magnus doesn't give a fuck about the environment or has never heard of LEDs—the door closes, and one of the giants sets a bag—presumably full of torture instruments—down on the table. Magnus approaches me and says, 'So, you think you can steal from me, huh?' The situation has now changed. I am annoyed at the hypocrisy here, but Magnus's accent is the worst thing about this. He looks and sounds like a budget Bond villain. I hate his ridiculous purple suit and want to hold him down and rip off his goatee.

The current situation is not ideal. I feel no fear other than the notion of leaving Ophelia alone. Despite my recent fuck ups, I am still a seasoned menace, and I reconcile with myself that I really ought to be thanking Magnus. I need information from him, and everything I need to obtain it is right here in this room. 'Thank you,' I say.

A punch to my gut startles me and brings me back to the fray. It's been some time since I was on the receiving end of a beating, and I don't much care for it. Torture is always an inconvenience, and it would seem that whoever applies it feels obligated to inflict a minimum amount of pain before asking any questions. *Why hit me first?* There are three people in this room—excluding me—and given that none of them will be leaving alive. I will happily tell them anything. There is no need for violence.

Another punch to the gut is followed by my first question. The punch winds me, and I can feel my rich Four Seasons breakfast returning. I struggle for breath, and now wasn't the time for a question. Was it, guys? A slap to the face is followed by Magnus asking, 'What were you doing in my house?'

This has gone from being an inconvenience to making me angry. I don't have time for this. I am annoyed that my *Braves* shirt is missing and vexed at the notion that I could be with

Ophelia by the pool. I open my mouth to speak, but before I do, Magnus removes a small blade from his belt and rams it into my midriff.

And *HOLY FUCK, THAT HURT!* Kudos to Magnus for being a grade-A psychopath. I was about to tell him everything, and *bam,* he sticks me. I look down at the blood that spurts from the wound. It lands on the plastic sheeting below me. It is a shallow wound, but it feels like an army of metal men is invading my cut. How am I going to explain that?

Magnus grabs me by the face and says, 'Are you ready to talk?' *I was ready to talk before you shanked me, you psycho.* I form my face into what I hope looks like contrition and nod sadly. He takes a step back, and I begin.

I am quite British, and since he paid goons to rob me—twice—he probably has some idea of who I am. I want to return to the pool, so I don't have time for pretence.

'Why did you rob me? Why do you have my flash drive?' I ask.

'Rob you?' he asks, 'rob you?' He looks at his two goons and laughs heartily. 'Look, fella. I don't know who you are. And I certainly didn't rob you.'

'Where is my other flash drive?'

'Your other flash drive? Buddy, you are crazy.' Magnus strolls up to within an inch of me and waves the USB stick in front of my face. 'This," he says, waving it angrily, 'this is nothing but footage of two idiots!' before chucking it to the ground.

'But my house,' I manage meekly. 'You stole—'

'I don't have time for this,' says Magnus echoing my thoughts. 'Take care of him.' And with that, he steps outside. This is not a Bond film, and I will not be subjected to an unnecessarily long death sequence from which I will eventually escape. If I am going to act, it needs to be now. Get it together, Arthur.

The door closes behind Magnus, leaving me alone with Hagrid and Goliath—I'm bleeding and weak on fictional giants—they approach me, and I drop my head. The sport is no fun without a little game, and as my head sinks, I whisper incoherently. My gibberish impresses even me. It sounds like I could be speaking English or even Aramaic.

Hagrid bites and the idiot approaches me despite the overuse of this in films—does he think I have tonight's lottery numbers—Goliath—or maybe Hagrid? I don't know. I've been stabbed—nears me and places his fat, juicy neck close to my mouth to get a better listen. As soon as he does, I pounce. I wrap my large legs around him and pull him in tight. Once he is close enough, I sink my teeth into his neck and gnaw at it like a rabid dog. As I pull him toward me, his frame pushes against the knife and *holyfuckingshit,* that hurts again. I scream internally—because my mouth is busy devouring Hagrid's neck. Human teeth can do some damage, and his attention turns away from me and toward saving his own life. He panics, and his preoccupation with living distracts him, and I am able to use him as a ladder and lift my hands from the hook in the ceiling. With my hands free, I loop the rope around his neck, and he is soon rendered useless between the strangling and the biting.

Having engaged in a bit of love-biting, *S and M,* autoerotic play with Hagrid, I roll off him and onto the floor. The pain in my gut—combined with hanging from the ceiling—is horrible, and I make a mental note to myself to do more stretching should I make it out of there. With Hagrid now either dead or very badly injured at the mouth of a savage,

Goliath looks far less confident. He pauses for a split second, allowing me to remove the knife from my middle and cut myself free from the rope around my wrists. But the minute I do, I realise why they advise you to leave the knife in. It comes out as well as what I assume is most of my blood, and as it drips onto the handy plastic, I wobble and feel slightly feint. I don't have a problem with blood. I just tend to fair better with mine where it should be.

Time moves at a million miles an hour and incredibly slowly simultaneously in these situations. Love Bite Hagrid is motionless on the floor, and Goliath looks at me, doing his best to appear menacing, but he clearly doesn't get paid enough for this. The *room/shed/annexe/torture house* is clearly sound-proofed—since Magnus hasn't reappeared—and he takes one more look at me and bolts for the door. Despite my stabbed state, I move quickly and catch up with him as his hand connects with the handle. *So close, Goliath, so close.* With the blade in my hand, I slice across his throat and throw him back into the room. I kick him into the middle, and he rolls around like a stuck pig.

Once I am happy that his blood has mixed with mine on the plastic, I turn and head for the door. The lesson here is always to be mindful of whom you are fucking with. The inept burglar might be an emotionless killer.

I step out into the world, and the sunlight warms my face. I spot Magnus standing all of ten feet away, smoking a cigarette. I am not pleased with being out in the open—I wouldn't be surprised if there were some cunty dogs lurking. My warm blood trickles down my body as I hold the wound with one hand and the knife in the other. I may have pulled a muscle during my tussle, and I limp toward Magnus, looking like an extra from *Dawn of the Dead*.

In my current state, I am less than stealthy. Magnus is standing at the bottom of his yard near the brush. The house is just out of sight, but I no longer am as he hears me approach and turns about. He no doubt has various security methods at his disposal. I think about Ophelia alone by the pool, and I summon what is left of my effort and charge at him before he has time to react.

I run, and we collide, and my god, does his stupid suit feel great against my bare skin. The impact sends us both tumbling. We roll together down a small embankment and don't stop spinning until we reach the bottom near a fence.

The knife must have fallen from my grasp during the commotion. Somehow, when we stop, I am the first to react. I climb atop Magnus and raise my fist above my head. I go to bring it down into his face when I notice that he is motionless, head back, pupils deep in his skull. It is then that I realise that there is blood pooling on the ground under his head, and he must have smacked it on something as we fell.

Rolling down a hill is very disorientating, but the first thing I do is check for a pulse. There is none. Fuck!

***

I sneak back to the torture annexe, wipe down any prints, retrieve my clothes, and USB stick, and leave.

I exit to the rear of the property into some woods, find a small creek, wash, change, and apply pressure to my wound. Magnus had little on him other than his phone—which he willingly unlocked for me—and, aside from taking a look at the maker of his suit, I largely drew a blank.

The sun is setting on a long and unpleasant day, and I am bleeding quite badly. The size of the hole in me suggests that it will require some medical attention should I decide I want to keep the rest of my blood inside of me. The wound will take some explaining to Ophelia, and I hope that Magnus keeps a record of his nefarious activities on his phone. Otherwise, I missed a day by the pool—and got stabbed—for nothing.

I could find something to cauterise the wound and then pass out. But it is one thing to explain a random knife wound. It is another entirely to talk my way out of why I burnt it instead of going to a hospital.

I can't use a hospital, which is why I currently find myself lurking outside a small suburban veterinary clinic.

My grandfather was a vet, and for some reason, they are chronically understated by the general public. A human doctor works on a patient who can tell them what is wrong, and vets get no such luck. In life or death, there's no significant difference. If your car breaks down in the middle of nowhere and the first passer-by tells you they are a lorry mechanic, you're not going to send them away, are you? I have faith that a kindly underpaid vet will look at me, then at my money and quietly go about patching me up.

I loiter in the parking lot outside the clinic. I wait until I see the last customer—is that the correct term?—leave before I stumble across the car park to the front door. Either the temperature in Atlanta suddenly increases as the sun sets, or I am beginning to feel a fever onset. I am putting my chips all in. Whoever is on the other side of this door can either help or hurt me, and I am powerless to change the outcome.

'Sorry, we're about to close,' comes the voice from the burly veterinarian behind a waist-high screen. His back is turned, and he has not yet seen me. I lock the door behind me and wait by the counter, almost physically propping myself up with it. There is a picture on the desk of my hopeful hero. He is in his yard with many, many cocker spaniels. And from the looks of his getup, most of his wage is spent on dog maintenance. He coughs, then sighs, and then turns about on the spot. The man is mid-thirties, dark-haired, and his face features many acne scars. His hair looks as though it was cut in the dark, and either he is the spitting image of one of his spaniels, or I am hallucinating from the loss of blood. Either is pretty possible. With the last of my strength, I remove my emergency roll of green banknotes and place it on the counter.

'I…I,' he begins. I tap the roll of money softly and lower my eyes toward it. I just about manage to gesture toward my wound before an unseen force steals my legs. I crash to the floor, and everything goes black.

When I come to and open my eyes, I sit up very slowly and take in the surrounding space. The room I am in features myriad portraits of just about every kind of Spaniel imaginable. Everything is dog themed, including a mug on the side with a dog bone for a handle. *Cute*. I am not a fan of spaniels in the slightest. It is nothing personal. It's just that their energy does not match mine, and I am far from certain that this is not hell. Panic sets in, and I try to stand before falling back to the table.

'Woah, woah, easy there,' comes a voice from beyond. I look down at my abdomen, spot a bandage, and immediately reach for it. 'Hey,' comes the voice again, 'don't make me get you a cone.' He seems to enjoy his dog-based humour, and I realise what is happening. I look up and see my rescuer move toward me, his spaniel eyes wide open, taking me in with the same misplaced excitement.

'Ww-what happened?' I stammer.

'Well,' says the man, 'you broke in here, shoved a wad of cash in my face, collapsed and then bled all over my floor.'

'Oh,' I say.

'You know,' he says, 'you really should go to a hospital. I've patched you up, but that is a nasty wound.' He moves toward a cabinet, opens, and closes it and then chucks a pill bottle in my direction. The bottle crashes into me, and I manage to grab it at the second time of asking. I raise the cap to my bleary eyes and read the label.

'It says these are for dogs.'

'Antibiotics!'

'But I'm not a dog.'

'Well, it's that or death from sepsis. Or you could go to the hospital.'

'I'll take the dog pills,' I say. 'Thanks,'

'Jesse,' he says.

'Thanks, Jesse, I'm—' Jesse holds his hands aloft and pats the wad of cash in the breast pocket of his lab coat.

'I don't wanna know,' he says. I see the bone-shaped tag featuring his name just under my wad of cash that sticks out of his pocket. 'I have a lot of tiny mouths to feed,' he says and shrugs.

Before I know what is happening, Jesse is ushering me to the door. I should tell him that his bedside manner needs work—the animals can't, but he has just saved my life, so I hold my tongue. He walks me as far as the double glass door and almost pushes me out. He half closes the door and then pauses. 'The knife missed any major organs but keep it clean and dry. Take the pills twice a day until they run out. And for Christ's sake, get to a hospital.'

The door closes, and I am alone in the dark. And as I stroll away into the night, I wonder if *Christ* would care if I went to a hospital or not.

THIRTY-THREE

Having been shaken down by Jesse for most of my cash, I was forced to dig deep into my super-secret hiding place for the last I had. I cannot use credit cards, as I don't want my trail to be bigger than it already is. I bought the only bus ticket I could afford back to town, got on the bus, and promptly fell asleep.

I was fortunate not to miss my stop when a kindly old lady woke me up, and I thanked her profusely. Not returning to my plush hotel and Ophelia would have compounded a rather shit day.

I step back into the Four Seasons, and my relief is palpable. Today was not a good one. I thought that what I needed was closure, Melissa. I believed I needed to get back to doing the things that make me, me. But not for the first time recently, I find myself bumbling, almost failing. Magnus did not die well. He smashed his head open on a rock as we fell and left his brains all over his yard. I have yet to get what I came for, and I will have to keep Magnus's phone off until we get home. I can't help but feel that something is wrong. My magic touch is missing, and for the most part, all I could think about was getting back to the hotel, to Ophelia.

My rumination continues as I stroll past reception and head to the spa. I remove my clothes and leave them to be laundered by housekeeping. Then I step into the monsoon shower and spray away the day's sins.

I shower for an inordinate amount of time until I finally must leave and face Ophelia. I don a soft white robe, gather mine and Magnus's possessions, and make for the elevator. The day is almost over, and I have missed all of it. I'm sure Ophelia will be fine, but that isn't my problem.

I spent the entire bus ride—that I was conscious for—as well as the time in the shower trying to think of a reason as to why I have a hole in me. It hurts, and I would be surprised if I could conceal it for the next few days or explain away a scar that wasn't there yesterday. My usually mighty mind is drawing a blank because I am not used to, nor want to, lie to the woman I love.

I reach the room door, enter my key card, and pause. I have no good excuse, and I am not willing to lie. Whatever happens, happens.

The problem with trauma, grief, and pain is that whatever made you feel that way becomes almost irrelevant. You can move on, forgive, forget, join the Peace Corps, or get really high, whatever you need to do. But you can't outrun your feelings, and you cannot begin to heal until you admit that you are *hurting*. It is not straightforward or linear, and you can be sad about something you thought you had recovered from. But I think the worst thing is doubt, which can (and does) happen to any of us. Trust is a big issue whether you are recovering from abuse, trauma, heartbreak, or failure. At first, you might not trust whatever or whoever caused your pain, but at some point, you wake up having lost faith in yourself. You no longer trust your mind, your instincts, or your decisions. And if you cannot trust yourself, whom do you trust?

The good news is it will get better. Regardless of whatever happened to you, you would need to be a colossal idiot to ignore that things will get better somehow. Most people know that. What is depressing is not knowing how or when. Time doesn't necessarily heal wounds; what does is how you use that time.

I wallowed at home, away from just about everyone, which was necessary yet counterproductive. I am getting there, but the reason I hid had more to do with my not wanting to be seen in the state I was in, something that I will admit was a little short-sighted.

I didn't want people to see me hurt, weak, and vulnerable. So, I hid. But the truth is the people that know you know it's temporary. They won't judge you if they are your friends. Look at Eeyore. The guy is duller than daytime TV, yet his friends always invite him to join in. Kudos to them. I would probably kill him and put him out of his misery if he was my friend.

The point is I was an idiot to act the way I did. Yes, watching reruns of *House MD* took away some of my pain, but it wasn't conducive to healing. But Melissa, you were my one and only. You knew the real me. I'd given everything to you. We even got married! I had thought marriage was the next step for bored or uninspired people, but I did it for you, Melissa.

As I loiter outside my hotel room, a sinking feeling washes over me as I wonder whether I can ever tell Ophelia my secrets. Is it possible for another human being to accept me for who I really am? As much as I miss you, Melissa, I miss knowing that you knew. What if there is only one person for you in life? What if I had that, and now it is gone forever?

I finally get my shit together and depress the door handle. The light turns green, and the door swings open. Ophelia is sitting on the bed, tissue in hand, tears streaming from her eyes. She sees me enter, looks up at me with her beautiful browns, opens her mouth, and says.

'Arthur, we need to talk.'

FUCK

My mind is fast-forwarding through a million different scenarios as I enter the room and sit on the bed next to her. I reach out and place my hand on hers, but she moves it away, and now I know this isn't good. My mind is racing, and it is like Silverstone on race day. I focus on keeping my mouth shut. 'Ophelia, I—' I blurt in panic. So much for keeping quiet.

'No, Arthur, let me,' she says. I bite my tongue, and a week-long silence ensues. I can feel my world crashing down around me, and the room starts to spin. It could be to do with the massive blood loss, but I don't like it either way. Everything has been going too well for too long with Ophelia. I just knew that there had to be a catch.

'I don't want there to be any secrets between us,' Ophelia says, shattering the silence. I look at her, then down at my stabbed abdomen, and wonder what I should tell her or what she already knows. I don't want there to be any secrets, but living a double life is complicated.

'I guess,' she continues, 'we all have things about us that we don't tell anyone else. And I don't want that to be us, Arthur.' Her lips tremble, and I am sure she quivers internally. I know this look. It is fear. Is she scared of me?

The tears stop, and her lips begin to move. I don't know what to do. Do I comfort her, or is there a SWAT team lurking in the bathroom, ready to take my head off if I get too close?

'Arthur,' she says, looking at me earnestly. 'There is something I need to tell you.' I go to speak, but she cuts me off. 'You know when there is something about you that you are scared will freak someone out?' I nod. 'Well, I wanted to tell you. I did, Arthur. I didn't want to scare you.'

'Hey,' I manage, now reasonably sure there aren't snipers aiming at my head. I place my hand on her leg softly and say. 'You can tell me anything, Ophelia. It won't change how I feel about you.'

'Okay,' she begins. 'It is about my last boyfriend. He didn't just 'die'; I killed him.'

***

If I had a drink, I'm sure I would have spat it everywhere. Ophelia's words hit my ears, enter my skull, and rummage around. Murderous impulses aren't a stranger to me, but it was a shock. I am sure I heard her right, but at the same time, I wonder if the Dog antibiotics are doing a number on my senses. I'm not a dog.

I don't know whether or not I'm freaking out. I have been stabbed today and lost a lot of blood. Of all the things I thought Ophelia would want to talk to me about, this was not a scenario I had played out in my head. I cannot judge—can I?—I decide that stolid calm is required, and I remain silent, smiling, and supportive as she continues.

'I'm sorry,' she says, 'I should have told you; I just didn't want to scare you off.' I nod, I seem to nod a lot, but it is a handy go-to. I am a little scared.

A slightly odd silence falls over the room. I realise we don't know much about each other, and I have just learnt that she, too, has blood on her hands. I am a little freaked out, and I know that is ironic and hypocritical. But I know what motivates me. I know what is wrong with me, and I deal with it. Aside from Theo—who probably deserved to die—I don't kill innocent people. I am not a monster.

I don't know if I have been silent for five minutes or five hours. I finally break the eternal silence and shuffle closer to her as I do. I want to be supportive and don't want to end up dead.

'Hey,' I say, finally taking my cue to calm her down. 'It's okay. I'm not going anywhere.' Ophelia takes a deep breath and opens her mouth.

'He wasn't always violent,' she says. 'Things used to be different. But it changed after his business collapsed and he started drinking. I guess I should have left, but you get trapped in a bad place, and before long, you forget that life shouldn't be this way.

'He would come home late, and he would be angry. It came out of nowhere the first time he got violent, then the next morning, he would be all apologies, and it would be fine until it wasn't. I guess . . . I guess one night I just had enough.'

'Hey,' I say, holding her tenderly. 'It was self-defence. It's not your fault!' She wipes her nose on my shoulder as she sniffles. I am amazed by how cute she is right now, even as she details how she took a life. Nose wiped, she looks me dead in the eyes and says.

'Not exactly.' Ophelia takes a deep breath and opens her mouth once more. 'One night, he came home drunk and had that wild look in his eye. He approached me in the kitchen, and I didn't think. I guess I had just had enough, and as he grabbed me, I hit him around the head with the iron. One blow, and that was it.'

I pause for a moment in contemplation. And I remember that you were her lawyer, Melissa.

'Did Melissa know?' I ask. Ophelia nods tentatively.

'Well,' I say, 'Melissa always did the right thing. I know that much.' And I consider my darkness. Can I tell her right now? Should I? It is a bit different. I don't get any more time to think before Ophelia throws her arms around me and breaks into tears. As she sobs down my back, she says.

'I'm so sorry. I wanted to tell you. And I never planned any of this. Melissa was a great woman. When I saw you that day in Southampton, I felt like it was meant to happen. She always said that you would understand.'

'Yeah,' I say. I pat her on the back as she cries on me, and I wonder if this is all a crazy blood loss, dog pill dream.

Ophelia relinquishes me from her hug, and we move apart. I go to speak when she says.

'Oh my gosh, Arthur, you're bleeding!' I look down at my plush robe and notice that the hug has persuaded my wound to bleed once more—goddamn white clothing—'Arthur,' she says in shock, 'what happened? Are you okay?'

I have had hours in my brilliant brain to find a convincing reason why I have a wound and why I am taking slightly dodgy dog pills. I have thought about it long and hard, and . . . and . . . I have nothing.

'Arthur?'

'I got stabbed, Ophelia!'

Her face is stern and serious, and I think I am about to crack. Tell her everything when she smiles and says.

'You're funny, Arthur.'

THIRTY-FOUR

We stay up late and talk the night into submission.

When Ophelia finally falls asleep, I gently move her from my arm, prise myself from the mattress, and tiptoe to the bathroom. The door closes so silently—thank you, five hundred pounds a night hotel—I slip inside and remove my bandage to inspect my wound. Whatever else the dog pills might be doing, they seem to be stopping the infection. I let the cut air, take a seat on the toilet, and finally look at my phone.

I have a queue of messages that have landed since arriving in Atlanta, and I use jet lag and time zones as my excuse for ignoring them. I don't think people realise how hard it is to lead a double life. I love my friends but don't have time for their banalities when I am out killing. I just don't. Add that to a new relationship and an actual holiday; it is hard work. Being a murderer is not for the faint-hearted. My messages are as follows:

A text from the garage: my Volvo is ready to collect. Good news.

A message from mum: reminding me about dinner. Bad news.

Rich Richard: wondering when we are going to play squash. Indifferent news.

And finally, Abdul's message poorly alludes to whether or not Ophelia and I have had sex yet. *We have*, I tell him, he will be happy. I reply to mum in lowercase, and I respond with *soon* to Rich Richard. Then I dress my wound, finish up in the bathroom and sneak back to bed.

It takes me a while to get back to sleep as I ponder Ophelia's admission. It will be Sunday in the morning, and we still have two more days of our trip. I know I am no monster. I just have urges. Something I realised the day I broke Duncan Fawley's nose in year six.

The kid had been calling me *Arthur Normal* for a few weeks, obviously alluding to the fact that I was not. He stood up and said it once in assembly, and I promptly sat him back down with a broken nose. I am not ashamed to say it felt good. Plus, no one ever dared call me *Normal* again. It was a swift way to dispel those notions. Regardless, I realised there and then that my abnormality was solved by violence, and I made a promise to myself to only take it out on those who deserved it.

If you think about it, that's all Batman does. He is angry that his parents died, so he puts on a suit and goes around Gotham, punching the lights out of anyone doing anything mildly wrong.

I think the unknown scares me; we all have our pitfalls as humans, and I suppose I had forgotten that I am not unique. I can't let my insecurities get in the way of something good, and I switch the light out and nestle into Ophelia's side.

I awake to find Ophelia missing. I have a moment of blind panic as I search the empty bed until I discover her note telling me she is in the gym. Early morning gym or any forced exercise is not for me. I stir and make my way to the freshly brewed coffee that she has made. I smile at the fact that I don't have to do it myself. I think that I am happy, and my grin widens. I guess deep down, we are all all-kinds of fucked up. It is what makes us human. And I suppose you were too, Melissa. You were happy being married to a serial killer. You were okay with defending a woman who had killed her husband.

We all have our problems. I have many. I am truculent, narcissistic, and a bit psychotic, and I talk to myself and my dead wife. I determine that I am finding fault in my next potential partner too quickly, and aside from *partner-cide* Ophelia is a wonderful woman. I can't let this ruin a good thing. I drink my coffee and settle down to read the morning paper.

The United States is fucking enormous. When I rented the Mustang, I must have had a half-brained notion that we could set off for a day trip to the beach. Because the reality is it would take hours to get out of Georgia. The nearest coastline from Atlanta is over two hundred miles, and when you consider that you are never more than seventy miles from the sea at any given place in England, it drives that perspective home. I have, in essence, rented a five-litre V8 to go from the airport to the hotel and back again. But boy, was it fun.

Atlanta offers a lot, including a subway, good public transport, and an oscillating restaurant with panoramic views. Somewhere we now sit. The panorama comes courtesy of the fact that the top of the building spins around while you eat. The view is fucking breathtaking, and in theory, it was a great idea. In practice, less so.

'Are you all right?' Ophelia asks me.

'Yes,' I reply. I lie. I don't know why. Perhaps it is some bullshit inbuilt masculinity that prevents me from being vulnerable. Whatever it is, I don't like heights and eating and drinking while spinning around the top of a building isn't sitting well with me. 'No, actually,' I admit, 'not really.'

'You look a bit off. Is it me?' Ophelia is an incredible woman who has been led down a path of self-doubt.

'Absolutely not,' I tell her. 'I'm just not too good with heights.'

'Aww,' she says, stretching out her hand, 'do you want to go?' I nod, and it feels surprisingly good, to be honest. I paid a lot of money to get these seats, and we have yet to order.

'I'd like that,' I say.

One thing I have noticed about Ophelia baring her soul to me is that, despite my irrational brain worrying that she might bash my head in with a kitchen appliance, I feel very safe telling her my insecurities. Many people consider that they only meet one person who truly accepts them and loves them for who they are. Soulmates, twin flames, whatever you want to call it, it happens, but it's rare. It's rarer still when they accept you for being a serial murderer. I have accepted now that any relationship post-Melissa can be great, loving, and accepting but probably won't be a hundred per cent truthful. I'm not sure that there can be more than one person who would love a mass murderer—aside from the true crime idiots who think Manson is super dreamy—but now and again, I get the feeling that Ophelia just might.

We get up to leave, and I tip the polite waitress handsomely. Not because I feel bad for abandoning our table but because the poor girl has to make a living in this equilibrium-shattering nightmare.

'So, you're afraid of heights?' Ophelia says playfully and sympathetically. 'I think we have just found the one thing Arthur Norman is afraid of.' *As well as never being loved again, I think to myself.*

'I'm not afraid,' I say, defending my honour. 'I just don't think we belong up there. It just feels off, even more so when you're constantly spinning. It's like eating on a merry-go-round.' Ophelia laughs. 'I'm serious,' I say. 'How often do you read the news about a Zebra falling to its death from a height?' Ophelia shrugs. 'Exactly, they aren't normally doing anything at height. We shouldn't either.'

'It was overpriced, too,' says Ophelia. 'You still wanna eat?' After my exploits with Magnus and his pals yesterday, I am famished, constantly. Something about having a hole in your abdomen is exhausting.

I nod. We leave. And we spot a steak house just down the way. Our eyes meet the building and then each others. Ophelia takes my arm, and we stroll down the road toward it.

I know what everyone is thinking. I have money. I have Ophelia, and I am having fun. I'm a lucky guy. Why not just give it all up and spend my days like this? I would, and I could, but that doesn't fix me. Nothing does. I need the thrill, the rush, and the adrenaline involved in a kill; I need to know that one is coming up. And I need something to look forward to—we all do. For me, there is no substitute. I have tried adrenaline sports, jumping out of planes, drugs, alcohol, gambling, etc. They help, but ultimately, I come undone if I don't get what I need. A train in my head is forever moving, and it may be inadvertent, but knowing that I am doing unseen good in the shadows salves my inner wounds. I don't think I am a problem. I have a level of control—sorry, Theo—and I am okay with who I am.

'Hey, did they ever find out what happened to Theo?' I ask Ophelia as I sip at my milkshake.

'No,' she replies, 'he never turned up. But the man was mixed up in some bad shit. He probably got himself in trouble and did a runner or got himself killed.' I nod, and I find it interesting that no one really cares what happens to you if you are a bell-end.

'Hey, if you think these people are so bad, why do you work with them?'

'Honestly,' she replies, 'I think it is a coping mechanism. I think it makes me feel better about myself knowing that I can tolerate them.'

'That's fair,' I say. 'How did you get into it?'

'It's stupid,' Ophelia says.

'Come on. Tell me.'

A waiter in a playful uniform passes by and places the bill on the table. The place is starting to empty, but to me, it has always just been the two of us. I look long into Ophelia's eyes. As I ask her questions, I realise we still don't know much about each other. We have essentially only really known each other for a few weeks. Yet here we are together in Atlanta, having dinner. It is strange how you can connect so quickly with some people—character matters, time less so.

'I wanted to make a difference,' she says. 'My plan was to PA there, learn a bit about law and then go on to study. There are so many injustices in the world. And, after what happened at my trial Melissa was kind of my hero.'

'Yeah,' I agree solemnly, 'mine too.'

'I'm sorry,' she replies, 'I didn't mean to bring her up.'

'It's fine,' I say, smiling at her. 'I think I've almost made my peace with it.' She grins, and our smiles meet.

'So,' I ask, 'what happened?'

'Life, I guess,' she replies. 'But I'm only twenty-three. I still have time.'

I almost choke on my drink when I realise that, to this point, I had taken no stock of how old she was. I was so wrapped up in myself that I didn't even notice when I had her passport in my hand to book the flights. No wonder I have been making mistakes lately.

‘So, what about you? What is Arthur’s dream?’

‘I’m living it,’ I say coolly. ‘I am an international man of leisure.’ She chuckles and touches my hand playfully. Her fingers dance along the back of my wrist, and she says.

‘But you can do anything. Don’t you want more?’

‘Oh, trust me,’ I say, looking long into her eyes. ‘I have everything I ever want. I love doing nothing.’

‘Hmmm,’ she replies. ‘The mysterious Arthur Norman, international man of leisure who goes on secretive business trips to Atlanta?’

She raises her eyebrows and purses her lips; we are both a little drunk and giddy. She stares at me in our bubble of comfortable silence and then says, ‘So, what did you get up to yesterday?’

‘What’s life without a little mystery?’ I say as I remove my wallet to pay.

‘Hmmm,’ she says. ‘Okay, but you’ll tell me one day.’

‘Hopefully,’ I say. I place some green money down on the table and stand up. I offer Ophelia my hand and say, ‘Mini golf?’

‘Fuck yeah,’ she replies.

THIRTY-FIVE

The rest of the trip was exquisite. We drank, we ate, we fucked, and we played. And it culminated in driving the mighty Mustang on the short journey back to the airport. It was, by all accounts, a fantastic trip.

We are back, and it is raining. There is no better reminder of just how shit the British weather is than coming home.

Now that the American sojourn is over, it is back to the impending realities of life. I still need to know what happened to Jarrod and Suzie, what Magnus wanted from my house and most pressingly, birthday dinner with my family.

I have so much business to take care of—a social life, among other things. I need to arrange a day to play squash with Rich Richard, see Abdul, Maureen, and Ophelia, and remember to eat. I also have a frankly ridiculous drum kit/music set to wrap. I have Magnus's phone to analyse, and as much as I don't have the time to do anything about it right now, it has become much like the *Tell-tale Heart,* and I have to look at it.

I kept the phone locked away in a Faraday bag until we got home. The urge to switch it on was vast, but I didn't want Magnus's goons or law enforcement tracking it. Magnus was at least reasonably efficient in hiding his business in plain sight. I almost gave up and considered smashing the phone when I thought I had drawn a blank. But it was somewhere between the smouldering rage and considering booking flights back to Atlanta that I noticed a series of emails between Magnus and a US Senator by the name of Riley Garcia!

The messages are ambiguous, meetings, double speak, coded language and what have you. And it means nothing to me. But I remember Shifty Steven from the party at Richards and Richards, and I wonder. Nothing in the text suggests any nefarious activity or maleficence, but that would be plain stupid. However, there is mention of Senator Garcia's upcoming trip to England.

Having just returned from Atlanta, I cannot fathom why any resident of Georgia in their right mind would want to come to the UK for pleasure. This cannot be a coincidence. As paranoid as it might seem, I want there to be no connection between myself and whatever this is. It runs deep, and tangling with a government official is dangerous. I have no idea who Garcia is, whether she is he, or what they look like. I want to take straight to my trusty search engine to find out. But my house was robbed, my car smashed, and who knows what else is happening. I must keep this under the radar.

I grab my coat and keys and head out to the one place you can still browse the web in relative anonymity, an internet café.

Jet lag is always exactly as bad as you remember. You essentially travel through time. Marty McFly made it look like an adventure. Except it's not! It is shit, confusing and tiring. The flight took off at eight in the evening US time. It flew through the night and landed just before seven in the morning. Only it wasn't seven. It was the early hours of the day. The remainder of the day becomes a competition to see how long you can stay up and level things out before you die of sheer exhaustion. I'm not too fond of it, and it puts me off flights that deviate too far from GMT.

We have been back just over twenty-four hours, and in another twenty-four, we are due to drive to Kent to celebrate the fact that my sister is still alive when I wish she wasn't. Add that to the jet lag, the four-day bender, the knife wound, and the canine drugs, and I am struggling. One small solace is the notion of the Army of Brats beating the crap out of an electronic drum kit.

I have things to do between now and then. Being back home brings with it certain anxieties. In Britain, we are very good at going away and leaving it all behind. Even workaholic Janice at the local council can fuck off to the Maldives for two weeks and leave the bin schedules well alone. But in coming back, so does the impending reality. Prior to my holiday, I attempted to kill two cat murders—only for some mystery killer to finish the job—and I killed two thugs—badly. Add that to Magnus, the stabbing, Garcia, and I have many thoughts swirling about my whirling mind. I need news, first-hand news. And this means taking a trip to see Carter at the police station. I also need to pick up the stealth Volvo I had almost forgotten about and find an internet café. I'm sure some still exist.

***

I collect the Volvo and consider it to look better than before. And I cruise around in my Swedish tank of anonymity until I hit the outskirts of Southampton. I drive until I find an operating internet café. As per the advancement of technology, they now primarily cater for something else—because you can no longer charge five pounds for ten minutes privilege on the World Wide Web—and this is an 'international shop' something which means it sells mainly Middle Eastern goods.

I purchase a can of *Mirinda* and half an hour of internet time and set myself down on a computer that looks like it should be in a museum. I stand out like a sore thumb, and I hope my purchase and affinity for a can of diabetes that is vaguely orange-flavoured makes me look less out of place.

I could perform a basic search for Senator Garcia at home, but it isn't worth the risk. No amount of deleting internet history means it didn't happen, and if they wind up dead, I don't want there to even be the most tenuous link to me. One of the last people I killed was in a bathroom at a well-attended party. Theo was an entitled douche. Garcia is a government official. I have a reason to live once more, and I need to be more careful.

A few taps of the sticky keyboard later, I find myself staring at various images of Senator Garcia. To my surprise, I discover that Senator Riley Garcia is a woman. My surprise at her being female doesn't come from the typical male—I don't want a woman in charge bullshit—quite the opposite. I think more women should be in power. Testosterone is not a hormone men control very well. Regardless of age, we like having pissing contests. And I wouldn't be surprised if most of the major conflicts in the world have boiled down to fragile male ego. No, I am amazed simply because, in my head, *Riley* was a man. One should never assume, Arthur. Regardless, Garcia has a look of power, and I certainly wouldn't feel comfortable engaging in a debate with her.

She is probably late fifties, covered in facial lines from excess cigarette smoke, but still very elegant. The greying hair looks enhanced and is perhaps only a few shades of grey lighter than her many blazers. I suppose that at least someone has found a practical use for the shades of grey. Garcia looks authoritative and also shady as shit, and I am determined to know more.

Senator Garcia's upcoming holiday to the UK is well documented. It has the feel of a publicity stunt, but I cannot fathom why someone who governs a state that is not much smaller than the United Kingdom could need to gain publicity here. I am sure the trip is duplicitous, and I am fortunate she has shared the details of her *vacay* with one of the awful celebrity gossip magazines. There is little in the way of fine detail, but the dates and even the name of her hotel are listed; that is all I need.

I make mental notes of the dates in my head, drain the remains of my drink, and clear the computer of any history. The sugary orange-ish drink enters my mouth, and I can feel my teeth degrading as I drink it. I will find out what Garcia was up to with Magnus soon.

I am sad to leave the *World Food's internet café*; it fills my brain with fond nostalgia. I miss the simplicity of the times when we *needed* internet cafés. I have also taken many 'business' trips to the Middle East, and I would be remiss to say that I don't have a genuine love for their culture. I appreciate any culture that doesn't revolve around reality tv or high streets consisting of *Greggs, WHSmith, Nando's* and, if you are lucky, a *Five Guys,* or *GBK.*

I leave the world food internet den, hop in the revitalised Volvo, and drive across town to the police station. This trip will be unannounced. But as much as Carter likes to pretend that he is still very much in the thick of the action—he is mid-fifties, grey, balding, and overweight—he spends most of his time behind a desk waiting to collect his pension. There is no world in which he won't be available.

I park outside the police station and walk inside. My baser instincts always tell me to run, but at the same time, there is a cheap, primal thrill for me every time I set foot in a custodial facility. I am like Dracula walking into Van Helsing's house and making a coffee. It is fun and naughty, like the R-rated version of *Secret Millionaire.* Surprise, I am a serial murderer. Now there is a show I would watch.

I approach the counter only to be sneered at by the desk Sergeant. She doesn't care that I know Carter and has me sit and wait in one of the chairs I assume they found outside. I glare at her from my perch.

A kid is brought in wearing cuffs, and he is high as fuck. I don't know what he has done, but I feel for him. Coming to and coming down from whatever he is on in a police cell would be a fucking nightmare. People blur past. I sit. I wait. I watch.

After what felt like aeons of waiting, Carter appears and lumbers down the hall toward me. He is a good twenty feet away, and I can already hear him wheezing. He parts what little hair he has on his pate as he approaches me, and when Carter arrives, he greets me with his classic detective smile. He nods at the robot desk sergeant and escorts me down the hall to a private room. Both our shoes squelch on the lino floor that hasn't been refreshed since it was installed in the late 70s. It was probably new when Carter started working here, and the floor, like him, should both have been changed long ago. It is perhaps no surprise when I say that I don't much like the police. But I do feel for them working in places like this.

The station itself looks like the setting for a mundane and depressing daytime TV drama. The décor is beyond dated, and I would expect the walls to be stuffed with asbestos were this building not likely to predate its use. The colour scheme is a sort of drab brown. American TV detectives work out of hip, bright, airy, modern spaces. This is not that.

'So, Arthur,' says Carter with sad sincerity as he shuts the door. 'How are you doing?'

'I'm good, thanks,' I reply. I like Carter, he is always very genuine, and I think to myself that if I ever got caught, I would ask for Carter to arrest me.

'Come on, Arthur,' he would say before patting me on the shoulder the same way I assume a loving father does to his son when he knows he has fucked up. My thoughts spin around my head in the time it takes Carter to pull out a chair and sit.

I have known Carter for many years. But he is a *man* from the past, and I am emotionally crippled. We don't share a deep and meaningful relationship. 'So, what can I do for you?' he asks.

Having sashayed through the pleasantries. I put on my best-*concerned* face and open my mouth.

'I'm just a little worried,' I lie. 'I went to the address you gave me, you know to get that guy's insurance details. But when I got there, it was a crime scene. I hope you don't think I had anything to do with it.'

Carter bellows heartily. Then scoffs. 'Don't worry, Arthur, you aren't a suspect. If that's what you are thinking?' My indignation peeks its head out when he disregards me wholeheartedly as a suspect. But I swallow my pride and remember that is a good thing. Carter shuffles on his chair awkwardly. 'I am afraid it is an active case, so I can't tell you anything about it.' He glances over his shoulder, presumably to indicate that he is about to spill something—why he looks over his shoulder, I don't know—and then says, 'But I'm glad you didn't get caught up in that. Two local druggies, very messy. It looks like they had a falling out.'

'Was it…murder?' I ask meekly.

'I can't go into specifics, Arthur. But I would steer clear of that part of town if I were you. Second drug-related violence we have had this month.'

'Second?'

'Yeah,' says Carter, 'some local drug dealer and his girlfriend were killed the week before.'

'Oh, gosh,' I say, 'there isn't a killer on the loose, is there?'

'Now, Arthur, nothing to get your knickers in a twist over. It's all very cut and dried, just druggies being druggies.'

I smile, and Carter checks his watch, the universal indicator he needs or wants to be elsewhere—presumably the canteen. He stands, and our hands shake. I look at his ill-fitted beige trench coat and wonder if he's ever replaced it. Carter escorts me back to the lobby, and we say our goodbyes. Two mysteries have been removed from my mind, no one is looking for me, and I allow myself to breathe a sigh of relief.

THIRTY-SIX

The day of reckoning has come! And despite knowing it would, I feel sick. There is no preparing for a situation like this. A chastening, soul-sucking feeling lives deep in the pit of my stomach. We are off to my parent's for Judy's birthday.

Ophelia is naturally quite excited about meeting my family—the poor, delusional girl—she has told me all about the great times they have at family get-togethers, and even if it is just a pretty picture that she paints, if the food is anything as good as Nikos's, I don't even care.

But here we are, in the car driving to the coast. We both have overnight bags, and she is elated. We are committed to this. There is no turning back.

Ophelia is driving—she insisted. And I am glad. I am still in quite some pain from my stab wound, and having my arms stretched out in discomfort only to drive in search of more pain doesn't appeal to me.

Ophelia is pepped up and grins every time she floors the accelerator, and there is something suitably sexy about a woman who enjoys Italian horsepower. I thought about bringing the Volvo, but then I remembered just how much my mother hates the noise of the V6, and it just had to come.

My mind is still a bit anxious, and I am a little preoccupied. As much as I am trying to enjoy these precious moments before we arrive in purgatory, I am still troubled. Carter was helpful. He was. But I can't shake the feeling that something is off. Could it just be a coincidence that Jarrod was killed when I was gone? Did I gift-wrap him and his girlfriend for some local criminal? If so, how many local thugs are there? I live in a Winchester suburb, not Brooklyn. Could someone have seen me? Or was I being watched? It seems thin to assume that some local rivals just happened to show up to kill Jarrod the same night I did. It is possible, but if it is, I really ought to reconsider my religious affiliations.

The business with Nicky and his friend Russell is less troubling, especially since Maureen is currently wandering about looking for my twin, who doesn't exist. But did Nicky really just die? Then I moved on from them to Magnus, who led me to Senator Garcia. I don't know what they have to do with Melissa or me. Is it possible that Garcia knows my true identity? Does the Mitchell case have anything to do with this? What information were they after?

Over the years, I have been as meticulous as possible, but one can only be so careful. We all make mistakes, and there are always variables that cannot be accounted for—but what—if anything— could Garcia possibly want from me?

'Are you okay?' Ophelia's sweet voice bounces off the confines of the car and registers in my whirling mind. I turn to her and say.

'Yeah, just preparing myself mentally for an evening at mum and dad's.'

'Ohh, it can't be that bad, Arthur. They are your family.' I smile and nod sardonically—if it is possible to display cynicism in a nod—and sink back into my mind again.

My family is hard to explain, but my parents are parents in title alone. Judy and I grew up far away from them, and we fled the nest as soon as possible. Judy is not me, and I am not her. We went to school together, but that is where the similarity ends. It was a co-ed boarding school in name alone. We took classes with the opposite sex, but our habitation was very un-cohabited. The girls lived at one end of the campus and the boys at the other. There was nearly a mile in-between, and sneaking across was as dangerous as it was difficult. Yes, teenage boys are horny, but a mile run at night, being chased by security . . . we are lazy too.

Judy left home five minutes after she met Tim and abandoned me to *holiday* at home for three years until I was old enough to leave. Mum and dad worked full time, so our holidays were spent at home, alone, friendless, and eventually sibling-less. Neither of our parents were present for football games, driving lessons, first loves, first heartbreaks, etc., and I can count the number of family dinners we have had in our history. They both made obligatory appearances at major life events, graduation, first wedding, and first child, but swore that one each was enough. There would be no do-overs. Neither of us was hugged enough as children, which is life. I don't resent my family; I just don't have much interest in seeing them. It is an odd dynamic and probably almost as bad as work *social* events.

I look at the satnav, and it declares that we have twenty-five miles to go—the directions aren't just for Ophelia's benefit. I don't know the way there either. As I accept reality and my impending doom, I climb out of my head and say to Ophelia. 'Thanks for coming.'

'You betcha,' she replies enthusiastically. 'I wouldn't miss it for the world.'

'You might regret saying that,' I say. 'You know, there is still time to turn back.' Ophelia grins and slaps me on the arm playfully as though I am joking. Having done that, she squeezes the throttle hard with her foot. The engine roars, and she shrieks wildly as the car snarls along the country lane.

'What did Melissa think?' Ophelia's words drift into my brain as we turn into my parent's cul-de-sac.

'About my family?'

'Yes.'

'Hmm,' I reply. 'Well, she and Judy hated each other.'

'Really?'

'Yes, but everyone hates Judy. Even her husband and children.'

'Stop it,' Ophelia says, hitting me playfully once more.

'I think it's best that you just see for yourself,' I say as the Alfa noses onto the driveway. Ophelia parks up, and I spot Judy's Fiat Multlipa on the drive.

'What did you buy her for her birthday?'

'Oh, a drumkit.'

'Holy fuck, is Judy a drummer?'

'No,' I reply, 'It's for the kids.'

We sit on the driveway for a few minutes, and I implore Ophelia to rev the engine a few times so that our arrival is noticed, and sure enough, I see an oval-rimmed pair of spectacles peer through the blind shortly after. We leave the engine running for longer than necessary, and it doesn't take long for the front door to crack open.

When we finally enter, we are greeted by the two gatekeepers. My mother stares at me, presumably to try and discern any notable changes that she can make comments on, and my father, who was no doubt in the study less than two minutes ago getting angry at the email server, dashes to the front door. Ophelia follows me in, and the man who is usually dour and silent gushes with welcome and addresses Ophelia before he does me—typical behaviour with any and all women I bring home.

'You must be Ophelia,' he says, immediately offering her a hug. They embrace, and I turn to my mother. I semi-hug mum, and she says.

'Good to see you've put some meat on those bones!' And she gestures toward the slight protrusion around my stomach. Last time I was too thin, now I'm too fat. I honestly don't know if it is a criticism or a compliment, so I take it as the latter and hug her tiny frame.

My father finally lets go of Ophelia and smiles at me before ruffling my hair playfully. Something I find odd. We do not, nor have we ever had, that kind of relationship. The four of us stand in the hallway, and the silence becomes deafening.

I am relieved when I hear the noise of the army of brats charging from the living room; the Legion of Doom appears and surrounds us.

'Uncle Arthur! I am so glad you are here,' says Maxine, running almost headfirst into me and wrapping her arm around my waist. I should add the disclaimer that I am not sure how much the kids actually like me; I know that any adult that isn't either of their parents is a marked improvement for them. That and I might be bearing gifts.

Maxine removes her arms from me, and as usual, I am surprised that I don't find a small, poorly written note in my pocket that says, *help me!* The rest of the children follow, with the twins—*thecreepyfuckingtwins*—bringing up the rear. I usher Ophelia away from the maddening crowd and down the hallway to the guest bedroom. We enter to find the bed made up, spare towels, slippers, and even gifts. I'd forgotten that the service here is far superior when I have company.

I turn back toward my parents and yell, 'We're gonna freshen up,' before I shut the door and throw Ophelia down on the bed playfully. She giggles, looks around the plain white room surrounding us and says.

‘Was this your room?’

‘God no,’ I shake my head. ‘I’ve never lived here.’

‘Wait, you don’t have a room?’ she asks.

I shake my head, ‘Nope, never really did.’ And then I warn her that everything she moves or uses must be immediately cleaned and returned to its original spot. She laughs once more, which is odd because I am not joking.

I am sure everyone’s parents have their quirks and pitfalls, and most parents mess up most children. But Judy is a sociopath, and I am a murderer, and I think it is mainly because this house, and all my parent’s houses, have been museums. It is like a guest house where the owners greet you the minute you arrive, loiter downstairs during your entire stay, and check the room every time you leave to ensure that you haven’t wrecked it. I am under no illusion that after we freshen up and depart the room, my mother will enter and make sure that the bags are on the case rack, no clothes are on the floor, and that anything that has moved is back in its place. The whole house is a similar affair. If you make toast, you must immediately ensure that there are no crumbs. If you shower, you must instantly remove every drop of water from the plexiglass, and if a single hair falls from your head, it must be gathered post haste! Okay, maybe I made that last one up, but it is not a functional place, and it is hard work being a guest.

We get ourselves *ready* for dinner, and I hear other people arriving as we simultaneously use and clean the bathroom. I delay leaving the hollow bedroom for as long as possible, but after five minutes of watching Ophelia do her hair, I get bored and decide to venture out alone.

I hadn’t inquired as to who else might be in attendance. I had enough reasons not to want to come. I figured Judy, Tim, and the kids were a given since it is her birthday, and I was already put off. So, I supposed it would be unwise to dissuade myself further.

Judy's birthday is in late June and always culminates in a BBQ party. My parents' house is lovely. The garden is a typical low-maintenance old person who travels all the time garden. It looks nice in pictures, but it is dull as fuck. The kids hate it and get bored quickly. I don't blame them. My attention span withers shortly after. I would offer to hold it at my house, and the little shits could try and drown each other in my pool. But that would involve having the *family* over, and I think I have suffered enough lately. I do feel kind of sorry for Judy's kids. I don't like them. I don't make much effort to be an uncle, and every gift they get is ironic or out of spite. The shame is, had they been raised by anyone other than my sister, they might be adorable little cherubs. They are not.

I loiter in the kitchen as I wait for Ophelia to get ready, she will divert attention away from me when we mingle on the patio, and the barrage of questions asked of her will spare me from banal small talk. My mother enters the kitchen and startles me. My thought bubble is broken, and not for the first time in my life. I don't know what to say to her. It is a strange feeling being awkward in front of your parents, but mine are basic strangers, and we have no normal conversation.

'Where's dad?' I ask stupidly.

'Oh,' she says tentatively, removing her glasses. 'he's been in the study since yesterday,'—that is probably not an over exaggeration—'Do you think you can go and have a word with him?'

Most things I say to the man tend to make him angrier. I cannot see it being a good idea. 'Sure,' I say, keen to get myself out of the hole I have dug, and I depart the kitchen for the study. I bump into Ophelia in the hallway; she looks genuinely magnificent in a Bodycon black satin dress. She is both ethereal and solid, dainty but yet firm. 'You look fan-fucking-tastic,' I say, grabbing her by the hand before she can speak. I almost drag her to the study door and knock loudly before inserting her into the room and following. If there is one way to disarm an angry dad, it is to present him with a beautiful woman. They are his kryptonite, and his anger will quickly fade.

'Oh, hi, Ophelia,' he chirps. I grit my teeth, knowing I would not have got the same response. I stand behind her and whisper, 'Ask him what he is doing?'

'What are you up to?' she asks.

'Oh, just this silly computer,' he replies calmly. 'It won't do what I ask it to.'

'Well,' she says, 'have you tried turning it on and off again? That's what I do at work.'

'You know,' he says, 'I hadn't tried that.' He probably isn't lying; I would imagine the sum of his efforts has been scowling and bad language. Dad reaches toward the computer—which I'm sure hasn't been updated since I was a teenager—and turns it off. It used to take six weeks to boot up when I was fourteen, so I can't imagine it is quicker now. As we wait in silence, I whisper in Ophelia's ear once more.

'Ask him if he is coming to light the BBQ?'

'Are you going to light the BBQ soon,' she asks.

'Yes, I'll be right there,' he replies and finally stands from the desk. He moves toward the exit, and we retreat into the hallway. The computer breathes a sigh of relief, and if it could wink at me, I'm sure it would have. He moves into the kitchen and pours either a vodka or gin, and he and my mother will no doubt embark on a short period of passive and aggressive talk in the kitchen. Ophelia turns to me and smiles. She always smiles. It lights up the fire inside me, and I take my Greek goddess outside to show off to the others.

We emerge onto the deck, and I am both surprised and relieved by the assembled crowd—surprised that anyone at all has come to celebrate Judy's birthday and relieved that the number is small. The gathered mass stops and turns toward us as we walk onto the wood that has probably been polished or wood treated within the last ten minutes, and there is a lull in the limited conversation as we do. I can only assume that all in attendance were informed that I was bringing a new lady. I suppose it is fairly big news after the death of one's spouse. The conversation stops, and Ophelia steps forward and smiles. It radiates into even the darkest of souls—Judy—and they all appear to beam back. I move behind her and place my arms around her waist, Ophelia exudes sunshine, and it is impossible to hate her. I raise her arm and use it to point as I move it around the crowd.

'So,' I say, 'moving from left to right, we have: Judy, Tim, and their children Maxine, Chloe, Oliver, Hailey, and Helen. Then we have Judy's friend Justine, her husband Mark, My uncle Phil, his wife Aga, and of course Jenny.' I finish the introduction and whisper to Ophelia, 'Aga is the only one worth talking to,' she giggles and hits my leg playfully with her hand. I remove my arms from her waist and my hand brushes against the black satin dress. I feel her warmth and the shape of her hips underneath, and I look forward to getting her alone on the solid wooden mattress in the bedroom later.

Aga approaches Ophelia, introduces herself, and they wander off together. Aga turns and winks at me before I approach Judy and say, 'Happy birthday, sis,'

'Thanks for the drum kit,' she says. I'm sure she is being sarcastic. But I smile regardless, and this is almost enjoyable.

'You're welcome,' I say, 'you know this is a vital time in their lives to develop their creative influences.' Tim—who is stapled to Judy's side—nods in firm agreement as though he has read some inciteful article on child development. And I wonder whether any of the children will ever be able to create anything other than chaos. I can't think of anything else to say to either of them, and I diligently move across to Justine and Mark.

Justine is Judy's best friend, much like Richard Hammond is Jeremy Clarkson's. They work together and occasionally socialise. Of the two, I cannot work out which I dislike more, but they give each other a run for their money. Her husband, Mark, has a smidge of character when he gets a few drinks in, but he is far too well-controlled ever to be likeable. They are both fairly nondescript, average height with regulation haircuts, semi-good shape, and neither is good nor bad looking for their age. We make some banal small talk before Mark comments on the Alfa. I *promise to let him take it for a spin one day,* but we both know that Justine will die before she allows that to happen—they own a Dacia Duster—I move on as I do the rounds, and before I know it, I find myself face to face with Jenny. I had hoped that she wouldn't be here, but in life, there are few certainties; death, taxes, the UK being governed by some halfwit from Eton, and Jenny being invited to a family gathering. She tells me *my hair looks nice,* and she got a *promotion at Home Bargains*. Anyone who uses *nice* as an adjective loses me as a friend instantly, and I cannot tell if she means that she got a promotion in a new position or if she just went shopping there. There is very little inflection when she talks, it could be either, and I am not interested in finding out which.

I finally escape Jenny and find myself coming full circle to Aga, Phil, and Ophelia. Phil is basically just a statue, and when I arrive, Aga and Ophelia are laughing wickedly about something one of them has said. I like Aga; we might have been friends if she were not affiliated with this family.

My parents finally put their differences aside for ten minutes, and they emerge with both food and wine. I realise that neither Ophelia nor I have had a drop to drink, and spending another minute sober in this place would be a crime against humanity.

I offer to open the wine and prise it from my mum's grasp. Dad sets the food down next to the BBQ, and I swear he uses glares to light it. I open the wine, popping the cork into next doors garden, which gets a *Yeeha* from Aga and a look of disapproval from Judy. With the bottle open, I take a long swig from the neck before handing it to Ophelia. I didn't see my mother roll her eyes, but I am sure she did.

Dad's glares seem to do the trick eventually, and we are all marvelled at the fact that the fire is alight. The food goes on, and the smell of BBQ food in the air stirs my hunger. The adults sit at the alfresco dining area, and we drink and talk while waiting for the food to cook.

'So,' says Judy to Ophelia, 'how did you two meet?'

'Oh,' says Ophelia, 'well, originally, I was a friend of Melissa's. But we bumped into each other shopping in Southampton, and I guess we just hit it off.'

'Shopping?' asks my mother, 'since when do you shop, Arthur? What on earth were you doing in Southampton shopping?'

'Buying gym clothes,' I reply meekly.

'What's wrong with the internet? You know you only get ripped off in town.'

'I guess I just wanted to try things on first,' I say. Thinking that attitudes like that are directly responsible for the decline in the high street.

'Well, I think it's great that you're going to the gym,' interjects Judy. 'It is never too late to better yourself.'

'Thanks, Jude,' I say, thinking that neither she nor Tim would know how to find the nearest gym.

'So, Ophelia,' begins my father, 'what is it you do for a living?'

'I'm a PA at Richards and Richards law firm.'

'Oh,' says my mother, 'well, at least you have a job, unlike Arthur.'

'Did you say Richards and Richards?' asks Justine.

'Yes,' replies Ophelia, 'how come?'

'Oh, haven't you heard?' Justine replies when it is clear that she hasn't. 'The senior partner was found dead. It was all over the news. What was his name, Mark?'

'Theo,' replies Mark, coming alive on command.

'What?' replies Ophelia. Justine sticks out her hand and thrusts her phone under my nose as if I'd asked. I look down at the unwanted screen. I can't quite believe my eyes. I zone out for a minute as the room starts to vibrate. I stare at the text and focus my eyes on reading. As incredulous as it might seem, old *Theo* must not have been quite dead. A site foreman had found an arm protruding from freshly set concrete a few days later. The irritating prick just had to ruin it. I calm my nerves and hand the phone to Ophelia. Aga looks at me and says.

'You okay, Arthur?' I nod, swallow, and say. 'Yeah, it's just a bit of a shock. We were at a party there a few days ago.'

'They are saying it looks like murder,' Justine says to Ophelia. *No shit, I think to myself, as though Theo had just climbed into some fresh concrete for a swim.*

'Come on,' says Aga, 'the table is no place for this talk.' And she is quite right. My mind is awash with thoughts. Did I leave any evidence behind? Did anyone see me? I dig deep inside and take a large gulp of wine to quieten my thoughts. I turn to Ophelia and, placing my hand on her shoulder, I ask.

'Are you okay?' She nods and smiles.

'I didn't really know him,' she says politely. And after an awkward pause, the conversation resumes.

The party winds up largely uneventfully; most of the talk is centred around everyone telling Ophelia embarrassing stories about my childhood. Some are funny, and I don't entirely hate reminiscing.

Mother starts cleaning up midway through the evening, and the guests slowly disappear. My father slinks off back to the study to continue his torture of the computer, and before long, the few who remain are me, Ophelia, Aga, and Phil. Phil may as well be a ghost, and once he had completed his talks on car detailing and how he could help me get the shine out of my Alfa one weekend, he doesn't have much else to say. It is both weird and comforting. His soul almost apparates through the wall; all that remains is his unmoving body. Aga and Ophelia get along well, and I smile as I sip my wine. It isn't long before Phil looks as though he might doze off, and Aga stirs him and tells him to 'Get the keys.'

Aga and Ophelia say their goodbyes and exchange numbers. I walk Aga to the door, and she pauses before she leaves. 'She is keeper,' she says to me.

‘I know,’ I reply. We embrace before she stumbles in the direction of their car. I look at Phil in the driver’s seat of his Vauxhall, and he waves. The car is very shiny; I will give him that. I close the door and make my way back into the house. Ophelia has moved from the deck into the living room, and I open the door to find her beaming a smile at me. She has a photo album in her hand that I presume my mother has produced, and she looks at me and says.

‘Can we?’

THIRTY-SEVEN

I wake up early the next morning feeling like shit. We were up late looking at photo albums with my mother and drank early into the morning. I then took Ophelia into the guest room and removed her clothes. The thrill of having sex in the guest room while your parents sleep upstairs never gets old.

The late night, hard bed, and the alcohol are part of why I feel rubbish, but also because I remember that I was drinking to forget. Theo's body was perfectly disposed of, buried in a chunk of concrete. It would never have been discovered in my lifetime. Of course, the prick wasn't quite dead. He had one more feeble escape attempt in him and managed to signal for help before he died. I can't believe it, and yet it happened.

His death was ugly, badly planned, and poorly managed. But my cover-up was good. I made him disappear on a bender like *Joe Goldberg* did with Benji. But his body has been found, it will be investigated, and those tweets will look a little suspicious. Now that they know where he was and where he ended up, the route between can be investigated. I wheeled him in a fucking cart, and there was every chance I made it onto a camera somewhere.

This is troubling, and I am powerless and can't keep haranguing Carter about random crimes. I will have to wait and see what transpires. I'm not too fond of that at the best of times, and I struggle to pull my mind away from it.

My life had slipped into darkness, sepia seeped in, and I was lost at sea. Ophelia came into my life and dragged me back into it. I cannot lose her now; I don't think she is ready to hear my darkness. We could run away together, but a life on the run is no life. My mind cannot deal with constant *what-ifs*. And you cannot get away from yourself by moving from one place to another.

I have been so sloppy and impulsive lately and need to get my shit together.

I think I am finally nearing acceptance, Melissa. I am almost ready to move forward. But I still need closure. There are loose ends surrounding me, you, and Senator Garcia's involvement. As dangerous as it is to go after a US Senator, I need to know where the rabbit hole leads, and I'm not sure I can move on until I do. I don't want to let you go, Melissa, but I need to stop clinging on. I have to put this to bed once and for all.

I *need* to get home, and I try to pack up and escape, but mum offers us breakfast. I say that *we will take it to go*, and we all make stilted small talk in the kitchen while she cooks some bacon in extra bacon. We finally get around to leaving, and my father makes an appearance when he hears that *Ophelia and I* are going. The computer is spared once more, and he comes to send us off. We say our goodbyes, and I smile. They are cold, dysfunctional, and annoying, but they are still my parents.

We finally make it into the car and pull out of the driveway. I see my mother stick her fingers in her ears and make a pained face as though a jet plane has just launched from the roof, and I dwell on the throttle for good measure. I mean, if she is going to make a face.

'That was fun,' says Ophelia, who has been quite quiet this morning.

'It was?' I ask. And I wonder if we attended the same party. She nods and then sticks her nose back into a book. I would wonder why she is being quiet, but I am pleased. I could use some peace. My head is in a million pieces and a billion places, and of all the things on my mind, her reaction to Theo's death looms large. The guy was a twat, granted. But she didn't seem to react at all.

I drive, and as the small seaside town disappears in the rear-view mirror, I smile. With Judy's birthday over, it will likely be many months before we gather again. We reach the motorway, and I look at Ophelia and grin.

I get us within an hour of home when the fuel light comes on. I tell Ophelia that we will *have to stop*, and I pull over at the next petrol station. I avoid the giant glaring, gaudy traveller trap they call services and head straight for the filling station. Despite my fortune, I only put in just enough to get home, and as I fill up, I consider whether it would be *just* to kill whomever it is that thinks it is okay to charge such a premium to people who are travelling. To top it all off, the toilet is out of order, and I am forced to pull the car to a semi-deserted spot and piss in a bush with all the other travellers who have a modicum of common sense. I get back in the car, give my hands the obligatory sanitation with the door pocket hand gel, and turn to Ophelia.

'How are you doing, beautiful?' I ask, given that she has been abnormally quiet on this journey. There is a slight pause in the silence of the vehicle before Ophelia turns toward me. Her beautiful browns burst as they take me in. There is a look of conflict on her face, and she hesitates before blurting out the words.

'I know, Arthur!'

'You know what?' I ask, slightly bemused.

'I know, as in I know, know!' she replies. I am still not quite following, and I cannot work out if it is my hungover head or if she is being unusually cryptic.

'I don't follow,' I say.

'Everything, Arthur, I know.' I pause, and I feel like someone poured vinegar into my heart. It is a strange feeling. I know that she could be talking about anything, but at the same time, I am certain she is not.

'How long have you known?' I ask. Ophelia pauses, and in that pause, my whole world begins to crumble. Her face is pained, tears have formed, and they run down her face taking her make-up with them. Fear is a horrible thing; I am not well acquainted with it. But right here, in the car at Fleet services, I am fucking terrified. Perhaps she worked it out. I mean, I was conspicuous in my absence the night Theo died. I left her on her porch. I went back to move his body; perhaps it was obvious. Maybe she called the police while I was filling up. An army of patrol cars might be about to descend on Fleet fucking services. If there is a God, please don't let my last moments of freedom be in the service station's parking lot.

Silence fills the car for an extended period until something unexpected happens. I feel Ophelia place her hand on mine.

'I'm sorry, Arthur, I should have told you I knew,' she says.

'How—'

'Melissa, she told me everything, Arthur. She told me EVERYTHING!'

'Oh, wow,' I reply. 'So, like you, know, know?'

'Yes, Arthur.'

I take a deep breath and sink my head back into the plush Italian leather. I can feel the logo push into the back of my skull, and it comforts me. I look up at the roof, and I feel oddly at ease.

I had been toying with the fact that I could never tell Ophelia. That I could never really be myself with her, and here she is, sitting next to me. And she knew all along. It might sound selfish to push this burden onto someone else, but it is not that, not at all. I just want to be loved and accepted for who I am, warts, deaths, and all. It is not that I expect her to join me. You never did, Melissa, but I don't want to lie about who I am, what I am, and what I enjoy. I have had many failed relationships because, as much as they had promise, I could never just be myself.

'And?' I ask nervously.

'And I don't care, Arthur. I love you.' A lightning bolt shoots through my cold heart and restarts it. And I don't care that she didn't tell me she knew.

My cold blood turns warm and flows through my veins. I feel a sense of belonging that I haven't known since you left, Melissa, and I feel at peace for the first time in months. Having to keep a secret like this from someone you love is devastating.

'I love you too,' I reply. 'Does it not—'

'I don't care, Arthur, I mean, I'm not thrilled, but I love you for who you are. You have a good heart, Arthur. That's all that matters to me.'

The following five minutes drift idly by. Life never seems to amaze me sometimes. I never really thought that I would get over you, Melissa. I know for sure that I didn't want to. When you left, I assumed the worst; not only were you gone, but I was alone and would be forever.

I start the car and smile to myself. I look at Ophelia, and she grins. Life restarts, only better than before. Ophelia loves me!

Floor it, she says, tapping the dashboard, and I ram the accelerator into the floor. All four wheels spin, and we get angry looks from passers-by as we shoot out of the car park and down the slip road. I look at Ophelia, and I'm not sure if life can get much better. Together we are a little like Clarence and Alabama in *True Romance;* Clarence doesn't care that Alabama was paid to spend the night with him. Their love is all that matters.

I like you, Clarence. Always have. Always will.

THIRTY-EIGHT

The following weeks drifted cathartically by. It is a clichéd adage, but life does move very quickly. With Ophelia's help, we cleared most of Melissa's belongings out of the house, and I even put the Maserati up for sale—something which was very, very annoying to sell—the police interviewed everyone who had been at the Richards and Richards party. Ophelia declared that we were together all night. The net had been cast far and wide. It would seem that many people might have liked to see Theo Richards dead. There were few *Justice for Theo* advocates, and like most wealthy semi-powerful twats people loved him for what he could give them, but now that he was gone, there was a void for them to fill.

I played squash with Rich Richard, ate with him and Cathy, and even took Ophelia to dinner at Abdul and Maureen's, which was far more palatable than dinner at the parents'. Slowly but surely, Ophelia became a bigger and bigger fixture in my life. We went to the movies, ate in restaurants, took to the arcade, and I even let her beat me at bowling. It is strange how fast things can change once you are ready for them to. The best part was having someone I knew I could count on, who knew the real me. It had quietened the longing in my head and salved my anxieties.

I know our tastes vary as we age, and we can worsen or improve, but fundamentally people don't change. There is no disabusing me of that notion. As much as I loved Melissa and thought everything was perfect, it wasn't. No relationship is. When something ends, it is easy to focus solely on what you miss, not what you don't. I cannot compare Ophelia to Melissa, but with each passing day, Ophelia waxes, and you wane, Melissa. I will never forget or stop loving you, but I am well on my way.

The months rolled by, and Summer breezed into early Autumn. I almost forgot about Senator Garcia; it has been months since I dabbled in death. But we all need a holiday; I cannot live solely this way, and to fully complete my transformation, I need to put the past behind me. Garcia needs to be addressed.

I have a vague plan, as they usually are. There is no manual for this. It is not as though I can start a Reddit thread on how to kill a US Senator successfully—although I suspect the CIA might have a few ideas, there is no forum to join.

As usual, I must do this alone and stay one step ahead of law enforcement and security. The latter is usually child's play, but I suspect a Senator travels with slightly better protection than most people. It is not a particularly elegant plan, nor does it need to be. I am reasonably sure that the Senator and her staff are not expecting me to be out to kill her, or are they?

There are many unanswered questions, and through the seven degrees of separation, the Senator and I know each other well. She has had my house broken into, after all. The Senator will be hard to reach during the day, but we are all most vulnerable when relaxed. So long as I can sneak into the hotel and wait, I should get my opportunity.

My urges are racing. Throughout this period, I have bungled two killings—technically, I didn't kill Magnus—completely, done half a job with Nicky, and almost entirely sabotaged my life impulse killing Theo in the men's room. I *need* to do it and do it right. I suppose most normal people wonder what that means, but it is an urge just like any other.

Some people get the overwhelming need to have sex, drink, take drugs, gamble, or drive really fast away from a set of traffic lights. For me, I need to kill, and soon.

I know from Magnus's phone correspondence—and the trashy gossip *mag*—that Garcia will be staying in the Park Lane Hilton—ironic since the chatter monger at Theo's party told me that she is building houses. I imagine a room there is expensive, and I can't very well check into the hotel where I plan to carry out potentially nefarious deeds. But there are two people in life that never get stopped wherever they go. People with clipboards and people in uniforms that denote that they have some menial job.

I am still slightly surprised by Ophelia's indifference to what I do, Melissa. I had always thought that you were a one-off. But I suppose it is all about perspective. Some spouses are immensely proud of their significant Armed Forces other. They attend ceremonies and parades knowing full well that the person they love is gainfully employed by their country to kill people from another, should the government deem it necessary. Perhaps it is all about how one sees it. Either that or love really does conquer all.

I am a little nervous about my trip to meet the good Senator. In two days, I will be driving to London, sneaking into a hotel in disguise, stealing a uniform, and hopefully getting to the senator in one piece. I am nervous for two reasons. One: everything I have touched lately has gone to shit. Two: I am torn between desperately needing to know and leaving it be. Part of me thinks I should start over with Ophelia and put all of this behind me, but it would be a question that forever nagged, and I would feel like I was living in fear and on my knees. Arthur Norman does not live on his knees!

***

I am on my way to see Abdul; Maureen is at work—hopefully not still looking for the version of me that doesn't exist—and I genuinely could use a friend. When you insert yourself back into life, it throws up many questions that didn't exist before. When I was a miserable moping misanthrope isolated from the world, I didn't have to deal with other people's feelings. I guess, in some way, it was what I needed just to shut myself away and deal with my shit without causing harm to anyone else. But I have an Ophelia now, and I must consider her.

Having a best friend I cannot fully confide in is challenging. It would be much easier if I could tell him all about the situation, my weekend extracurricular plans, and how my lifestyle might affect Ophelia. He might understand, but it is a huge, potentially irreversible risk. I hope I am never exposed for the sake of the people in my life like Abdul. Imagine being the unwitting friend and confidant of a mass murderer for years. You probably don't recover from that.

'Hey, Bro-ceans Eleven,' says Abdul as I walk in through the front door and take a seat. As always, Abdul's homemade colloquial greetings are a nuanced delight.

'Hey,' I say as I sit on the well-worn but comfortable sofa. I look around the living room, and even after all these years, I still can't quite grasp the theme. The place is never clean or tidy. The décor is modern and well-appointed, mixed with a Middle-Eastern flea market. It appears that when they decorated, they bought every item of furniture in a different place. But it is what it is. Plus, what do I know about home décor? I can decorate with blood, that's about it. I sit, Abdul gets me a beer, and we talk.

'So, what's up, my man?' Abdul asks, 'it's rare I get you to myself these days.'

'Har-har,' I reply sardonically. 'You couldn't be more of a husband.'

'I'm happy for you, I am. Ophelia is—'

'Hot? You were gonna say hot.'

'No,' replies Abdul, 'I was gonna say cool. But she is hot too!'

'Tell me about it,' I say. 'Anyway, that's kinda why I am here.'

'Go on.'

'Well, what do I do next?'

'Dude,' replies Abdul, 'bro, you were married for years.'

'I know,' I say, ignoring his double pronoun, 'that's exactly the problem. I met Melissa. I married Melissa. Years have passed. It's a brave new world now.'

'Dude, relax. She likes you. I can see it in her eyes.'

'But what do I do? I don't know whether to buy her a toothbrush for mine, give her a draw, or go looking for a house together.'

'What's wrong with your place?'

'It would be weird. Plus, there are the Wellingtons.'

'Yeah,' agrees Abdul, 'they are a bit much. Inviting you to dinner, how dare they.'

'Hey,' I say, throwing one of the gaudy scatter cushions at him. 'You don't know how they are. The inside of the house is like a Stephen King movie adaptation. It looks normal, but something is off.

'Anyway, I planned to grow old in the place with Melissa. I dunno, it just doesn't feel right.'

'For someone who was married for so long, you know nothing about women. Just talk to her and skip the guessing games. You're both adults. Engage in an open and honest dialogue.'

Ignoring the part where he said *open and honest dialogue*, Abdul gives sage advice. It is why I need a friend like this. My brain entertains so many thoughts it often can't see the trees for the wood.

'You're right,' I say.

'I know,' he replies.

'So, what were your plans for your evening alone,' I ask. Abdul reaches behind him and digs into what I can only assume is a hidden compartment in the sofa. When his hands return, he is holding a comically large joint.

'Ha-ha,' I laugh out loud. 'I bet it took you longer to roll that than it will to smoke it?' He grins,

'Worth it. Fancy joining me? I was gonna smoke it and watch the *Iron Man* films back-to-back. Maureen is on a double shift.'

'Do you even have to ask?' I reply. 'I just hope we are high enough by the point we watch number three that we don't care how bad it is.'

'That's the plan,' he says, smiling and reaching into his secret compartment for a lighter.

THIRTY-NINE

I spent the night on Abdul's sofa and woke up a little groggy and thirsty but otherwise feeling quite good. Drink and drugs dull my intellect, and I always have to be careful not to admit to anything I shouldn't. But when you have a brain train that never stops, there is a time and a place for such things.

I have just twenty-four hours until I make my way up to London and hopefully put the whole *JarrodSuzie-NickyRussellIMagusSenatorGarciaMeliss*a thing to bed. Ophelia knows I am going for *work*, so she will not accompany me. But I need to see her before going, firstly, in case something goes wrong, and second, to follow Abdul's advice about honest and open dialogue. The thought of the words almost makes me nauseous, but he is right. I do need to find out where she wants to go with this. After tomorrow, Melissa, I hope to lay you to rest; as such, it seems prudent to have a plan for life after you.

I have a text from Ophelia that is just a simple smiling emoji, and I text her back, asking her if she wants to get dinner. I have to wait less than two minutes for a reply, and as ever, I appreciate her lack of bullshit. As much as I want to plan our potential future together, I also know that she is back at work—most staff were given time off to mourn the loss of someone they didn't much care for—and that the police might still be involved.

I have garnered over the years that investigations into a death like the one that befell Theo are usually very insidious. They move slowly, creeping up on you until law enforcement inserts themselves into your life one day and asks awkward and invasive questions. I have also learnt that it is a switch, their job is to find the truth, and until they do, everyone is a suspect. It is nothing personal. There isn't much of a rush to find Theo's killer, but I know this is far from over, and I do not want to put myself in the crosshairs of the police.

The evening rolls around, and I pick up Ophelia to take her out for dinner, and when I say *out,* I mean quite literally. The summer is rolling by, but the sun is still high in the sky, and the weather is pleasant. Despite my money, I am still much more of a fan of sitting in the park and eating alfresco. I pick up some takeaway gyros and a few cans of beer on the way to get Ophelia, and then we ride into the city and find a small park.

We sit and eat. Ophelia is as beautiful as always, ethereal and charming. The birds chirp in the trees as the sun throws its warmth over me. I feel as though a new dawn is coming, and for the first time in a long, long time, I smile a smile that isn't saccharine. I loved you, Melissa. I did, but there is a different feel to things with Ophelia. The once white-hot, violent rage dims with every word she utters. I feel a sense of peace and order, and after all the fuck ups and mistakes I have made recently, I wonder if I am still cut out for this life. I was young, and I wanted to set the world on fire. I met one of the loves of my life, and I lost you, Melissa. I can't and won't let that happen again.

'What do you want to do?' I ask Ophelia.

'Right now, I could murder another kebab!'

I laugh.

'No, I mean life in general.'

'I dunno,' she says ruminatively. 'I haven't really thought about it. My life kinda stalled, you know.'

'All too well,' I reply. Ophelia takes a sip of her beer as she washes down a mammoth-sized bite.

'I guess I would like to go home to Greece one day,' she says, 'My grandparents are still there, and they aren't getting any younger.'

'How's the investigation going into Theo's death?' I ask cautiously.

'It's moving slowly,' she replies. 'I don't think they suspect you.'

'Well, that's a relief,' I chuckle.

'Yeah, they seem to think it happened after the party. Theo pissed a lot of people off. I don't think he will be missed.' Ophelia pauses for a moment, then says. 'Do you ever think about pursuing a different career path?'

'I hadn't until lately,' I say.

'Well, I'll support you,' she says, 'whatever you do.'

'Hey,' I say without really thinking. 'After I take care of business this weekend, do you wanna get away for a bit?'

'I have work, Arthur.'

'Fuck work,' I reply. Ophelia laughs. 'I'm serious. I'm thinking of selling the house. I think it is time for a new start.'

'Where would we go?'

'I hear Greece is great,' I say.

'You hear correctly,' she grins. 'Are you serious?'

'Why not,' I say. 'You only live once.'

'Well,' she says, 'I'm game. You're paying, though.'

'Honestly,' I reply, 'I have more money than I know what to do with.'

'You're not kidding, are you?' I shake my head sincerely.

'I'm really not.' I reach into my pocket, remove my wallet and hand her one of my credit cards.

'What are you doing?'

'You're the expert,' I say. 'You book it, and we'll go.'

‘Holy shit! For real?’ I nod. ‘I’ll need some new clothes,’ she says, looking at the card.

‘I was hoping you wouldn’t need any,’ I reply. She hits me playfully, and we tussle on the grass. When we tire of our antics, we fall back against the floor and stare up at the darkening evening sky. ‘I need to get an early night, but we can go as soon as I’m back from London.’

‘I’ll get packing,’ she says. We lie on the floor, and Ophelia presses against my side. Her head rests on my chest and rises and falls gently with each of my breaths, but she is unphased. Quiet contentment oozes out from both of us until she says.

‘Arthur, where shall we go after Greece?’

‘Wherever you want, my love,’ I reply, ‘wherever you want.’

FORTY

I rise early the next morning and almost jump out of bed. I get down on the floor and push out fifty push-ups before almost skipping to the shower. Despite being up late—packing—and not getting much sleep, my mood and mind are clear. I had resigned myself to letting a bad chapter end my story. It was short-sighted. You wouldn't want that, Melissa; in truth, neither do I. For the first time in a long, long time, I am excited to see what the future holds.

The Wellingtons are going at it in the garden, but I have no time for them today. I waste no time at home. I get my shit together. I leave.

I am on the road early to avoid the inevitable crash on the M3 and the perpetual, reasonless queue that is the M25. I remember reading once that Chris Rea wrote the song *The Road to Hell* about the M25! I have no idea if that is true or not, but it damn well ought to be.

I push the hard-working Volvo to the edge of the speed limit and halt it there. Today I am the early bird, and this early bird shall draw as little attention to himself as possible.

There is no crash on the M3—for a change—and I make good time until I meet the M25. There is the obligatory queue near Heathrow, and I finally make it onto the M40—I don't wish to torture myself by driving in actual London—the standard of driving in Greater London isn't much better than it is in the centre and by the time I have acclimatised to driving like a massive twat I am at my destination. I park in the vicinity of Wembley stadium and make for the tube at rush hour

The queue for the train at Wembley early on a Saturday morning is as hectic as ever. Thanks to constant capitalism, there are just as many weekend warriors now as there are Monday-to-Friday-ers. The grubby old Piccadilly line train arrives, and the crowd moves as one toward the open doors. It reminds me of the schools of fish that clump together when a predator appears, and thanks to being a part of this much less weird human centipede, I make it onto the train.

The next forty minutes are spent in a constant tangle of bodies, and for once, I am pleased to be of superior height as I don't have to spend the journey with my head in the armpit of a taller human.

At some point in the ride, a seat becomes available, and many eyes dart about, checking for the legitimacy of their seat claim in the most British way possible. As soon as the pecking order of need is established and all are clear that there is no sweet old lady in need of a seat or anyone with a visible ailment, it goes to the youngest person in proximity. Alas, with trips to the centre of the constant city, the car never empties, and by the time I reach my destination at the corner of Hyde Park, I already feel as though I need to go home and shower.

Having moved as one with the departing mass, I finally unlink myself from the human chain and take the short walk to the Hilton.

I still don't have a solid plan, but my brain is superior to most people's, and I am very good at winging it. I have learnt that trips like this cannot involve too much planning. There are just too many variables. And on the basis that I am not able to easily infiltrate the security detail of a US Senator, I am left with just the element of surprise and my trusty mind.

I walk by the Statue of Achilles and am glad I do not have a well-known weakness. I glance at the Greek warrior. As much as Greek mythology interests me, I cannot fathom why we have the statue of a mythical Trojan warrior in London to celebrate Napoleonic victories. Still, each to their own, I suppose.

I don't break stride as I arrive at the Hotel. I take a deep breath and stroll in with purpose. I learnt long ago that if you act as if you belong somewhere, no one will stop you—it is even better if you have a clipboard, sadly I don't—I power past the reception and loiter before finding somewhere to sit.

The place is enormous, and it reminds me of a Megacity from *Judge Dredd*. It is such a hive of activity that no one notices Anonymous Arthur sitting alone. I survey the scene for a while, and it doesn't take long to figure out where the staff come and go.

I rise, continue my sense of purpose, and follow an elderly Hispanic woman through a pin-coded door and into the staff area. She notices me behind her and holds the door. Either my sense of belonging works, or she is too old to care. Once through, I continue on my quest until I find a jacket, a name badge, and a key card. It is surprisingly easy once you are inside.

I shaved most of my hair last night and wear a long dark-haired wig in a ponytail. I have thick-rimmed spectacles that hide most of my face, and I don't look much like myself. I take note of the badge on my chest and commit the name *Jeff* to memory should anyone use it. Once prepared, I step out of the changing area and find the most disinterested member of housekeeping who is taking a break.

I explain to the man with cat-like features that *I am new and need to find the housekeeping trolleys*. Fortunately, my feline-featured friend doesn't care much, and he points me in the right direction. I keep my head down, find a trolley, and move into the kitchen to find something with which to garnish it.

I load up my trolley with fruit and an expensive-looking bottle of wine and then head to the reception. I tell the flustered and busy woman at the desk that the Senator's staff had demanded some complimentary goods, and she multi-tasks surprisingly well and finds me the senator's room number.

With 101 committed to memory, I push my trolley through reception and toward the lift.

I move through throngs of people, and I scan the faces. It doesn't take me long to spot a member of security who presumably belongs to the Senator's detail. Security guards are always easy to spot. They are essentially bodybuilders in suits and don't blend in at all. No one wears a full suit in London and stands rigidly to attention with their hands clamped around their waist unless they are part of a protective detail. No one stands still in London, period.

The man-beast clocks me as I head to the lift, our eyes meet, and I offer him the standard head nod. Something about his face makes me dislike him, almost like a premonition. And he returns the nod in an " I'm watching you " way. I guess the feeling is mutual, and I continue toward the lift.

The elevator arrives, and I step in. Fortunately, hotels such as this are well-signed because I don't have a fucking clue where I am going. The lift is empty, and when the doors close, I exhale. A mild pang of nerves hits me, it is a strange sensation, but I think I know I have mishandled everything I have done lately. As a painful reminder, I even have a tender scar on my abdomen.

The efficient lift delivers me to the first floor, and I eye the signs before I exit. I trundle in the direction of the Senator's room, and as I near it, the security presence increases. There is one man by the lift and two outside the room door, including a woman who looks like she could kill me with her stare.

I approach the door timidly and announce that I have complimentary gifts from the hotel. The once motionless goons spring into life, and the man immediately frisks me before death-stare-woman searches the trolley. Once they are confident I carry no threat—I do—they allow me near the door.

I don't always bring a weapon to a kill. I know it would seem like the classic serial killer move but bringing your own weapon (BYOW) adds to the challenge. You put yourself at risk before and after the crime just by having it on you. And as much as I am no Jason Bourne, I am quite adept at using my hands as killing instruments. That being said, I was a tad nervous today—and I knew I would tangle with rent a mob—so I did bring a particularly sharp scalpel from home, which is happily hidden in the false bottom of one of my shoes.

I pause for a moment in hesitation before knocking on the door. I announce that I am *room service with complimentary goods from the hotel*—some shrivelled fruit and champagne is a paltry offering, but you work with what you have—and I am relieved when I hear the Senator call back in a husky tone, *the door is open, and I should enter, set it down and leave*! Thank goodness no one ever says no to free goods from a fancy hotel.

The door is open, and I subtly use the sleeve of my jacket to push it down and enter. The room is incredible, and it is only outdone by the view. I have to shelve my appreciation for a lavish room and refocus on the task. It is clearly Ameliorate Arthur day today, and I am in luck when I enter the room. Garcia has her back to me and stares out the window—fair —as she ponders her thoughts, which is good because I would very much like to know what is on her mind.

I leave the trolley in front of the door and quietly reach into my shoe for the blade. My muscle memory returns, and within seconds, it is in my hand, and I am upon the Senator. I sneak up behind her and place one large hand over her mouth and the other with the blade at her throat. She barely has time to flinch as I press the cold blade into her neck deep enough to draw blood and say, *try anything, or even make a sound, and I will kill you where you stand!* I adlib. It sounded convincing.

I can feel the weight of Garcia's body tremble against mine—I bet she didn't see this happening today—I ensure she cannot catch my reflection in the window. I press her against the glass and don't allow her to see my face.

'I'm going to ask you a series of questions,' I say menacingly. 'And I want you to answer them honestly. I am going to move my hand away from your mouth now.' I move my hand a few inches from her lips and then say. 'If I even suspect that you are lying, you die. If you move, you die, and if you make a sound—'

'I die?' she says in a low murmur. 'I got it.' To the Senator's credit, she has balls. I'll give her that. 'Please,' she says, 'If this is about money, it's yours—'

'I don't want money,' I say, pushing the blade deeper into her throat. 'I want answers.'

'Okay,' she says, 'ask away.'

'What was your connection to Magnus?'

'Magnus?' she asks. I add a small amount of pressure to the blade and say.

'I said, don't lie to me!' A drop of blood trickles down her neck onto her blouse, reminding her that life is both ephemeral and in my hands.

'Okay, okay,' she says. 'Magnus was the kind of guy that people like me use to do the jobs we can't be seen to be doing. Do I assume it was you who killed him?'

'You assume correct,' I say, 'and unless you want to be next, I suggest you keep talking. Why did you get Magnus to rob my house?'

'Your house? No one robbed your house. What are you talking about?' she asks, sounding genuinely confused, 'My dear, I don't know who you are?'

'My house, just outside Winchester? The one that Magnus hired Nick and his friend, Russell, to rob. The same guys who stole my flash drive and nearly destroyed my Volvo.' I was getting angry at the length of time this was taking, and in truth, I am still bitter about the Volvo. 'Why were you after me?'

'Oh, my dear,' she says, 'I think we have a misunderstanding here. No one robbed your house, and it wasn't you they were after.' I pause.

'What do you mean?'

'Those boys were just cleaning up their mess.' My anger and confusion peak and collide with each other. I take the knife and drag it slowly down her neck, making a small but bloody cut. She will have a nice scar to remember me by, if nothing else.

'What are you talking about?' I whisper angrily into her ear. She pauses, and in hindsight, I realise that the penny must have dropped in her head, and she was reluctant to say anything else. 'Tell me,' I repeat, 'or the next cut won't be easy to repair.'

'Okay, all right,' she says, 'but you have to realise it was just business.'

'What was,' I growl.

'The lawyer, she was digging into our operation. I couldn't have it falling apart. I launder money for some dangerous people. In return, they support my campaign. You have to realise that I had no choice.'

'We always have a choice. What did you do?'

A tear rolls down the face of Garcia, and her voice begins to tremble as she speaks.

'The lawyer—'

'MELISSA,' I roar.

'Yes, Melissa. She had worked out that we were buying property here to wash the money. I couldn't have it falling apart. I couldn't . . . so I paid Magnus to stop her. But she had some hidden evidence.' The words rush out of her mouth, bounce off the stunningly clean glass, and hurry into my brain.

'You…you had Melissa killed?' The thoughts mix in my brain, and I feel sick. The knowledge replaced the bittersweet feeling that Melissa didn't kill herself and was murdered for the sake of some houses and to further the campaign of a corrupt Senator and her dodgy disciples.

The news and sensations were overwhelming, and time became muddled. It was like I was outside of myself looking in. My order of events disappeared, and everything began to spin. The news that Melissa was murdered tore through me like a tornado. I was confused and angry, and I acted on impulse. My response was an emotional one, and when that happens, things don't end well . . .

. . . And this is how I now find myself lifeless and face down on the cold concrete on the floor of a grubby alleyway, gun pressed against my head, waiting for death.

***

It all transpired very quickly, but I think it happened like this:

I must have loosened my grip on both Garcia and the knife. She sensed my hesitation and seized upon the moment. With the knife no longer digging into her throat, she threw her elbow back hard into my gut. The blow hit me like a freight train, and I staggered backwards. I know it was just an elbow to the stomach, and the movies make out like that can happen, and the polite protagonist moves on. But in reality, the smack sucked all the air out of me, and Garcia managed to turn, bolt for the door and yell for help.

The situation spiralled out of my control. The winding and the news struck me like an axe, and I was warm melty butter. It spread through me, and it took me a few seconds to get it under control. Fortunately, the trolley blocked the door, and I had applied the brakes. I turned to see Garcia wrestle with it as she fumbled at something in her hand.

I presumed it was some kind of panic button because it wasn't long before I heard a commotion outside. I had to act.

With the knife in my hand still, I sped toward Garcia with renewed vigour and caught up with her as she fervently struggled with the trolley. I grabbed her by the arm and spun her around so that she saw my face before I raised the knife and opened her throat like I was unzipping a jacket. A warm blood rush fell over me as she emptied onto the floor and ruined the carpet. I ducked and dodged an arterial spurt before pushing her to the ground. The door then hammered hard against the trolley, and I knew I didn't have long before the beefcakes outside flooded the room.

I crouched down on the floor beside the door and waited. The door bucked hard against the trolley and then once more before it dislodged it from its way.

The enormous woman entered first and saw the spurting senator on the floor. She made straight for her. She was followed swiftly by the man who entered cautiously with his gun raised. He took a sweep of the room but made the mistake of assuming the attacker would not be huddled on the floor, and I had the time to slice at his heel before he got the chance to—thank you, Achilles—he made a pained *yelp* as he fell to the floor, and I bolted out of the room.

I scuttled out, keeping low like a demonic toddler, and made for the staircase at the other end of the floor. The third guard by the lift had heard the commotion and was bolting for the room. He removed his gun as he saw me and quickly let off two shots. Despite my erratic movements, the first missed, but the second winged the back of my arm as I made it into the stairwell. Fuck, these guys were pretty good.

I hurtled down the stairs as fast as possible and took the first exit. I was fortunate to depart on a level that featured the health club and took a detour into the toilets. Once there, I calmed my breathing and checked to ensure the bullet hadn't caused serious damage before removing my uniform, wig, and glasses. I rolled them together, composed myself, and stepped out of the cubicle.

I deposited my disguise in a nearby bin and then walked toward the lift calmly. I was not keen on leaving potential DNA evidence to be found at a later date, but my DNA is not in the system, plus I had bigger priorities.

The hotel floors must have been well soundproofed because as I exited the lift in the lobby, business was very much as usual. I walked casually across the foyer with such reckless abandon that I didn't spot the guard—I knew I didn't like him—from earlier, who was now stationed at the exit.

He surveyed everyone and everything, and as I approached him, our eyes met once more, and a look of familiarity flooded his face. It took him less than a few seconds before he realised he had seen me earlier, albeit looking slightly different. And then the shit situation got even shitter.

FORTY-ONE

I had seconds to react before the giant penny dropped, and the security-oaf realised where he'd seen me before and pulled a gun. I was no longer in disguise. His facial recognition skills were good. I'll give him that. He clocked me as I approached the door, simultaneously removed his gun, and shouted, 'Hold it right there!' I was fortunate that the lobby was fairly full, and coupled with his histrionics, the mass went into a frenzy at the sight of a gun—I mean, come on buddy, this is England, that like never happens here.

I have a problem with authority in general, so I didn't *hold it right there*. Can you blame me? Instead, I seized upon the moment of madness, bolted through the door into the street, and started to run.

I probably could and should have made better use of my gym membership because running in a panicked state of confusion is exhausting. And kudos to anyone living in Central London who goes for a jog. It is nigh on impossible, more urban assault course, less relaxing run.

I sprang from the hotel and ran, but the man followed, hot on my tail like a bloodhound. Looking over your shoulder while sprinting is difficult. It is even more challenging in London while dodging people, cars, Ubers, taxis, and Bloody Boris Bikes. To the man's credit, he was fast for a big man, but fortunately, I was faster.

I managed to put some serious distance between us. I turned the corner into a very *London* back street. The street cum alley was largely empty and allowed me to turn my head and take a good look. I had made it a hundred yards down the street before I saw the large, bald, sweaty head appear around the corner. His gun was still in his hand, which I thought was a mistake, it must be challenging to run with a gun, and I bet it was tough to shoot and run simultaneously. Apparently, it isn't.

I saw him appear, and I was confident I could reach the end of the street and lose him in the next one. The smile returned to my face, and I spun around just in time to see a fucking cat do that annoying thing where it loiters underneath something, waits until someone or something is coming, and then decides to dart across the road at the last possible moment.

I saw the cat move too late, and before I could do anything, it raced across the road and smacked into my trailing leg. I wobbled, teetered, and remained awkwardly on my feet for a few moments before losing it and stacking myself all over the floor. I hit the ground, and it hurt, but I was undeterred and pulled myself back to my feet, kept moving, and made it to the end of the alley before the first bullet ripped through my right shoulder.

I have never been shot before, and fuck did it tear through me. It felt as though some enormous giant had smacked me on the back of the shoulder.

The whack sent me off balance and hurtling forward, the pain was exorbitant, but I could still see the end in sight. And I kept going until the second bullet tore through the back of my leg, and it probably took a large chunk of my femur with it. I stopped dead and collapsed to the floor. The pain was immense, and I fell forward onto my face. No amount of adrenaline cures a shattered femur.

***

So, here I am, Melissa, lying on the grubby ground in some anonymous alley riddled with bullets. It all happened so fast; it is still a bit of a blur. The mystery I came to solve is bigger than ever; perhaps I should have let it be. On the upside, I don't think it will be long until we are together again, Melissa.

My mind is awash with physical and emotional pain as I lie face down on the cold concrete. I can feel blood pouring from my body and the unsanitary floor filling me with infection. As far as I know, neither bullet hit any arteries or major organs, but I suspect I have a hole in my rotator cuff to go with the one in my femur. I cannot move my right arm or leg, and even if I had the energy to get up and fight the man walking toward me with a gun, I don't know how I would.

With my head tilted to the right, I can hear his footsteps approach. I do not doubt that Senator Garcia is dead, and I am sure he is wired for sound and is well aware. The alley is deserted, and he is a US diplomat charged with protecting a senator, and he just failed.

The footsteps get closer, and I know my life will likely end when they arrive. Time slows down for a moment, and I get clarity of thought. I don't fear death, but this was far from my preferred option for ways to die. The news that Melissa was murdered is fresh in my head, and the mystery that I wanted to put to bed is wide fucking open. Who else was involved? What evidence is on that USB stick? Why didn't I look at it? How did I miss this?

My mind flicks to Ophelia, happily packing away, ready to start a new life. I know we didn't know each other that long, but I have felt the pain of having the person you love plucked from your life. I know it hurts, and I would imagine it comes with a higher toll when the person you loved is splashed all over the *Daily-Fucking-Mail* as a murderer. I can see the headline now, *Senator Slasher.* Poor Ophelia.

I know that there is never really a good time to die. But dying at the hands of a trigger-happy meathead, fresh after coming out of heartbreak and depression and having made plans for a new life, seems like a pretty shitty way to go.

The footsteps stop, and I feel the cold metal of a gun barrel press against my head. I cannot see my would-be killer from my position on the floor, but I can hear and feel him. I can smell his diplomatic cologne. So, I close my eyes and wait for the darkness to come for me. It won't be long now.

A third bullet is fired, and the noise is deafening. I hear the sound, and I squeeze my eyes shut. Then something strange happens.

Either I am dead and am having an out-of-body experience, or my concept of physics is way off because I am pretty sure that when someone fires a gun that is pressed against your head, one should expect pieces of brain to be exiting through your eye sockets followed by permanent nothingness.

This is not that, and I am not dead! I keep my eyes wide shut for as long as I can before I dare open them. Is it possible he missed?

My question is soon answered when the body of the meat head drops to the ground next to me. We are face to face, and I am no coroner, but from the bullet-shaped hole in his temple, I would say that was the cause of death. Either he changed his mind completely and shot himself, or . . .

My ears are still ringing. The noise of the gun is just awful. But amid the shrill tilling sound, I can make out the sound of another set of footsteps, but not just any steps—the unmistakable sound of heels on concrete.

I lie on the floor in my bloody heap as the footsteps approach and stop. There are two options here, either an opportunist heel-wearing gun toter has spared me, or there is a second assassin out for my blood who didn't want the spoils to go to *Meaty McMeathead.*

The footsteps stop, and all I can hear is my breath and my slowing heart rate. I shut my eyes and prepare to meet my maker once more . . . my maker never comes. I wait in limbo for what seems like forever, but no matter how much I stall or how tight I close my eyes, I don't seem to be getting any deader.

I dig deep, find what energy I have, and attempt to roll myself over on the second attempt. I am hardy, but three bullets, one old knife wound, major moving parts of my body being destroyed, and a long run is pretty much my limit, it turns out.

I struggle to flip myself, and after much ado, I roll onto my back. The shift in pressure makes me bleed more of my blood. I look up from my position on the floor and take in the figure before me.

I am giddy, lightheaded, and weary as I blink and focus. Despite my state, I recognise her immediately. How could I not?

As inconceivable as it is. My brain stumbles as I stare in disbelief at the unmistakable woman looming large over me.

My mind finally engages. I find my words, and I stammer as I say.

'Melissa?'

Arthur Norman will return in:

You're Back.

Thank you very much for reading. As an independent author, I very much appreciate and depend on reviews (both good and bad), so if you enjoyed the book (or didn't) and can, a review would be greatly appreciated.

John

The characters and scenarios in this story are entirely fictional. However, the depiction of mental health, be it depression, anxiety, heartache, and low self-esteem, are based on my own experiences. I don't mean to add the humour to make light of it, simply to try to bring some light to the way a lot of us feel.

If you are feeling low, I know (and Arthur knows) that platitudes can be annoying, but it will get better; you are not alone, and it is not your fault. There are people whose worlds are better off with you in them. No matter how terrible life might seem or how much darkness seeps in. Make sure that the first thing you do is TALK to someone.

Writing things down can bring about a real catharsis. After a poor year, I fell back in love with writing and channelled a lot of my dark thoughts into creating something new, and I if can, then so can you.

Acknowledgements:

I want to thank every single one of my friends for listening to me drone on endlessly about my stories. For responding to messages in the middle of the day, asking for ideas about names, and whether I have used the word 'fuck' too many times. For thoughts on characters, giving up portions of their day to help design covers, suggestions, feedback, basically everything ever.

Everyone who has bought, read, downloaded, reviewed a book, or liked a post. Thank you. It makes a huge impact (and gets me really excited).

And finally, to my brother, Jack. For being my number one fan (and sometimes only one) since day one and for reading all of the unedited versions fervently.

Printed in Great Britain
by Amazon

18645694R00161